THE
OMEGA
DOCUMENT

THE CANAAN TRILOGY:

1. **The Omega Document**

2. **The Rahab Link**

3. **The Jordan Intercept**

MARK BRUMELS

THE
OMEGA
DOCUMENT

J. ALEXANDER McKENZIE

Bethany Fellowship INC.
MINNEAPOLIS, MINNESOTA 55438

For Patricia, beloved wife and mother . . .
whose family is
known in the gates

The Omega Document
J. Alexander McKenzie

Library of Congress Catalog Card Number 79-53442

ISBN 0-87123-416-5

Copyright © 1979
J. Alexander McKenzie
All Rights Reserved

Published by Bethany Fellowship, Inc.
6820 Auto Club Road, Minneapolis, Minnesota 55438

Printed in the United States of America

Prologue

At 4:30 in the morning, the sprawling horseshoe complex of Los Angeles International Airport was operating at its lowest ebb. From his elevated vantage point, Cleve Lambert ignored the sparse flow of airport traffic below him, concentrating instead on the deserted overpass leading to the second floor of the nearby terminal. The meeting place was as secure as any he had ever arranged. He had personally alerted the airport security people to keep clear of the roof-level parking lot for two hours. The unmarked van he was now in had been borrowed from the DMV pool less than an hour ago. And, he was there totally incognito, using the ID of one of his agents on the pretense of huddling with an informer on an unrelated routine case. The precautions, to that point, might not have been fully justified.

Unless, what he had to report was actually true . . .

The known facts seemed to be indisputable, carefully catalogued in a sealed manila envelope under his bucket seat. Yet, the sheer improbability of it all still made him wonder.

Impatiently checking his watch again, he verified that the Chicago flight should have touched down over ten minutes ago. He reached out the open window then to slowly rotate the rear-view mirror, tracking the vacant area behind the van. I'm getting a little paranoid, he thought after a moment, and he turned the mirror to stare at himself in the bland mercury-vapor light. Cleve Lambert was aware of his ability to size up a suspect quickly by what was revealed in his face. And he was troubled by what he saw now. There was the familiar erosion of nearly thirty years' active service in the field. The twice-broken nose, cleft on the bridge. The right ear nearly flat next to his close-cropped hairline, shrunken in by the impact of a half-dozen buckshot pellets. The stoic, impassive look around the eyes, the more grave consequence of a man having lost his wife too early in life. And, of late, the underlying more subtle lines of resentment against the changes taking place around him about which seemingly he could do nothing. The bad light helped now, but it couldn't entirely hide the overlay of worry, the anxiety . . .

Distracted by movement on the overpass, he leaned forward to squint through the windshield, focusing on the slowly moving figure coming his way. It was an older man, with a great mane of nearly white hair, and there was no mistaking the familiar military gait. Relieved, Lambert quickly pulled the van's light switch out one notch, leaving the parking lights on until he saw that the other man had spotted the signal. A few moments later, Jerome Mason, the Director of the Federal Bureau of Investigation, climbed into the passenger seat beside him.

Cleve Lambert extended his right hand. "It's good to see you, sir," he said as convincingly as he could, doing his best to sound casual, because confronting Jerome Mason was a little like sitting down with a latter-day General Patton.

"You should know," said Jerome Mason evenly, "that your untimely call caught me smack in the middle of running a beautiful bluff on a busted flush."

Lambert forced a small laugh, thankful for his superior's apparent magnaminity. "Five'll get you ten you were in the poker game within an hour after you touched down at O'Hare."

"That's a cinch bet and you know it."

Lambert hit the starter and as he backed the van into the exit lane, he was again aware of the awkward timing of the clandestine meeting. The annual Police Chief's convention was Jerome Mason's one fling for the year, a tradition, where he not only could relax among old buddies for a few days but also manage to gather field intelligence he could never acquire from his Washington desk.

"I'm sorry to have hauled you away," said Lambert gravely, "but this is the only way I could figure to handle it." He reached down between the two bucket seats, pulled out a thermos. "Black coffee. Or, if you want, a pint of sour mash in the glove compartment."

Mason made a wry face, shaking his head. "Coffee's fine."

There was an extended silence then as they worked around Sepulveda to turn onto Imperial Boulevard toward the beach. Finally Cleve Lambert decided he must get to the point: "I presume you remember the ETC Corporation."

"Uh-huh," grunted Mason after a moment. "Our friends,

the national good Samaritans. Did we ever find out what the ETC stands for?"

Lambert had to dig into his memory, before answering, "Negative; I recall checking their incorporation package, and the ETC title was simply listed as non-explained initials."

Jerome Mason grunted once again, his manner decidedly suspicious. "They're playing games," he mused.

"Probably so," Lambert agreed. "You may recall, we got onto them originally during the kidnap case of Mayberry Courtland's boy."

"I remember the ETC coughed up half the ransom money."

"A cool million and a half, in less than two hours."

"Probably out of petty cash," Mason suggested dryly as he turned to watch the last of the airport slip by on their right. "That was two years ago last month," he said reflectively. "Let's see, a little over a year ago, Dick Martinson ran a report across my desk."

Lambert was silent, allowing his boss to collect his own thoughts on the subject. Dick Martinson was the chief of the Bureau's Special Litigation Section, the little-known group assigned to investigate and keep an eye on the various terrorist and more radical groups around the country.

"It was in response to a secret-committee request from the foreign relations people," Mason was saying guardedly. "Something to do with the ETC allegedly helping finance an anti-Allende chain of newspapers, or some such nonsense."

They were at the beach now, and Lambert pulled the van into the nearest public parking lot fronting the sand. The lot was empty, except for a vacant sedan parked about fifty yards to his right, apparently belonging to the two early-rising fishermen working the surf another fifty yards down the beach.

"They were given a clean bill," Mason added as an afterthought.

"Almost, but not entirely," Lambert said. "They were clean on the Chile deal, but Dick recommended we dig a little deeper because of the highly secret nature of the ETC so-called executive committee. You may recall, it bugged him that he couldn't turn a single item linking the executive committee to the day-to-day business of the company."

"I remember now," said Mason. "I sent you a copy of Dick's report, with a memo attached—"

"Exactly," Lambert confirmed. "Your recommendation was that we try to develop a contact, on a very low-key basis, with our only objective to get a handle on the ETC executive committee." He paused then, watching the two men down the beach. "I got in touch with Dick right away because even though a year had gone by, I suspected we still had just the contact we needed."

"Once in a while we get lucky."

Lambert chuckled with the same touch of irony. "You remember how we busted the Courtland kidnap case?"

"Through an informer, but I've forgotten his name."

"Joshua," said Lambert. "Joshua Bain. He was a student at Berkeley at the time, there, from what I could gather, to get his head screwed back on straight. He was a POW, about eighteen months, I think. And, he was living with a broad who was hooked on drugs, the hard stuff, heroin. She was a real radical one, typical subculture all the way. Showed up at all the demonstrations, anti-war, farm workers, you name it. And the worst of it, of course, was that she was an active soldier in the Weathermen for Action and Revolution—"

"According to Dick," said Mason, "the WAR people are still around."

"Just barely," Lambert said deprecatingly. "There's maybe a handful of 'em left down here." He looked aside to see Mason checking his watch. "Anyway, Joshua Bain called me up a couple weeks after the Courtland case broke in the papers. You should remember that old man Courtland was giving us fits, insisting we stay out of it."

"Don't remind me."

"Well, Bain sounded straight, so I set up a secret meeting between the three of us, Bain, Courtland, and myself. Bain gave us the information leading to the WAR hideout where they were holding the boy, but only after I agreed to keep both him and his woman completely out of it." Lambert was shaking his head then. "It was sweet the way Bain pulled it off; I mean, there was Mayberry Courtland leaning on me, and he was a witness besides."

"It was a good trade."

"Oh, yeah, and Bain told me the reason he was coming forward was because he was trying to get the girl out of it all, off the drugs."

"You find it hard to accept decent motives?"

Lambert snorted through his nose. "All I know is that she escaped prosecution, and she was in it up to her eyebrows, and you know how I feel about making deals with criminals." He noticed again that Mason was checking his watch, so he started up the van, backed around to head back toward the airport. "Only I and old man Courtland knew about Bain and the girl," he went on. "A couple days after we busted the WAR hideout, a man by the name of Calvin Price came to my office to pick up the ETC share of the ransom, and he had the gall to ask me the name of the person who had helped us out."

"The Calvin Price from Dallas?"

"Yeah, the Texas biggie. At that point, all I knew was that he was on the board of directors of the ETC Corporation. And he was a personal friend of old man Courtland, who had suggested to him in confidence that there was an informer involved. Price's pitch was that the ETC wanted to reward the party pulling the string on the WAR kidnappers."

"And you of course refused him."

"Absolutely, and as soon as he left my office I called Courtland and gave him the official word, reminding him that our agreement was to keep Bain's name completely secret. Both he and Price were cooperative and the matter was dropped."

"So when the ETC memo hit your desk last year," Mason speculated, "you realized you had a ready-made pipeline."

"Couldn't have been prettier, and Dick agreed to let me run with it. Joshua Bain was in his last semester at Berkeley. I flew up and had a long chat with him, and he agreed to go along, so long as the girl could accompany him."

"Was he having any luck with her?"

"Apparently so, and the timing was good. She had pulled out of the Weathermen. And Bain figured a move away from the environment up there would help her kick the habit. So I had Courtland leak Bain's name back to Calvin Price, on the pretense that a year had gone by and, after all, the man did deserve a reward. Price offered him either an outright gift of fifty grand or a job of some kind with the ETC."

"Naturally you insisted he take the job."

"He took it without my advice. Moved down to the Coachella Valley, right next door to the ETC headquarters, and took over a small forty-acre grape ranch as resident manager."

Jerome Mason was nodding appreciatively as they turned into the airport. "Okay, Cleve, what do you have?" he asked flatly.

"Two days ago, in one of his routine reports, Joshua said he had picked up something solid suggesting a strong possibility of a connection between the death of Senator Bradford Turner and the ETC."

"Come on, Cleve," Mason responded quickly, "both we and the Secret Service agreed; old man Turner died of a heart attack. He had a long record of heart trouble, and he simply over-exerted himself playing racquetball."

Lambert was nodding as he pulled into park in the same parking place. "It was a pat deal all right. He dropped dead in the locker room of the Las Tunas Country Club. And, night before last, I made a covert entry into the locker room."

"Without a warrant?"

"A judgment move, okay. I had to verify." He took a deep breath as he reached under his bucket seat. "It's all here," he went on, handing Mason a sealed manila envelope. "Turner was zapped and no question about it. And, it was super slick, as you'll see."

Taking the envelope with his left hand, Mason placed his coffee cup on the dash. He then thoughtfully slipped the sealed report into his inside jacket pocket. There was silence for a moment while both men watched the halo of condensation form on the windshield above the coffee cup.

"I've put together everything that Bain has given me," Lambert continued, "plus I've done a whole lot of checking in the past couple days on my own. And, I'm recommending that you personally run a top-secret check against the details included in my report. I'm telling you, sir, it's spooky. The entire upper end of the ETC is sealed off. We know it's there, from Bain's reports alone, but it's like a gigantic no-man's land." He turned to face the terminal, and he heard the glove compartment coming open, the soft clatter of a bottle coming out.

"My trusty gut tells me," he went on soberly, "that the Turner connection tied in with the super secrecy spells probable conspiracy. If there is something coming down, and if it's only half as big as I suspect, then they've got to have records, probably in that Indian Wells fortress they use as their headquarters. So, I'm asking for your permission to penetrate the ETC upper echelon as soon as possible.

"You've got my tentative approval," said Mason cautiously. "Until we can produce some hard evidence. You know, like with a warrant. Your trusty gut does not qualify as probable cause."

"We've got suspicion of murder—"

"Don't fence words with me, Cleve."

"Okay," said Lambert judiciously. "But please protect my man. Only you and I know about Joshua Bain. If we ever have to refer to him in the open, use the code name Anzio. If this turns out to be a heavy scene, we'll not have the time to replace Bain if he washes."

"The time?"

"Yes, sir," Lambert said soberly. "I'm positive we've reached out and just touched the tip of this iceberg."

"How far along is Bain?"

"That's another problem," replied Lambert worriedly. "He's done pretty well up until the last few weeks. He's still on the grape ranch, and, with my pushing him, he's made plenty of points with the ETC management."

"So what's the problem?"

"Bain's girl, Jerrie McKennan," Lambert complained bitterly. "She's pregnant, a few months along, and Bain is making noises like he wants her out of the combat zone."

Jerome Mason reached up to adjust his dark glasses before cracking his door open. "How sure are you of Bain?"

Lambert shrugged, looking aside. "He's a natural, probably the best free agent I've ever run across. We've had the time to work together, and I've trained him myself. But, that broad has got him boxed, and as weird as she is, there's no telling what she might get him to do."

Mason got out, walked around the front of the van to stop by his elbow. "You don't mean he might pull out?"

Lambert shrugged again. "I don't think so, but . . ."

"You'd best get on the problem, Cleve," Mason said evenly. "You've given me a whole bunch of 'ifs' on this dreary morning, and I'm going to give you just one in return. *If* the ETC did in fact murder Bradford Turner, then not only I but the Attorney General as well are going to insist you have Joshua Bain screwed in there tight." Without waiting for a reply, he turned to start toward the overpass. He pulled up after three or four steps, turned around. "By the way, Cleve," he said more casually, "tell me about those two guys fishing down at the beach." And he was smiling for the first time, a little knowingly, Lambert thought, as if the last item of business

12

had to be one of his own contribution.

"A couple of friends," said Lambert.

Jerome Mason nodded once as he turned to walk more purposefully toward the overpass. Watching him, Lambert couldn't help counting cadence, one-hop-areep, three, four, your left. Sixty paces per minute, exactly. He presumed Mason's parting gesture was one of approval.

Settled comfortably in his assigned seat, Jerome Mason figured he was home free now. He had thus far escaped recognition. His ticket reported the name, "J. Claypool," the AKA suggested by Lambert. The early-bird flight to Chicago was a kind of businessmen's special, and with most of the seats taken, he was just another one of the bleary-eyed flock. It really didn't matter now, anyway, so as the 727 reached its flight level, he exchanged his dark glasses for a pair of more utilitarian horn-rimmed reading glasses. Seated forward in the first-class section, he put his order in quickly for a cup of coffee, declining the on-board breakfast.

With the coffee on the tray in front of him, he removed the heavy envelope from his inside jacket pocket, broke the seal carefully. Attached to Lambert's formal report was a small map and a 5 x 7 aerial photo. The map was a photo reduction of the greater Coachella Valley, which he knew was located about a hundred miles inland from Los Angeles. From Palm Springs at the north, he worked his finger curiously down Highway 111, through Cathedral City, Rancho Mirage, then east across Palm Desert, Indian Wells, to end up at Indio. Desert country, hot as Hades this time of the year. Between Indian Wells and La Quinta was a small blue square marked, "See aerial photo." He pulled the photo around in front of the map, turning it to get the shadow fall correctly aligned. The ETC building was enormous. Split level, into two, maybe three offset floors. Literally built into the side of a mountain. It occurred to him that the designers might have borrowed the Norad floor plan. A formidable abode for the nonprofit company which on the surface seemed dedicated to helping mankind and whose activities ranged from sponsoring hundreds of overseas missionaries to providing substantial grants to as many worthwhile causes and individuals.

He shook his head, again baffled by the vagaries of human nature, by the apparent Jekyll-and-Hyde conduct of an organization like the ETC, which during the day went about its humanitarian business while at night skulking about playing out some deadly, sinister role. It ought to be illogical that crime should exist at such a respected and sophisticated level. Yet, here they were, starting out again to put the pieces of this new puzzle together, and no matter how bizarre and grotesque the final picture, it had to be done by someone.

He spent the next twenty minutes carefully going over Cleve Lambert's detailed report. Finished, he promptly ordered a double Jack Daniels, straight up. His first impulse was to put Dick Martinson on the project, since the Special Litigation Section specialized in just such cases. However, in view of the chance for compromise, he would retain Lambert until the situation demanded otherwise.

They had to give Joshua Bain the chance.

My thoughts are not your thoughts,
neither are your ways my ways,
saith the Lord.
For as the heavens are higher than
the earth, so are my ways higher
than your ways, and my thoughts
than your thoughts.—Isaiah

Chapter one

The sun was coming up now, and she looked out to the distant edge of the ranch, where the first harsh light was filtering through the picket line of date palms, making the heavy, dense trunks look like spindly match sticks. Between her and the palm trees, the flat and endless rows of grapevines were still in deep shadow, sun-tipped only here and there. Shortly, she knew, and then only for a few moments, the vine rows would be furrowed to look like a deeply ploughed field. Right now, she wanted to freeze it all, so that there would be nothing past, nothing to come. Why not, she thought dreamily, like taking a picture with a camera and the image on the film is fixed, preserved for all eternity. She closed her eyes briefly against the tree-filtered glare of the new desert sun, hearing behind her the soft wet sound of Joshua hitting the water, and with that subtle distraction she smiled to herself.

It was Joshua who ordered the sun to stand still.

Do it now, please, please . . .

Jerrie McKennan waited longer, hoping, listening to the silence of the ranch they called Canaan, savoring the precious moment, and it came to her that there was nothing else she could possibly want for at the moment . . .

Why can't it just stay this way?

And she slowly opened her eyes after another passing moment, but the sun was less red now and higher among the drooping fronds. Such is life, she thought resignedly, and she moved her right hand across the wet bathing suit over her lower stomach, feeling her body tense with disappointment. She carefully started to relax again, controlling herself back to normal, knowing that if she didn't the frustration would surge out of control until it became unmanageable. She had to remain calm, unruffled. In the past year, with Joshua's constant help, she had managed to master the mental state and attitude enabling her to kick the habit, hopefully, once and for all. Turning away toward the side of the house and the walkway leading to the pool, she took a deep liberating breath.

The 30 x 60 elevated swimming pool was really a reservoir

for their main water well, so formally identified by the county assessor, a write-off ploy used by all the local gentlemen farmers. It occurred to her in a still dreamy sort of way that a year ago that kind of rich man's dodge would have caused her to bristle, but now she didn't seem to care.

As she drew up next to the end of the pool nearest the house, Joshua surfaced a few feet away. Seeing her, he stroked once to the pool's edge, then lifted himself out of the water cleanly, turning in one graceful motion to sit on the coping, his legs still in the water. He shifted once, straightening out his bathing suit under his thighs.

Jerrie pulled up beside him, shoulder to shoulder, facing the other way. She supposed that on this early July morning the desert was at its coolest hour, yet all about her things were still warm, even Joshua's shoulder just out of the water. "We're being terribly out of order," she suggested quietly.

"Not really," Joshua said after a moment. "It's a little like the tree falling in the forest. If there's nobody there to hear it, does it really make a sound?"

"I see," she said then. "Because there's no one here to see us, are we really out here swimming before breakfast?"

"Something like that."

"Can you imagine the look on Alan's face if he were to come traipsing around the corner of the house right now? I mean, like he usually beats us out of bed by an hour."

"Nothing shakes Alan."

She chuckled appreciatively, conceding the point.

They were both quiet then, and Jerrie thought about the baby. "You will help me," she said, her voice low and concerned, and she turned to look at his profile, thinking again that when he came out of the water with his hair down over his face he looked much younger than his still boyish thirty-two years. When dry, his thick dark brown hair is a rebellious curly mass. "You will help me," she offered again.

"Sure," he was saying somberly, "you do the eggs and I'll take care of the steaks."

She had dropped her head to nuzzle into his left shoulder where the muscle came over thickly to run down his arms. Realizing he was teasing her, she bit into his wet skin.

She felt herself looping backward then, headfirst into the pool whose temperature now was so like the outside air she had little sensation of being under water, and in her first feeling of weightlessness she was aware he had her by the ankles, pushing her upward. She was out of the water then, and he flipped her backwards into a somersault. Surfacing, she lunged at him, trying to catch his bathing suit, but he was gone, stroking furiously away toward the deep end. Laughing then, she moved haltingly to the nearby coping where she lofted herself out. Pulling her coppery-red hair around her right shoulder, she started to wring it out again.

"You're a sneak, and a coward!" she screamed after him. He pulled up under the diving board, dog-paddling, with the pool's light behind and under him. "The Coachella chicken!" she taunted him then, and he leaned forward toward her, stroking powerfully. Laughing again, she turned deftly on the coping to drop to the patio level, thinking that one dunking was enough for the morning.

She dashed to the patio sliding glass door, turning to see him standing straddle-legged on the coping, tottering a little unsteadily, and he started to sing, bellowing really, as he always did in the shower, shattering the heavy silence around them:

"Went down to the river,
Thought that I would drown—"

She shushed him frantically, waving at him to knock it off, and she was relieved then to see him fighting for his balance, reeling backwards. And he fell flat into the water, sending up a shaggy plume of water into the new sun slanting in from the east. Watching him recover to start a lap down the length of the pool, Jerrie McKennan relaxed contentedly against the jamb of the door.

Turning away into the kitchen, she realized that she was about to cry, something she hadn't done since she was in the eighth grade.

The next hour moved all too quickly. They showered and dressed, and as he had promised, Joshua helped her with the breakfast, insisting on broiling the breakfast steaks on the patio gas barbecue. She fixed the eggs, fussing around the kitchen doing wifely kinds of things. With the food finally on the dinette table, Joshua belatedly suggested they eat on the patio.

"You're on some kind of outdoor kick this morning," Jerrie noted idly as she helped him move the food outside.

Joshua didn't answer and was quiet for the next few minutes until they were seated opposite each other across the redwood table. Jerrie remained silent while he started to eat, guessing that Joshua Bain might be slipping into one of his moods. A normal enough reaction for a man whose memory included the harsh and brutal reality of eighteen months confinement as a prisoner of war.

"You know it's just now starting to get hot here," Joshua was saying.

"Uh-huh," Jerrie agreed warily. Now in their second summer at the ranch, they both were well aware of the temperature averages.

"I understand," Joshua went on, "that it's tougher with the first baby. I mean, the morning sickness stuff," and he waved his fork, "and whatever."

"That's what they say."

Joshua was nodding as he methodically cut through his steak, eating it European style. "Last week, when I took the Avion up for the instrument check," he finally went on, "I made an unscheduled stop at the San Juan Capistrano airport."

Jerrie sat quietly, not eating, chewing on her lower lip instead, waiting for him to get to the point.

"While I was there," Joshua was saying, "I had a talk with a local real estate agent."

"So?"

"Well, I called him yesterday, and he's found a place down by the beach at Dana Point. He claims it's a dynamite unit—"

"I don't understand."

Joshua put his knife and fork down, looking directly at her for the first time. At that moment, Jerrie figured that the Joshua of old might have very well looked like the man sitting opposite her. Joshua Bain was not a strikingly handsome man. His cheeks were a little full, making him look years younger. But nonetheless in his swarthy face was an authority, a solemn, certain kind of countenance that suggested he knew precisely what he was doing. It was mostly in his eyes, she realized then, as she blinked once herself. When he wanted it to, like now, his stare could almost punch holes through someone. The indirect light falling on his face was from the darker western quarter of the sky, giving to his normally grey eyes an even lighter shade of blue. The contrast against his sun-darkened skin was vivid.

"Why don't you fly over there this morning?" Joshua was saying. "You need the solo time, anyway. Be good experience. And you can look at the place yourself."

"What for?"

"We can take it as a summer house."'

"Joshua, the baby isn't due for six months."

"I know, honey. But you know how this place is in the summer. The grapes are going to be coming in. The dust, gnats; it's really rough around here." He looked down to her plate. "You see, you haven't even touched your food."

And in his voice, too, she thought. The smooth, persuasive manner, so subtle that he could take your socks off without removing your shoes. He would make an incredible attorney, and, with an all-woman jury, baby, you'd never lose a case. "All right," she said reluctantly, "so how's it going to work? I mean, do we go down there together on weekends?" And she was frankly suspicious now, feeling her Irish obstinance.

"We can work that out later," Joshua said off-handedly, obviously evading the question.

Jerrie lowered her eyes, toyed briefly with her fork. "It had better work out so we're together."

Joshua was smiling now. "Fair enough," he said easily. He pulled his legs out from under the table. "I'll give you the broker's business card. He'll be at the airport at ten o'clock."

Jerrie sensed that she had just lost one sock. "You already had it arranged."

"No, I've got to call him."

She got up then, and they met at the end of the table. "I'm sorry," she said. "But you're not going to get rid of me that easily."

He kissed her hard.

"You know better than that," he told her then, his voice warm on her ear. "Besides, everyone knows that Irish red-heads are con-proof."

She pushed him away. "What's the schedule for this glorious morning?"

He turned to walk up to the edge of the pool, looking out across Rancho Canaan. "I've got to meet this guy at the Riverside Raceway at ten o'clock." He checked his watch. "He wants me to road test the car before we settle the deal."

"You're going to buy it, anyway."

He turned to face her, and his voice slipped an octave lower. "Oh, yeah. But he's asking five and I'm only offering four, so he wants to show it off, try to nail down the higher number."

"In the end," she suggested idly, "you'll probably pay whatever he asks."

"A correlation, then," he said softly, "between how badly

you want something and the price you're willing to pay for it," and, he too, was smiling now.

The small talk was less significant now, she thought as she moved toward him. Before, their being close was more of a game perhaps, a provincial intellectual exercise with each of them playing out a role. Of late, though, the role playing had diminished, and she caught herself thinking there was more truth than fiction to the notion that a man and a woman could in fact become as one.

It was as if he could read her thoughts, that she loved him so much. As she folded into his arms she shivered once, inexplicably.

"What's wrong?" he asked gently.

It worked both ways, she thought, not knowing what she really should say. She looked up to his face then, directly into his smoke-gray eyes. "Do you really understand that I'm carrying your child, Joshua Bain?"

Chuckling once, he laid her head down against his chest. "The baby will have flaming red hair," he mused softly. "It will be a girl, and when she gets older she'll have a patch of freckles across her nose, just like her mother."

"No, it'll be a boy."

He chuckled once again, and with her ear on his chest the sound was a deep resonant roll of thunder in the early spring over the desert. "You think I'm taking it all too seriously," she said then.

"Not half as serious as I am," he assured her.

"So why do we have to go to Dana Point? Or, anyplace, for that matter?"

"You're taking advantage of me at a weak moment," he complained.

Relaxing against him, she elected to let the matter pass for the moment. It was possible, after all, she conceded to herself, that Joshua was just concerned about her health.

Joshua left for Riverside at a little past nine o'clock, after calling Dana Point to firm up the realtor's meeting with Jerrie. He took the Ford station wagon, one of the two company vehicles owned by the ranch; the other, a GMC pick-up, was used by Alan Hunt, the handyman and only other person living on the ranch. Jerrie was left with their vintage Plymouth sedan, one of the few relics remaining from their Berkeley days, which she could use to drive to the nearby Bermuda Dunes Airport.

It took him only a few minutes to make the Highway 10 Freeway connection. As he turned northbound, Jerrie's remark that "you're not going to get rid of me that easily," lingered warmly and affectionately in his mind. The trauma and hysteria of Berkeley was more than a year in their past now. But the memories went down hard. So much so that they both were having difficulty in finally accepting the peace of Rancho Canaan.

It had been reasonable to assume, up until a few days ago, that they were about to pull it off. Rancho Canaan was a reality not even she could deny.

It was as though their sheer power of love for each other had finally overcome even her skepticism, so that by her own admission, "We've gone beyond just being lovers."

The remarkable conversion of a liberated free-spirit to "a righteous kind of heavy one-on-one relationship."

If you only knew, angel.

And they now even had the marriage license to prove it.

Enter Cleve Lambert.

The Piper come to collect.

So the correlation still held. A high positive shot, really.

And there was indeed no price too high for this package, especially a lousy one-year lease on a beach house at Dana Point.

He angrily slammed the steering wheel with his right fist, frustrated because he knew he could not tell her about his undercover role and the danger it likely would soon involve. She would never leave. Not without trauma. Not without risking a relapse into the old way of dealing with her hang-ups. He sighed heavily then, shaking his head to clear his mind once more, and in a few moments he was thinking ahead, out beyond the present reality to the time when he would have paid his debt. The dream was a recurring one, of Joshua Bain and his family at peace.

As she finished cleaning off the patio table, Jerrie McKennan realized she had to accept the miracle of their being together, of Joshua's position as resident manager of Rancho Canaan, which she understood would ultimately become their own. She was delighted to see Joshua interested in the racing car because there was simply not enough around the forty-acre ranch to keep him busy, since all the producing acreage was leased out to a local cooperative. With one full-time handyman to help him, Joshua actually spent only about an hour a day fussing around the grounds.

She pulled up in the kitchen, shaking her head, once again perplexed by the whole arrangement. And all Joshua would tell her, or could tell her, perhaps, was that it was all via the pleasure of a mysterious benefactor, Calvin Price. Her intuition told her that Britt Halley was also involved. In the many times she and Joshua had been to the Halley estate, Jerrie had on each occasion become more suspicious that the widow Halley enjoyed the close company of Joshua Bain.

She was startled out of her thoughts by the ringing of the telephone, which she answered, using the kitchen wall phone. The man's voice on the other end informed her that there was a large package marked perishable and addressed to the ranch waiting to be picked up at the ETC receiving dock at Indio, and would she please pass the message to the foreman as soon as possible. As she hung up, Jerrie was smiling to herself, thinking that Alan Hunt, the resident jack-of-all-trades, must be passing himself off as the "foreman" among the local merchants. Already dressed in her white flight suit, she checked her watch to see she still had nearly twenty minutes before leaving for the airport. She was on a special kind of high now, a little excited, as she looked forward to her solo flight to the coast.

Outside and on her way to the barn, she was conscious of the day's already fierce heat, conceding for a passing moment that maybe Joshua was right about taking the place at Dana Point. Inside the barn, she moved directly to the tack room, Alan Hunt's spartan living quarters. The door was ajar, as usual, and she peeked inside to see he wasn't there. She now rejected the assumption that Alan Hunt could be passing himself off as the ranch's foreman; the pretense was too much out of the man's character. Like many other things connected with the ranch, Alan Hunt didn't seem to fit. He regularly trounced both her and Joshua at Fan-Tan, displayed Olympic style at ten-meter board diving, politely but firmly refused strong drink of any kind. And, in addition to praying regularly over his food before eating, the usually composed Alan Hunt always managed to thoroughly disrupt Joshua's concentration at nine-ball by quoting scripture in a manner and with a relish suggesting imminent judgment upon them all. Such was his edge on the pool table.

Returning to the barn's open front door, she knew there was the more serious side to Alan Hunt, that underlying and more profound part of him totally committed to Jesus Christ, as he once had described it. That part of him that apparently was at peace. Like the Jesus people who used to accost her at Berkeley, who now, in retrospect, had possessed a sureness of personal conviction. She remembered, too, being angry with them, resenting their tranquillity and their peace. But she could not now imagine herself being angry with Alan Hunt, nor resenting him in any way. She supposed that her affection for the man derived from the understanding that he too was struggling as she had had to do, and though they were poles apart in their method, they were close together in their hopes and dreams.

She finally located Alan in the shady lee of the barn, tinkering with something under the upraised hood of the GMC pickup truck.

"The top of the morning to you, ma'am," Alan offered, standing away from the truck. No more than a couple inches taller than she, Alan Hunt was athletically slender, with the classic build of a swimmer, and he was now dressed only in shorts, barefoot as usual, wrench in hand. He was smiling broadly, embarrassed. He wore his straight black hair longer than Joshua's.

There was something purely comical about Alan Hunt, as inscrutable and as typical a Cahuilla Indian as could be found in the entire Coachella Valley, trying to make with the Irish brogue.

"And the same to you, sir," she replied, smiling to herself now. She gave him the brief message from the receiving dock.

"Perishable, huh?"

"That's what the man said."

Alan had been carefully wiping off the wrench on his weathered shorts. "It won't last long in this heat, then, if it's sitting on the dock. Kind of strange, though. We usually don't get freight on Monday. Must've come in air express." He shoved the wrench in his back pocket, wiped his hands on his shorts. "I think I've got this thing fixed; it shouldn't take me more than twenty minutes."

Jerrie nodded. "Take your time; I'm leaving for the airport anyway."

Back in the comfortable coolness of the refrigerated house, Jerrie heard the truck leave. Alan Hunt was a very careful man of his word, which meant he would be back in precisely twenty minutes. She shut down the kitchen, moving then leisurely through the other rooms, turning out lights, closing drapes. Almost ready to leave herself, she idly pulled her billfold out of her purse, checking it before slipping it into the right thigh pocket of the flight suit. Flying was Joshua's first love, and they did a lot of it together now, especially since they could use the ETC Avion at almost any time. If it were not for the time Joshua spent at the airport, he would be climbing the walls by now for sure. It had been a successful part of her own therapy, learning to fly. And, being with him was important now, and she wondered what more she could do to make him understand.

In the master bedroom, she moved to his night stand to turn off the lamp. Joshua's Bible was open. Curious, she looked more closely at the page. Solomon's Song. An odd name for a book of the Bible. The underlined verse caught her eye:

> Let us get up early to the vineyards;
> let us see if the vine flourish,
> whether the tender grape appear,
> and the pomegranates bud forth:
> there will I give thee my loves.

She turned the corner of the page before closing the Book, thinking she would later on copy the verse down and have it put on a plaque. Yes, he would like that. The Bible had been a gift from Alan on Joshua's last birthday, and Jerrie was not sure of her feelings over the fact that Joshua had of late started reading it. She had for too many years ridiculed the notion of any kind of god, living or otherwise, and she remembered then that she had once condemned love, too, as another kind of opiate. And, especially, marriage.

She closed her eyes, compressed her lips into a tight angry line, resenting the fact that the Book under her hand had opened the door just enough to let that part of her past start to seep through. She pulled the image of Joshua into focus, his face, his whole being. The present. So forget the rest, woman. She felt herself starting to relax. After turning off the light, she remained a moment longer, stroking the Book's grained cover, holding the picture of Joshua in her mind against the backdrop of the room's darkness.

The front doorbell chimed once.

She came out of her thoughts abruptly.

Irritated at someone's poor timing, she hurried to the front door, checking to make sure she had her car keys. Opening the door, she stopped short, putting her right hand to her throat in a defensive gesture.

She stared uncomprehendingly, only sensing that coming at her with the morning's heat were harsh and unwelcome memories of a time she desperately wanted to forget.

He was alone, smiling slightly. The long hair, stringing past his shoulders, a black headband keeping it back away from his eyes. Sleeveless shirt, gaudy. Dirty, well-worn denim trousers. Barefoot.

"You've changed," he said easily, shifting his feet, lifting his hands to his slender hips. "You've put on weight."

"Tony Seastrom!" Jerrie exclaimed, her voice now carefully controlled. "What in the world?"

"A couple of us drove down to help out," and he jerked his thumb toward the sedan parked off the driveway. "You know, the Huelga fight." He was smiling broadly now, showing his bad teeth. "In the fields, sister, like it used to be."

"Oh, no, Tony," Jerrie started to explain, "I'm just on my way to the airport, something very important and—"

"No sweat," he said. "Couple of friends in the car; we thought you could pass us out something cool, you know."

"Hey, come on," she said reassuringly. "Bring 'em in. You guys can live it up here until I get back."

Gesturing for the other two people to come in, Tony Seastrom took a tentative step inside the house, stopping astride the door jamb. "Looks like the fat of the lamb," he said good-naturedly, surveying what he could see of the house. "Is it all yours?"

"Not exactly," Jerrie replied, seeing the couple now walking onto the porch.

Seastrom stepped inside. "Are you sure it's all right?" he said cordially. "I mean, like leaving us all alone?"

"No problem," she again reassured him. "The man who works for us will be back in a few minutes anyway. Just tell him you're friends of mine."

Following Jerrie toward the recreation room, Tony Seastrom introduced the two strangers: Fred Bingston, white male, age about twenty-eight. A big man, heavy boned, dense hair tightly curled, sallow complexion, small brown eyes widely spaced and out of proportion to his heavy flaccid face. The woman was introduced as his wife, Sara Bingston. Black female, age about twenty-two. Heavy full Afro hair style. Slender, slight build, flat chested. Face narrow, thin. Her expression was guarded, sober. Despite the July desert heat, both were unaccountably dressed in the familiar black leather jackets and matching pants.

"That's far enough!" Sara Bingston snapped, shattering the easy silence of the closed-up house.

Almost to the patio door, Jerrie turned around slowly, facing the trio. She studied the group for another moment, and then realized that the Bingstons were not the type to stand up in the fields. They were soldiers of a different sort. "What's going on, Tony?" she demanded quietly. The sliding glass door behind her was locked on her side, and she calculated that she'd never get it open in time.

Tony Seastrom was moving away now, back toward the front door. "I've done my part," he said nervously over his shoulder, and he was gone.

Fred Bingston stood still in the middle of the room, his right hip near the pool table. Sweating heavily, he was obviously uncomfortable in the heavy leather gear. As he reached into his outside jacket pocket, Sara Bingston moved sideways to block the kitchen entry. Fred Bingston now had what looked like a small 3 x 5 card in his hand.

"You are Jerrie McKennan," he said in a monotone a scale or two higher than would be expected of a man his size. "Also known as Nita while in the service of the People's Army, the Weathermen for Action and Revolution?"

Jerrie knew her only chance now would be to stall them until Alan returned. "You talk like you should be guarding a harem," she said, trying to put all the contempt she could into her voice.

Fred Bingston lurched forward, a look of rage on his fat face. At the same time, he reached under his leather jacket.

"Read it, Fred!" Sara Bingston shrilled at him.

He pulled up three feet short of Jerrie, who simply stared at him with a look of contempt and disgust.

Wavering under Jerrie's glare, he brought the small card back up to eye level, not bothering to conceal the eight-inch switch blade in his right hand. "We are directed to hereby inform you," he said in a formal, falsetto voice, "that on Friday last, July 6th, before a duly convened People's Court, you were tried in absentee . . . " and he faltered, causing Sara Bingston to step in close enough to snatch the card away from him. Stuffing the black-bordered card in her purse, she pulled out a small pressure spray can, handed it to him. Her voice was harsh, "Get on with it."

Fred Bingston lumbered to the nearest wall, shaking the can clumsily.

"All right, Nita," Sara Bingston said formally to Jerrie, "you have been tried and convicted by the People's Court. The charge says that you ratted on your special action group, causing the death of one of your brother soldiers as well as permitting the escape of a political prisoner."

Jerrie McKennan stared on through her, as if absorbed with a more distant object.

"The sentence is death by execution."

Fred Bingston had finished, and he turned heavily back toward Jerrie, leaving behind him on the opposite beige wall the three-foot-high black letters, "WAR" above the word, "TRAITOR." Pushing the spray can into his companion's hand, he shoved her roughly aside. He popped the switch blade, the knife held low at hip level.

"Punishment time!" he said shrilly.

"Kill her!" Sara ordered. "We're running outa time."

"Time to show you who the man is," he said thickly. "Take off the fancy suit, redhead."

Sara grabbed his arm. "Get to it, you sadist!"

"Don't push him," Jerrie said calmly, her eyes coming back into closer focus. "You see, this pervert can't go any other way," and she grinned at him. "Isn't that right, jelly-belly?"

Fred Bingston exploded with a siren-like scream, lashing out with the knife, the scalpel-sharp blade arcing across the narrowing distance between them.

At the same moment, Tony Seastrom was in the driver's seat of the car. He had had the engine idling for the past few minutes, waiting impatiently in the stifling heat. He got out now, leaving the engine running, to start up the incline toward the front door. As he hit the higher elevation of the porch, he glanced out toward the front of the property. He was astonished to see a car at the entrance to the long access road!

He delayed another second, his heart thumping wildly. The car was a Caddie, one of those black limo jobs, but it wasn't really moving. Just parked on an angle off the main road.

He punched through the front door, resolved that the two executioners had about five seconds to run with him, or they were on their own. He was compelled to give them the chance because he knew otherwise that his name might very well appear next on a black-bordered 3 x 5 card.

Chapter two

It was pushing early afternoon before Joshua could get away from the raceway. Moving south toward Indio on Highway 10, he was still caught up in the excitement of road testing the Jaguar. They had finally settled on a purchase price of forty-seven hundred for the car, after haggling for over an hour, and Joshua was satisfied that he had made a good deal. He had paid for the car with a check drawn against his and Jerrie's joint checking account, and he figured he would put the coupe in both their names. He had managed recently to quietly shift all their assets into both their names. A useful precaution, considering the way things were developing. Passing the Highway 111 turn-off for Palm Springs, he checked the road behind him as he slowly pushed the wagon up to seventy miles per hour.

He was anxious to get back to the ranch, wanting to get Jerrie's reaction to the Dana Point house. She had to get out now, he thought again. The gut feel. Cleve Lambert had set him straight a long time ago. *Act on the gut feel like you would on a written order from headquarters! That inner feeling is a valid response. We are each like a computer. We receive, we store, we analyze, and we read out. And the brain sorts and arranges all its input, both because of its tendency for orderliness as well as ultimately to help its carrier survive. Thus, once in a while we experience a readout that we haven't consciously called for. It seems to come through the belly. And I don't care if you think it's coming from your tail, you act, and quickly! You'll save your neck or bust a case wide open.*

Gut feel, sixth sense, or whatever, Joshua knew he had to move Jerrie away from the ranch and all he was presently involved with. His own priorities now tempted him to walk away from Cleve Lambert, the ETC, the whole lousy game.

But his conscience refused him that simple way out.

So, he would compromise. First, he had to get Jerrie out of the danger zone. With the baby coming, he had justification to satisfy any ETC curiosity. He could then more efficiently carry out his penetration, perhaps hurry it up by months. Besides, with Jerrie away during the week, at least, it would be easier for him to do what he had to do with Britt Halley; he would rather take another route, but with the heat from Lambert, the apparent urgency now—

Preoccupied, he didn't notice the police car until it was right on top of his rear end. Disgusted with his carelessness, he obediently pulled over to the side of the freeway. The uniformed deputy sheriff was beside the door before Joshua could get his wallet out.

"Your name Bain?" the deputy asked him in a surprisingly cordial tone.

"Yes, sir. Joshua Bain."

"Follow me and stick close," the deputy told him, wheeling immediately back toward the patrol car.

Joshua thought he should be demanding to know what was going on, but before he could collect himself the patrol car careened around him, blazing off down the highway toward Indio, its siren wailing. Joshua started the wagon, snapped it into low drive. With the gas pedal on the floor, he sideslipped off the sandy shoulder to steady out on the pavement, wishing for a passing moment that he had the Jag under him.

In just under ten minutes, he was escorted into the manager's office of the Bermuda Dunes Airport.

Joshua imagined the worst. Coming in, he had already noticed that the Avion wasn't in its usual tie-down place next to the ETC hangar. The blood pounded in his temples. He saw Britt Halley standing next to the desk, and he vaguely noticed that it was a business hour for her, yet she was informally dressed in white sailcloth, hip-hugging pants. Powder-blue midriff, matching sandals. Even in her casual clothes, Britt Halley was still a disarmingly beautiful woman. Shorter than Jerrie by two or three inches, she was more delicate in her features, her slender tanned face the work of an artist concerned with fine detail. She looked at Joshua inquiringly, her almond brown eyes expressive of some inner strain. Now, with her mouth slightly open, her full lower lip moved as if she was about to speak.

Seeing that Britt was there, Joshua hoped that maybe Jerrie had had mechanical trouble and was stuck at Capistrano, and maybe he was going to get chewed out for authorizing the flight. But Jeff Capstan, the airport manager, looked grim.

Britt Halley had felt her own respiration quicken as Joshua entered the room. She tried to speak now, but one look at Joshua's stricken face caused her to back down.

"What's happened to Jerrie?" Joshua asked evenly.

Britt looked aside to Jeff Capstan, who was biting on his lower lip, running his fingertips in an apparent unfeeling path over his desk blotter.

"I'm sorry," Jeff finally offered, his voice barely audible, "but we have it confirmed that the Avion—" His voice broke once, and he had to clear his throat "—that the Avion went in at about seven thousand feet."

"She crashed?" exclaimed Joshua incredulously.

"Yes, she did, Josh," Jeff went on. "About a thousand feet below the summit of Mount Diablo, at ten-o-five hours," and his voice was more authoritative now.

Joshua had his head down now, his left hand over his eyes, as if he was trying to escape or ward off a blinding light.

"It's true, Joshua," Britt confirmed, surprised at her own voice. "I sent the helicopter up myself. Gino was over the crash site for ten minutes."

Joshua finally looked up. "Any chance she could've survived?"

"None whatsoever," Jeff told him gently. "She must've impacted at full cruising speed, right into a tight vee," and he sighed heavily before adding, "It's a total burn."

"Yeah," Joshua commented slackly. "I was always telling her to be sure to take off with full tanks," and his voice trailed off.

"Gino tried to set down," Britt said, "but the terrain was so bad he had to give up."

Joshua was nodding now, pulling himself more upright, obviously trying to compose himself, and Britt wanted desperately to console him. She too was fighting for control of herself now, knowing she must be careful in how she responded to this morning's events.

"What about Jerrie?" Joshua said slowly. "I mean, how do we get her out?"

"A rescue team from Idyllwild," Jeff told him. "The coroner will handle the details."

"What happened, Jeff?" Joshua asked then, his voice now almost back to normal.

"We don't know. I made a quick check with operations, but we had no hint of any trouble from the time she took off until we received the flash from the forest service people. Her initial heading was visually toward the coast. Take-off normal. No radio transmission, nothing."

"The forest service?" Joshua said idly.

"Yes; one of their lookouts spotted the fire almost as soon as it happened."

Joshua nodded he understood. "The FAA, now, I guess," he noted under his breath.

"Yes," Jeff said. "They will investigate it thoroughly, and I imagine they will want to talk to you."

"Good," said Joshua. "Because I'm gonna want to talk to them."

Britt Halley eyed him a little more closely now, searching for some further meaning in his last statement. She knew Joshua Bain to be a man of intense curiosity, and she supposed that was the motive behind his remark.

"I guess there's nothing more I can do here," Joshua was saying. He extended his right hand to Jeff Capstan. "Thanks. You've been helpful and considerate."

Britt followed him out the door and down the hallway to the entrance. Outside in the intense heat, she caught up to his elbow. "Please, Joshua," she said carefully, "let me drive you back to the ranch."

He pulled up. "I'd rather be by myself."

"You will be, but I must talk to you first," she insisted. "It's very important, otherwise I wouldn't ask."

He shrugged. "All right," following her to the Mercedes limo. She handed him the keys. As they pulled onto Jefferson Street, heading south, Britt also remained silent, arranging her thoughts. She realized she was nearly exhausted now, after a most trying morning.

"What's so important?" Joshua asked.

"I placed a call to Calvin from the airport," Britt began. "You know, Joshua, that Calvin Price cares a good deal for you, and he'll be calling you later on. And, he agrees with me that you must now keep busy, get moving, be active."

"What am I supposed to do," Joshua said, a tinge of sarcasm in his voice, "take up needlepoint?"

"As of tonight," Britt went on, "you will be nominated to the council as an elder." She looked aside to his profile, expecting at least some reaction but he continued to stare forward, his eyes narrowed against the sunlight.

"Did you hear me?" she finally asked.

"Yes, and I'm sorry. My mind was wandering." He turned his head briefly to look squarely at her, a small smile touching the corners of his mouth. "That's quite a surprise," he said then, turning back to the roadway. "I'm deeply impressed."

They turned right on Avenue 52 toward La Quinta and the ranch. Britt was encouraged by his apparent quick return to normal, that he seemed to be taking Jerrie's death in stride. Or, as it then occurred to her, Joshua Bain might have an exceptional ability to mask his feelings, and she was aware that she too was playing a hiding game of sorts herself, that her interest in him was far more personal than professional. She moved away from the door, a little closer to him.

"Well, then," she said cheerfully, "that's my contribution."

"What's next?"

Good, she thought. The snappy reaction. And she braced herself as they swung into the long access road leading to the ranch house. "You'll be busy for the next few weeks. As soon as we can arrange it, you'll start on a crash training program. You'll be screened by the executive committee. Have to undergo some routine tests." She had been studying him closely, noticing the easy, confident way he handled the car, thinking he was some kind of latent machine. "You can handle it," she reassured him affectionately as they pulled in to park beside the house. She looked aside to see Alan Hunt standing in the open front doorway. "You must keep this to yourself," she cautioned him. "If Calvin or anyone mentions this, please act surprised."

"I understand," Joshua said warmly.

There was an awkward moment as Joshua turned off the ignition, set the handbrake. Britt put her left hand on his shoulder, unable to keep from touching him any longer. "I'm truly sorry," she said. "What can I do? I have some pills."

"No; I'm all right now," he assured her, taking her hand from his shoulder, holding it briefly. "You've done enough." He pressed the back of her hand to his cheek before placing it on the console between them. He got out then, to stand by the open door.

"Can you get back okay?"

"I can take Alan to the airport," she suggested, "to pick up your car. Gino can follow him back in the other one."

Joshua hesitated, as if he had forgotten about Jerrie's car. Closing the door, he told her he would send Alan right out.

Moving up the easy incline to the front porch, Joshua Bain felt as if he was scaling some far steeper slope. His legs were weary, and he felt spent, dragged out, beaten down. Stepping aside to give him room, Alan Hunt looked like a man who had just been kicked in the solar plexis, the lines in his face drawn tight by the inner pain, and Joshua was briefly taken back by the obviously heartfelt reaction of the man whom they really hardly knew at all. He also saw that Alan Hunt had his Bible in his hand.

Not now, Joshua thought numbly. He moved away unsteadily into the living room, thankful that Alan had said nothing. He noticed the odor in the air then.

"What's the smell?" he asked indifferently.

"Paint," Alan explained. "The recreation room. She . . . she wanted me to have it finished before you got back."

Joshua accepted the explanation without a second thought. Jerrie had done such things regularly to surprise him. A new piece of furniture, a picture. And plaques; she had been addicted to immortalizing their favorite sayings. He fumbled in his pockets, looking for his car keys, remembering then that in his hurrying at the airport he must've left them in the Ford. He turned to Alan. "Would you mind going back to the airport with Mrs. Halley?"

"Of course not."

"Bring the Ford back; the keys should be in the ignition. There's a spare key on the ring for the Plymouth. Give it to Gino."

"Nothing else you need?"

Joshua shook his head no. He watched numbly while Alan moved through the door, closing it behind him carefully. Joshua stood stock still in the middle of the room, at a complete loss as to which way he should turn. Thinking for a frightening moment that she would come walking into the room, he moved mechanically into the recreation room to the bar behind the pool table. The heavy, oily smell of enamel was over-whelming, and he saw that Alan had been able to finish only the one long opposite wall. Green. The Kelly variety. That figured. And he felt his eyes starting to burn. He took a half dozen lemons out of the small bar refrigerator. With a full quart of tequila under his arm, he detoured through the kitchen to pick up a salt shaker.

On the patio, he stopped to look down the length of the swimming pool, and there was something inevitable forming in his throat as he remembered back just a few hours.

Why, he asked inside. Why?

It didn't make any kind of sense at all.

He lifted his eyes to the nearby barren mountains, now burnt greyish brown, on up to the even more implacable bleak, thin summer sky. "She had everything to live for, God," he said haltingly, feeling his anger finally at this most inexplicable injustice. "Don't you hear me, God!" And a thermal breeze moved across Rancho Canaan, rustling the upper mantle of vine leaves to touch the pool's surface. "It doesn't make any sense!" and he was screaming hoarsely, forcing the air out his tightening throat, and he kicked savagely at the nearest patio chair, sending it crashing into the heavy redwood table.

His rage gave way as quickly as it had begun, and Joshua Bain stood in the fierce afternoon heat, broken to his core by some force or some thing he did not understand, only that his tears were hot on his face, that he was staggering blindly in some direction of escape, until after a while he realized in a kind of daze that he was down on his knees somewhere in the rows of grapevines. Wiping his nose, he turned clumsily into the nearest shade, sitting now in the sandy Coachella loam. He had lost his lemons and salt, but he still had the bottle, which he opened. Taking a long scalding drink, he told himself that he would force himself to forget, for a while anyway.

Chapter three

On Wednesday morning, early, the radio-dispatched message caught Cleve Lambert just minutes after he had pulled away from his west Los Angeles apartment. Terminating with "Claypool," the terse message included only a telephone number and the words, "urgent and confidential." On his way to his downtown office, Lambert drove slowly past the intersection to the shopping center in the next block, where he pulled in beside a pair of empty pay phones. The name Claypool had been the AKA used by Jerome Mason at the LAX meeting. Getting out of his car, Lambert realized he didn't recognize the telephone number, beyond the more obvious fact of its area code, which told him it could be from Washington. Using his credit card number, he asked for the number station-to-station.

Jerome Mason came on the line after one ring.

Lambert quickly identified himself.

"Where are you?" Mason asked him.

"Pay phone."

"Good," Mason told him. "I'm on a secure phone in Bill Morrison's office, and we're on tape."

It disturbed Cleve Lambert to know that the Director of the Bureau had to resort to a CIA telephone in order to guarantee a clean line.

"The subject is the ETC Corporation," Mason was saying mechanically.

Cleve Lambert was not at all surprised.

"Last Friday," Mason went on, "after our LAX meeting and upon my return to Washington from Chicago, I began a preliminary top secret and fully guarded investigation based on your report re Senator Bradford Turner and the ETC. To minimize compromise, I conducted the bulk of this investigation myself. I brought in just one man to help, Ben Caplan from Dick Martinson's section."

Lambert listened with an impatient ear, convinced that the higher one got in the Bureau the longer it took him to get to the point.

"We checked out the registries on the Lear jets reported by Anzio," Mason finally began to explain. "Also started name and background check on all persons listed as being associated with the ETC. And, you were correct in assuming that the upper end of the organization is staffed by some high-powered and influential people. Adding in and using what Ben had already accumulated, we are now also of the opinion that there is much more going on within the secret level than we had earlier suspected." There was a following pause.

"What about syndicate connections?"

"That was also Ben's first reaction when he first started snooping last year. However, he had been very reliably able to determine no connection with major crime or criminal elements. In fact, the ETC publicly has been heavily anti-crime, even active in supporting general law enforcement."

"Could be a smoke screen."

"Anything's possible," Mason replied, "but we are for the time being ruling out syndicate activity."

"So it's either out of the country or it's political," Lambert surmised half aloud.

"Ben Caplan suspected it was political because of Senator Turner, so I let him run with it a couple days ago. He started out with the same profile as Turner and ran it across several other personages who had died recently either by natural causes or by accident."

Realizing the circumstances of the telephone meeting, the urgency and secrecy, Cleve Lambert was prepared for the next comment.

"By noon yesterday, Ben had turned two probables out of the six or seven that he checked," Mason told him. "By midnight last night he had confirmed the first."

"So I was right," Lambert exclaimed under his breath.

"Score one for your trusty gut," Mason went on. "You recall Professor William Hadden?"

"Yeah, the China expert. Pacifist type, the one who led the demonstration at the Pentagon a few years back."

"And he fits the profile on significant points. Enjoyed left-wing support, very popular with liberals, but we'll get to that later."

"He died of some disease," Lambert said, "about six months ago."

"After he was nominated and confirmed as ambassador to China."

"After a senate fight."

"But he was confirmed," said Mason. "And, prior to departing the country, he underwent the usual overseas vaccination series, which included typhoid fever. Two days later, he keeled over in his office, and he subsequently died of complications attributed to massive typhoid infection. It was a fairly routine prognosis."

"Wasn't there some stink raised about the vaccination procedure, its safeguards, or something?"

"Yes, but it petered out, because that kind of thing is expected to occur once in every so many thousands of cases. Hadden was a feisty, independent character, and he was thought to have just waited too long to report the reaction."

There was a pause, and Lambert waited, figuring he could already fill in the gist of what had to follow.

"At any rate," Mason continued, "his case got our attention because his old apartment is less than five miles from here. His widow moved out two weeks ago, and the place is still empty. Ben hit it with everything. He scored in the bathroom. In the P-trap under the sink. Typhoid bacteria. The specimens taken from the P-trap showed without exception traces of a benign sodium fluoride derivative."

"Toothpaste!" Lambert interjected.

"So simple, it's appalling," Mason noted. "The lab has enough to figure the killers chemically neutralized a commercial toothpaste, treated it with supportive nutrients, then packed it with enough active typhoid bacteria to knock down an army. The wife, as expected, used her own brand of toothpaste."

How utterly bizarre, Lambert thought, yet so practical. Professor Hadden stuck his toothbrush in his mouth one morning and thereby ingested the equivalent of one Hong Kong cesspool. He drew a deep reflective breath. "But it's the same as with Turner," he heard himself saying. "There isn't a thing we can prove conclusively beyond the probable fact that he was murdered."

"Evidence, Cleve, remember."

"Yes, sir."

"You've got just two weeks."

Two weeks, Lambert repeated disbelievingly to himself.

Mason didn't allow a lengthy pause to develop. "While Ben Caplan was doing his thing for the past few days," he said gravely, "I was out doing some digging myself. The ultimate owners of those three executive jets you reported come right out of the top ten of this country's wealthiest families. And, while I haven't got the time to report what I've collected, I can tell you that it's enough to escalate my attitude from one of suspicion to actual incrimination. But, to this point, it's all circumstantial." He then allowed a meaningful pause to develop. "Do you get the picture, Cleve?"

"I think so."

"Either you score in two weeks or I move a task force in.

Ben Caplan thinks we should go that way right now."

"Just keep him off my back."

"For two weeks."

Fourteen days to score, Lambert was thinking.

"I've got to know," Mason insisted; "what are you doing?"

"I'll type out a complete schedule as soon as I get to the office. An original only. I'll use Burt Ingstrom."

"He's the resident at March Air Force Base."

"Right. I'll manacle the report to his wrist myself. There's a daily courier flight from the base at oh-nine-hundred hours each morning for the Pentagon. You can either meet him there or at Andrews."

"Give me some basics now."

"As of the last couple of days," Lambert began after a moment, "things are breaking well, and we should be turning the location of the records soon, a week at the outside, hopefully. As to getting them out, who knows, sir. Two weeks isn't much time." And he's thinking worriedly that it's been two full days since he had last heard from Joshua Bain, even though that too had been expected.

"Don't blow it now," Mason was saying. "If they get onto us, they either destroy the records or else bury them so deep it'd take an army of moles a hundred years—"

"We're as airtight as we can be on this end," Lambert assured him pointedly, and there was a following pause. Lambert figured his boss had the message that if there was a leak, it would have to come from the Washington end.

"Now you understand," Mason finally said, "why I'm going direct to the old man himself."

Only once before could he remember feeling so unalterably horrible, when he had experienced firsthand the punishment a human body and soul could withstand before the numbness set in: a combination of bacillary dysentery, jungle fever, crushed ribs, broken right arm, and the debilitating humiliation of knowing he had fallen into the hands of the enemy.

He opened his eyes, which felt as if they were breaded in cracker crumbs.

There was light about him, not much, but some, and he was satisfied he was at least still alive. He turned his head slightly to the right.

An oriental face?

And he closed his eyes, not moving, fearful for a passing

moment that if he reached out he might touch bamboo bars.

"Welcome to Rancho Canaan," Alan Hunt observed somberly.

The familiar voice was a trigger opening the gate inside his mind, and he remained still for a moment longer, sorting out the torrent of released thoughts. "Would you believe," he mumbled hoarsely, "you scared the hell out of me."

"A worthwhile catharsis," Alan said slowly, "but that kind of hell has a way of returning quickly, hoping the premises have been tidied up." He looked away reflectively. "I wonder if any of us in this life will ever admit we've had the 'heaven' scared out of us."

Joshua chuckled once, then groaned. He sat up on the couch, turned to put his feet on the floor, looking around to confirm they were in the living room. Gravity relieved the throbbing in his head only momentarily, and he clasped his hands to his temples. "How long has it been?" he whispered.

"About thirty-six hours."

His mind in some semblance of order now, Joshua was wishing it were thirty-six days. So, today must be Wednesday. While the memory of the day before yesterday was a little fuzzy, a little remote, it was still with him. He looked at Alan, who was sitting near his knee on the ottoman. "She is really gone, isn't she?" he said bleakly. "I mean, you're going to have to tell me that."

Alan Hunt spoke in the same placid manner as the expression on his face. "Yes, my friend, she is gone."

Joshua stared blankly across the room. "It happened so quickly, without any warning."

"It's in the nature of calamity to surprise its victims."

"The sage saying of one's tribal ancestor?"

"Hardly," Alan answered good-naturedly. "I'm told the saying is consigned to a WASP missionary neck deep in the Yunan at flood stage, there to escape a cloud of locusts."

That was characteristic of Alan Hunt, Joshua noted to himself. His quickness, both in body and mind, especially in countermoves, as if he might have trained himself in such an art form.

"Where is she?" Joshua asked.

"At the county morgue, in Riverside."

Joshua pushed himself unsteadily to his feet, vaguely aware of the mess he was in. He could smell himself as he unfolded to stand up. "You got the address?" he asked, and he felt his weight shifting to his right and he tried to move his feet to catch up. Alan was on his feet, supporting him by his right arm.

"Don't go there today," he warned him.

Joshua pulled away, his own eyes narrowing.

"You were in the war," Alan went on gently. "You know what it's like after a bad wreck. And believe me, this was one of the worst."

Yeah, Joshua was thinking. The rubber bag bit, with what they could find of her. "I want some answers," he said then, "and that's as good a place as any to start."

"Use the telephone."

Of course, Joshua thought confusedly. That was the logical thing to do. Feeling his belly starting to knot up, Joshua sensed he couldn't cope with the situation. He fell back heavily onto the couch, his mind tumbling aimlessly and in the jumbled montage were the close intimate visions of Jerrie pulsing in and out. Pulling listlessly on his chin with his right hand, he felt his anger rising again.

"Tell me, Alan Hunt," he said accusingly, "how could your God let it happen?"

Alan grunted after a moment, a little more appreciatively than Joshua liked. "It is natural at a time like this," Alan proposed carefully, "to ask about the Lord's role in the situation, maybe even to blame Him."

"Don't con me with double talk," Joshua said harshly. "If you can't give Him a proper defense—"

"Don't ever ask me to defend the Lord," Alan told him, his voice heavy with a surprising note of authority.

"All right," said Joshua just as sternly, "so you're copping out."

Alan took a deep breath through his nose, exhaled slowly. "So you want it straight, huh. Okay, for starters, it's a common enough known fact, a general law really, that no two objects can occupy the same space at the same time. Even a small child learns that lesson soon enough when he falls out of a tree and hits the ground." He held up his right hand. "This hand and this table cannot occupy the same space at the same time," and he slapped his hand on the coffee table for emphasis. "We can say with gratitude that the Lord has given us this law, as a product of His creative genius. We know about it, don't we? Well, don't we?"

Joshua nodded once, waiting.

"So is it God's fault when *we choose* to flaunt that law?" and Alan paused briefly on the rhetorical question. "Joshua, we both know that *a person* tried to fly that airplane through Mount Diablo. Was the Lord's hand really on the controls? Either deliberately or through carelessness, *a person* arranged the circumstances. Can you really blame God? I mean, after all, you can hold God responsible for the pure physics of the collision, but, my friend, I'm afraid you're copping out if you look to Him for the liability of arranging it."

Joshua's mouth had compressed into an obstinate thin line. "I can accept that kind of logic," he finally said, "but you know that's not what I'm driving at."

Alan had shifted his weight on the ottoman, turned his head to stare down at the carpeted floor. "I guess I can only answer for myself," he said softly. "You see, up until a little over a year ago, nothing made any sense to me either. Oh, I put up a good enough front, made it look like I was really flying high. You know, the good-time bit, the glad hand, the big smile, the good humor." He shook his head then. "But it was mostly put on, an act, and not a very good one at that." He chuckled then under his breath. "Worst of all, I didn't even realize how much of an actor I really was. After a while, after you've pretended so much for so long, it all becomes natural to you, so that you start believing in the role you're playing. And, of course, I was doing it all on my own. I was the master of my own fate. I was calling the shots." He paused, looking out the front bay window, out across the lawn to the rows of grapevines.

"And?" Joshua said.

"And I was the most miserable of men," Alan went on. "Each time I'd take a shot, the score seemed to get lower and lower, until . . ."

"Until?"

"The moment I came face to face with Jesus Christ," Alan answered solemnly, and as he turned back to look at Joshua, he was smiling. "And I wasn't alone anymore, nor have I ever been alone since. And, that, my friend, is the best answer I can give to you. It seems to me you ought not to be alone now either."

Joshua realized he was biting hard on his lower lip. Sensing he was being drawn into a confrontation he didn't want, he pushed himself up from the couch. It was nearly noon. Wednesday. And he had to get moving. He had to reach Cleve

Lambert sometime today. He was conscious then of the two days' heavy growth of beard on his face. "I need to get cleaned up," he stated, putting an end to the discussion.

"Wait'll you see yourself in the mirror."

"I can imagine," Joshua said lamely. "While I'm at it, you can help speed things up. Get on the phone and get me the numbers for the coroner, the FAA unit handling the investigation, and also, check with the ETC operations and get the name of the duty mechanic for Monday. Okay?"

Alan nodded once. "You better put Mrs. Halley on the top of your list; she called four times already."

"Okay," said Joshua resignedly. "Call her right now and tell her I'm steaming out in the shower and will get to her first."

Joshua Bain strode more purposefully toward the guest bedroom, unwilling to be around even her things now; and while he could not yet comprehend how he was going to handle himself, to bear it, to ultimately somehow or other keep on going, he knew for certain that it didn't make any sense at all that as good a pilot as Jerrie McKennan arranged the circumstances of trying to fly an airplane through a mountain.

He begrudgingly had to admit that Alan Hunt might be closer to the truth than either of them realized.

Alan Hunt passed through the kitchen to open the door to the recreation room, which he had isolated away from the rest of the house. The sliding glass door opening onto the patio had been left open now for nearly two days in order to vent the room, and he pulled up near the pool table, sniffing inquiringly in the oppressive heat. Satisfied that the hundred-degree temperature had finally boiled off the smell of paint, he slowly and reflectively pulled the heavy glass door closed.

He walked slowly around the room then, opening the air-conditioning vents, ending up next to the living room door, which he pushed open. Feeling the cool air of the house flowing in around his ankles, he stood in the doorway for a moment, staring listlessly across the room to the patio and on out to the pool. Being in the room again did not upset him as much as he supposed it should. But as he turned away he was aware that he had carefully avoided looking at the tiled floor.

Alan Hunt had put the matter to rest in his mind, and he was unwilling to resurrect it now.

He stopped briefly by the roll-top desk in the living room,

before deciding he would use the extension phone in his own room to make the several inquiries for Joshua. He started for the front door, but he didn't get halfway across the room when he realized that something was again nibbling at him inside.

Stopped now short of the door, he knew that walking away from the situation was not going to help Joshua Bain. Two years ago, he would have taken the two steps forward, turned the knob, and hit the road without looking back. You'd better believe it, and with no regrets. And he had had two nights and the better part of two days to turn that tempting option a dozen different ways, but no matter what the angle the answer still kept coming up the same. He had put his hand to the plough, and there was no looking back.

"So what now, Lord?" he asked, staring blankly at the solid oak door. He felt himself turning around to face the roll-top desk. The house was quiet, except for the hushed background of water running in the guest-room bath, and he looked to the opposite wall and on through it as he imagined Joshua standing in the shower. So, dear God, he said inside, do I tell him that it was the will of the Lord, that it was in your plan for some higher celestial reason that Jerrie McKennan was chopped up?

Or, how about a little bit of 'as ye sow so shall ye reap'?

Talk about a king-sized stumbling block—

And really burn him off, Lord, and probably lose him, forever, and that is a long, long time. Feeling ashamed then, he dropped his eyes to stare at the carpet near his feet.

"I'm sorry," he said after a moment, hearing his voice as a whisper.

He moved back across the room to sit down resolutely in the stiff-backed chair facing the desk. During the past few seconds he had admitted he did not understand why it had happened or what he was supposed to do about it. So I will pray, he told himself determinedly as he pulled out the phone book. And I will read scripture. But mostly I will pray, enough so, maybe, that I just might move Mount San Jacinto into the Salton Sea.

He paused for a moment, taken with his own intensity, thinking that rearranging the local geography probably wouldn't help solve a thing. He relaxed into the chair then, smiling to himself, for he had again realized that what he really was talking about was faith. He'd been jammed, and he had let himself get sidetracked, with the result that he had struck out again on his own. The old ego bit . . . So, it was back to basics, or, more appropriately, back to the one basic—faith. And, that was what it was all about.

A few minutes out of Indian Wells on Highway 111, on a line below the Bermuda Dunes golf course, there was a small hardly noticeable metal sign beside the private road leading south. The sign said simply, "ETC CORPORATION." The well-attended concrete access road wound for about a half mile, losing itself among desolate dune elevations, to lead to the massive tri-level building erected by Morgan Halley.

Designed to blend with its natural surroundings, the structure's exterior was plain, even stark, a subtle joining of slumpstone and granite, working up through three levels, each offset and separate of the other in order to escalate the eighteen degree ascending slope providing its foundation. The first and broader level, with over seventy thousand square feet of floor space, housed the administrative offices of the corporation, including a fully equipped computer processing center, an automated printing plant, a cafeteria, even a medical operating room. Above and behind, the second level was partially underground and housed the Operations Center, the Planning Department, and the executive offices. The third level, almost totally underground, was called the Sanctuary, the private and exclusive domain of the executive committee and a handful of selected attendants.

At the top of the short list of those especially selected was Gus Holliman, male secretary, man-Friday. In the employ of Morgan Halley for eighteen years. Trusted confidante. And for the past two years carrying on both in position and tradition the same function for his former employer's widow, Britt Halley. Officially, the public corporation records reported Gustave L. Holliman as the Executive Vice-President for Operations. By corporate statute, he was required to be present at all board meetings, though he was not entitled to vote.

One of Gus Holliman's several additional duties was to play the devil's advocate in the screening of all nominated elders, a task he took most seriously, since it was his conviction that the twenty-four-man board of elders comprised the backbone of the secret level of the organization. While the executive committee passed on the critical decisions, it was up to the elders to execute within their operational districts. There were six elders assigned to each of the four regional district headquarters, in New York, Chicago, Dallas, and here at the home office representing the Western operational district.

Early that morning he had been informed by Britt Halley personally that Joshua Bain had been nominated to the Western board as a stand-by elder and was to be voted on at the next quarterly executive session. He had been given until one-thirty that afternoon to put together a screening plan.

A meticulous and careful man, Gus Holliman prided himself on his attention to detail, and he thus entered the private office of the corporate president, Britt Halley, at exactly one twenty-nine with the completed screening plan under his arm. At her suggestion, he settled his slight frame into a chair near her desk. As usual, he was dressed in a vested, conservative suit, and as he moved into the chair, he nervously released the bottom two buttons on the vest. He self-consciously pushed his glasses higher on his thin nose, aware now that he was about to promote a surprise confrontation. He was pumping his nerve now, for the first time in many years, and he could feel the sweat forming on his forehead. Despite ten years of close association, the woman before him was still a mystery, still an enigma. And he had no specific plan, no strategy, to try to reach her now. He had only been able to calculate that she still needed him enough.

"You have the screening plan?" Britt was asking him.

"Yes, ma'am," he said, clearing his throat. "But I have to, shall we say, unofficially lodge a protest."

He flinched at the quick change in her face. From the indifferent, almost bland, executive expresson to one on the alert, wary, yet the small part of a sinister smile near her mouth.

"You owe me, Britt," he went on bravely, aware too that he had used her first name, in itself enough of an outrage. He swallowed once; the movement in his throat was galvanic.

"We owe each other nothing!" she snapped venomously.

He had thought earlier to blackmail her, to tell her that he had a record hidden away of their own private conspiracy, but the temptation had passed, since she probably would turn him over to Gino, knowing his aversion to physical pain. Then, too, there were the drugs. Or, even just another accident. Now, he hoped to simply bluff his way through, a tactic so out of character that the move might just throw her off balance. "Must I remind you why we killed the old man?" he said boldly.

Britt Halley erupted out of her chair. Her face was contorted now, outer evidence of her inner rage, and Gus knew she was into another one of her angry storms. "You stupid fool!" she exclaimed. She then glanced furtively around the room.

"It's clean," he assured her. "I made sure myself, this morning."

She leaned forward at the hips, her palms flat on the desk top. As she continued to glare menacingly at him, obviously gathering her thoughts, Gus Holliman noted that she was no longer the poised and lovely woman she so much of the time pretended to be. His own nerve level began to sag as he realized he was face to face with the real Britt Halley. Ironically enough, the old man had made the same discovery, too late.

"Why did we kill Morgan Halley?" he repeated abruptly.

She chuckled acidly. "I won't lower myself, Gus."

"We killed him because he was an obstacle to the Omega plan," Gus said. "And that, at least for my part, was the supreme kind of sacrifice."

"But not for me?" she said angrily.

It was his turn to chuckle. "I've come to realize that you couldn't have cared less."

She sighed heavily, looked up to the ceiling, began to shake her head. "You are bitter, Gus. You need help."

"No," he interjected. "You need the help, and that's why I'm here now. You're throwing yourself at this man."

She laughed then, cutting him off. She relaxed into her chair, catching her breath. "You are aware," she mocked, "that Gus Holliman is the last person in the world I'd come to, seeking advice on what should take place between a man and a woman."

Gus came slowly to his feet. Her blatant insolence had finally overwhelmed him, causing him to blurt, "You've got to be the most callous person I've ever known!" He hesitated briefly, surprised at his own vehemence. "You are totally without feeling!" He sucked in a deep breath, searching for the words. "Under that makeup, under that mask of beauty, there's nothing but . . . but dried grass. You hear me, rotten dried grass . . ." and he looked aside then, feeling his chest heave with the exertion.

After a passing moment of silence, broken only by his labored breathing, he tentatively glanced up to see that she was studying him intently.

"I hurt you more than I thought," she finally said, her

voice now returned to its usual level of confidence.

"You made a promise."

"The statute of limitations has expired," she pointed out. "Besides, there has been compensation. Omega is really your first love, so much so that anything else would be no more than a passing affair."

"I figure you still owe me," he insisted stubbornly.

"I have to warn you," she said, and her voice was even, her eyes immutable, "that you must not be against Joshua Bain."

Gus Holliman drew a deep, reflective breath. What good is it all? he thought resignedly. He tossed the screening plan onto her desk, a gesture of his surrender. He then turned to sit back down in his chair before telling her, "It's an awfully tight schedule, since the executive session is set for weekend after next," and he was relieved to see that Britt Halley at least had the wisdom to avoid exploiting her advantage.

"Joshua can handle it," Britt said briskly, as if nothing at all had happened. "We've had twelve months to check him out," she went on, opening the folder. "And, unless you've come up with something concrete—"

"No, ma'am; he is clean."

"And qualified?"

"Seems so, to this point."

"Come on, Gus," she said then, looking up at the qualification in his last statement. "I don't want any surprises; neither does Mister Price."

"Well, if you check on interim report number three," he began carefully, "Doctor Truesdale's profile suggested an emotional instability factor."

"And his association with the McKennan woman was a part of that diagnosis?"

"Yes; in fact, very integral."

Britt was now staring hard at him. "She's out of the picture now, isn't she?"

"Yes, ma'am."

"Okay, then, get Truesdale to file a follow-up report as soon as possible." She read rapidly through the schedule, looked up to her desk calendar. "Today is Wednesday. Starting tomorrow morning, he runs for seven days with Blaisdale."

Total isolation, Gus thought. Seven days of rigorous training which normally took two weeks. Joshua Bain was going to be pushed to his limit. It was to his advantage that he was already skilled in the use of small arms, explosives, hand-to-hand combat, field survival.

"All day next Thursday for his final physical exam," Britt continued. "Then you'll have him all day Friday for field testing."

And Gus Holliman sensed he was smiling a little now.

"So that by Saturday, ten days from now, he'll be ready for the final interview by the committee."

"If he's still able."

Britt was smiling now as she handed him back the folder. "Don't pull any punches on him, Gus. But, you know of Mister Price's personal interest in him also," she cautioned him.

Getting up, Gus Holliman took the warning with a sober expression, concealing his own belief that Britt Halley was usually not so transparent, because they both knew whose personal interest was really at stake.

Back in his office, he dropped Bain's folder on his desk as he turned it to sit down heavily. He opened the right upper drawer of his desk, pulled out a piece of paper. He smoothed the teletype tape out, studying the classified report dated four days ago. According to their Las Vegas contact, and in response to a routine name check, Joshua Bain and Jerrie McKennan had been married in that city on June 2. Over a month ago. The corporate routing stamp in the upper right-hand corner indicated that the report came to his desk first, that he had routed it to only one other officer, the president herself. The initials, "B.H." had been dutifully entered in the prescribed box, followed by the brief and indifferent and certainly commonplace enough office term, "File."

He obediently placed it inside the folder.

He settled back into his chair then, folding his hands under his chin as he tried to assess what he might have accomplished in his confrontation with Britt Halley. He gave up after a moment, sensing at best that he might have broken even. For better or for worse, he had finally forced himself to admit that while he had fancied himself in love with her, he was in fact much more afraid of her now. The next step, perhaps, would be to hate her.

As Joshua passed through the dining room to the kitchen, he again noticed the four empty tequila bottles on the connecting counter, apparently arranged there by Alan, representing a bizarre kind of box score. As he dropped a small, letter-sized envelope on the sink, he figured he didn't need the reminder, since both his head and stomach were complaining enough already. He pushed through the back door to call out to Alan, who was working out in the pool.

A few minutes later, they were both seated at the dinette table. Alan was still in his black nylon workout trunks, a bath towel around his neck. Joshua handed him the sealed envelope, which showed a man's name above a Riverside address.

"That's for my new attorney," Joshua explained. "I got his name out of the yellow pages and gave him a call, and he had agreed to represent me at the coroner's office. There's a couple of documents in there, plus a retainer check, and, he's expecting you first thing in the morning."

Alan took the envelope, frowning slightly.

"I'm sorry," Joshua said then, realizing Alan was completely in the dark. "I called all the numbers you worked up for me," he went on. "First, I've got to leave town tomorrow morning early on ETC business. Be gone about a week, so you'll be alone here. If you need help, call Martinez at the coop' and he'll send over a temporary man. Okay?"

"No problem."

"After Mrs. Halley, I checked with the coroner and got no place. Some garbage about having to be a close relative or appointed trustee."

"Can't Mrs. Halley help?"

"Sure she can, but I want this kept solo for a while."

"Should I just drop this off?" Alan asked, holding up the envelope.

"Yeah, and introduce yourself personally to him. Give him your phone number, and tell him to call you immediately if he runs into any developments."

"How do I get to you?"

"You don't; I'll have to work out some way of getting to you once or twice while I'm gone."

Alan nodded that he understood. "What about the FAA?"

Joshua shrugged. "Almost as bad, but not quite. That Riverside number you gave me led to the Palm Springs field office, where they're putting the plane back together. It'll take at least a couple weeks to finalize the investigation. However, I did find out that the plane's controls were on automatic pilot."

"That's not unusual, is it? I mean, I've seen you guys use the auto pilot plenty of times."

"That's true," Joshua admitted, "but normally on the longer flights, like to Vegas." He shook his head then. "But

Jerrie loved the feel of the controls; you know, she was a natural. The auto pilot took a lot of the fun out if it for her. And, especially on this flight, because it was fairly short."

"Okay, so what does it prove?"

"Nothing, but it's just one more unusual thing that keeps me wondering."

"Wondering what?"

"I don't know yet," Joshua said warily, getting up. "But I've got a call into Jeff Capstan, and he's trying to set me up to get a look at what they've got tonight." He moved through the recreation room doorway. "How about something to drink?"

Alan followed him, absently dropping his towel on the pool table. The smell of paint had all but disappeared from the room. He grunted affirmatively as Joshua asked him if he would take his usual plain tonic and ice.

"There's something I want to talk to you about," Joshua said reflectively as he started working up the two drinks, careful to pour himself tonic only. "You can understand I've got to get out of this place as soon as I can." He put the filled glass on the bar in front of Alan, who was now perched on the end bar stool. Joshua then walked slowly down the pool table, running his hand along the side rail, trying to arrange his thoughts. He turned back, retraced his steps.

"Yes," Alan finally said, "I guess I understand."

Joshua had stopped at the near corner of the pool table. "Where's the pool table cover?" he asked absently, for he had only now noticed that the green plastic cover was missing. Jerrie had been fussy about the table, insisting on keeping it covered when they weren't using it.

"Behind the bar, maybe," Alan suggested. "Isn't that where she kept it?"

Joshua poked around behind the bar and under the counter. "It's not here," he said under his breath, and he was frowning now, for some reason perplexed with the small detail.

"She probably threw it out," Alan said then. "It was old, wasn't it? Maybe she was going to get a new one, a different color, maybe, to match the paint job."

"Maybe," Joshua mused quietly. "But I can't see why she'd throw the old one out before replacing it."

"I'll look around for it tomorrow," Alan said. "If I can't find it, I'll pick up a new one myself."

Joshua downed his tonic in one gulp, knowing that the fire inside would eventually have to burn itself out on its own. "As

I was saying," he began again, "I've got to move soon. When Jerrie and I came down from Berkeley, I was given my choice between this place or the Fuller Ranch. You know the place up on Highway 74, where we went quail hunting."

"I know."

"Beautiful place," Joshua said meaningfully. "High desert, and cooler. Used to be a dude ranch that Morgan Halley bought up when it went broke. And it's just sitting there, with a caretaker family. It's got a half-mile asphalt runway, with a Butler-hut hangar. The main house and guest quarters are still in perfect shape." Chug-a-lugging directly from the quart tonic bottle he continued: "I've got a ten-year buy-out option on this place, and I figure to trade it straight across the board for the Fuller Ranch. Britt Halley told me this afternoon that she'll start the paperwork through tomorrow."

"What are you going to do with the Fuller place?"

"I don't know," Joshua admitted, "but we sure can do something."

"We?"

"Yeah; that's what I want to talk to you about. If you want, you'll be in for thirty-three and a third percent. I would offer you half, but I figure we should hold out the last third for contingency purposes."

Alan looked down to his glass, not answering right away. "I appreciate the chance," he finally said. "But that place; it's got to be worth what, a quarter of a million?"

"I didn't say you had to buy in; we'll go equal partners on the buy-out contract. We'll both start from scratch." He lifted the bottle one more time to drain it. "All we have to do for now is make interest and tax payments on the original principle."

Alan was looking at him now, a strange, perhaps bewildered look on his face. "How strange are the ways of the Lord," he said softly. Slipping off the bar stool, he walked over to the sliding glass door to stare out across the pool, as if he might be trying to put some space between him and what appeared to be an embarrassing moment.

"It's even got an olympic-size pool," Joshua pointed out.

"Please forgive me," Alan said, "for you see I'm most grateful to know you could even think of such a thing."

"Do you want to think about it?"

Alan was looking at him again, his face more composed. "I suppose she would have approved of such a venture."

"She already did, in a way," said Joshua, and he turned the bar counter to step up beside him. "Over a month ago we agreed to ask you in for a third on this place. She was the one who first suggested it, and we just hadn't gotten around to legalizing it."

Alan Hunt looked away, closing his eyes, and Joshua noticed that his shoulders were trembling.

"Is it a deal?" Joshua asked.

Alan turned back to face him, extending both his hands. "It is a deal, my friend."

Clasping his forearms warmly, Joshua too was smiling broadly. "What shall we call it?"

"How about Canaan?" said Alan quickly.

"Beautiful! She would've liked that too."

Chapter four

It was at a time like this that a man had to reach down to some deeper level, down to that plateau where the basic reflexes could be depended upon to punch out the orders to an exhausted brain that just didn't care anymore. Cleve Lambert moved woodenly along the walled runway of satellite number 5, LAX, wondering what it was that kept him going. As he approached a row of pay phones, he resolved that he would be in bed in thirty minutes, barring catastrophe, and that he would stay there for a hundred years. He couldn't remember when he had slept last, setting aside one or two cat naps. Two days, or was it three? Today was Thursday. Point of reference. Ten days since the death of Jerrie McKennan. Seven days since Joshua Bain had flown off in some unknown direction on an ETC assignment. Three days, instead of two, since he had climbed on board an American Airlines flight for Washington, D.C.

Punching a dime into the nearest phone, he called his office. He was advised that he had a package, among other urgent items, marked with the return name of Benjamin Scott. Not a catastrophe, as such, but first contact with Joshua in a week. As he headed for the baggage area, he realized the message had started the juices to flowing. Perhaps he had enough left to make it for another two or three hours before he collapsed.

It took him nearly an hour to get to his office, where his first order of business was to open the Benjamin Scott package. According to his secretary, the Indio courier had delivered the pouch at a little after noon, meaning it was still fresh. The pouch contained a tape cartridge and a crude hand-drawn map. He inserted the tape into his desk machine, switched it on.

"So here I am, under the same palm tree, and it's about the same time." The taped voice of Joshua Bain started out in a dull monotone.

So maybe he's tired, Lambert thought appreciatively.

"I started this habit pattern per your advice, you know," the voice went on, "to enable me to make this drop without arousing suspicion." There was a pause, then, "I'll bet you've never seen the sun coming up on the desert. It's something to behold. And it's about as cool now as it ever gets this time of the year."

Will you get to it, Lambert thought impatiently.

"But we didn't really count on Jerrie, did we, Mister Lambert—"

Cleve Lambert straightened up, wide awake now.

"—because she started getting up with me in the last few weeks. Yeah, and she'd come out here to watch with me. And maybe we'd take a swim—" and there was a longer pause, "—she had a way of moving into my habit patterns, you know."

Lambert relaxed back into his chair, feeling his pulse pounding in his temples.

"Do me a favor," the voice was saying, "and erase everything up to this point. Start of report. It is now 05:40 hours, Thursday, July the twentieth. And the first official thing I've got to say is for you to try to relax, because it's getting close to countdown for kick-off. With any luck at all, I'm a cinch to be confirmed as an elder sometime this weekend. Which means among other good things, that I'll have a chance to get into the Sanctuary. The way things are adding up, it looks like we just might make it within your deadline. It's a bit early to pin down the actual day but I figure another week to ten days will see it finished."

Lambert shut down the machine for a few seconds, while

he reviewed Joshua's voice, seeking clues to the man's attitude, his mental demeanor. Switching the machine back on, he was satisfied that Joshua was alert and normal enough.

"Now for a quick recap on the past week. Thursday morning last, at about this same time, they flew me out in Britt Halley's Lear to Phoenix. I was blindfolded at the airport but can say I was oriented enough to know our destination was between twenty to twenty-five miles south to southwest. A ranch of some kind, probably horse breeding. The enclosed map shows the ranch layout and is referenced to the nearby road. We had a heavy thundershower last Sunday at fourteen-twenty hours. Also a helicopter pad. The only authentic name I could pick up is Blaisdale, apparently the guy in charge."

Lambert studied the map briefly, thinking they could locate the ranch easy enough with what they had. He set it aside, putting it out of his mind, for they were now after the head of this rat, not the limbs.

"—only hitting the highlights," Joshua was saying evenly, and Lambert noticed that the syllables were flowing more quickly now, suggesting that Joshua Bain was anxious to get moving. "—and I can best describe this place as a high-class school for assassins, but on an exotic and sophisticated level. Not the expected hard stuff, with guns or explosives. Not at all. The first three days is on theory, classroom and lab time. Films, training aids. Minimum fall distances to guarantee fatal impact. How long can the brain survive without oxygen. Killing times of various far-out drugs and poisons. How to read and interpret medical records, clinical reports, X rays."

It figured, Lambert was thinking. The MO was the trademark of the ETC killers. Cause of death was always either accidental or natural.

"The last four days are given to application," the voice hurried on, "under field conditions. Emphasis is heavy on covert entry. Detection of security systems, lock picking, even safe cracking, and all without leaving traces of tampering. If you can't make it all the way in without detection, then pull out. You can't believe it. This place would turn Willie Sutton green with envy. Disguises, phony papers." There was a pause. "Let me wind this up by saying these people are slick, super suede shoe, and believe me, it's been quite an eye-opening experience. If nothing else, I've learned in the past week to be careful now. Nothing like a little time in the trenches to wise up the troops."

Lambert grunted to himself, appreciating Joshua's last comment.

"Now to two other quickies," the taped voice continued. "First, get me everything you can on one Alan Hunt," and he spelled the name out carefully. "The only thing I can tell you is that his last job, about two years ago, was at the Japanese Deer Park in Anaheim. He's Indian, age about twenty-eight. May have worked in Vegas before the Anaheim job. Has been on the ETC payroll for nearly two years. Knew Morgan Halley, but how well I don't know. This is important and I want the info by early next week. But don't start snooping around down here; with what I know about these clowns now I can tell you to be careful. But get it done."

Lambert was perplexed by the Alan Hunt inquiry. Perhaps Joshua intended to use Alan Hunt in some way.

"Secondly, Mister Lambert, and this is the most important item. I need help re Jerrie's death. I'm now positive it wasn't an accident."

Cleve Lambert again came upright in his chair.

"Late last night, when I got in from Phoenix, I contacted my attorney in Riverside, and he told me that the pathologist's report says she had heroin in her blood. Probably enough to have OD'd her." There was another brief pause, and Lambert realized he was on the forward edge of his chair, listening intently, thinking that it couldn't get fouled up now, not with only a week to go.

"That I can't accept," the taped voice insisted. "Granted, it's possible. But where did she get it? We didn't run with the local crowd, and I know she never had a chance to set up a local source. It's possible that maybe some of our friends from Berkeley were down for that Huelga demonstration. The farm workers bit. There was quite a rhubarb at the Indio courthouse the Saturday before, and there were some college kids there according to the news reports. So, I'm asking you to use your influence to get me a list of the outsiders in Indio on that weekend. I know you guys cover this kind of thing, taking pictures and what not. Now, don't take this as a threat, but if you don't help me, then I'll run it solo. One way or the other, I'm going to get at the truth. And this ends this report. I'll be in touch."

Joshua Bain's voice ended with a different edge, one which Cleve Lambert couldn't really interpret beyond its deadly soberness. He switched off the recorder. He was as perplexed as Joshua Bain was as to what or who had flown Jerrie McKennan into that mountain.

He got up, pulled his jacket on wearily, thinking it was the same with any case; the closer you got to the wire the more complicated it all became. In a way, it was like life in general, the more you learned about something the more you realized how much you really didn't know. A discouraging paradox. But that was the way it worked.

Right now, on top of the local barrel of snakes, was the problem developing at the other end of the chain of command. He had just spent seventy-two hours sequestered in a small dingy apartment somewhere on the outskirts of Washington, D.C., doing his best to convince Jerome Mason and an assistant to let him run the show at least until they could reap the profits from the last year's labor. He had obtained his one week. And it galled him that a fuzzy-cheeked attorney named Ben Caplan, a hotshot out of the Special Litigation Section, had sat in judgment on his capability to produce. The kid was probably adept at the prosecution of IRA gun runners or in gathering evidence against the Jewish Defense League for buying firearms from a Mexican supplier. Textbook play. Bush league. And his only consolation was that Ben Caplan would remain locked up for the next week, mapping out strategy, kept busy with the grandiose plan which would please Jerome Mason. On paper, anyway.

Like Joshua Bain suggested, it took a little time in the trenches to wise up the troops.

On his way out, he stopped by his secretary briefly, giving her the urgent request for a background check on Alan Hunt. As for the Jerrie McKennan situation, he had already decided the matter would have to be thought over in more detail.

The Jaguar didn't seem to be as important now, to Joshua, as he walked slowly around the sleek racing machine. The car had been as much for her, because knowing the way she took to the flying had told him she would enjoy driving a competitive car as well. They were in the barn, and Alan stood behind him silhouetted in the open doorway. Joshua stopped next to the left front fender. Model XK120, vintage year 1950. Drop-head coupe. Wire wheels with knock-off hubs. It was all there.

"When'd he leave it?" Joshua asked.

"Monday morning."

Joshua nodded as he ran his hand along the long, sloping hood. "What do you think?"

Alan walked up to the front end, bounced the right fender. "A little loose in the front," he suggested.

"You drove it?"

"Yeah, a couple times. At high speed, it floats a little on the local roads."

Joshua looked at him, realized they both were grinning. "I think you're right. He had it slung for city streets."

"I stopped by the hangar yesterday," Alan told him. "Picked up some bungee cord. We can tie it down with that."

"You should've done it. We'll have to experiment with the number of turns, anyway."

"I'll do it later tonight."

They walked back together to the main house. It was pushing seven o'clock, and Joshua's empty stomach reminded him it had been nearly twenty-four hours since he ate last, a necessary outcome of having submitted himself to the day-long series of physical exams by the ETC doctors. He needed a good meal, along with a full night's rest, to be ready for tomorrow, Friday, when he would be examined for a different sort of health and vigor. In the kitchen, he pulled two sirloins out of the freezer, tossed them to Alan.

They worked quickly getting the meal together, not saying much except to discuss the Jaguar, and Joshua was pleasantly surprised to learn how much Alan knew about racing cars. In a little under an hour, they were finished eating. Relaxing on the patio, they had left behind them a spotless and well-ordered kitchen. In front of Joshua was a heavy manila envelope, and he opened it to remove a sheaf of papers. He pushed them across the redwood table, next to Alan's coffee cup. "Sign those and we're home free," he said cordially, and he realized then that he was about to fall asleep.

"The Fuller place?"

"Uh-huh. And the instant you put your name to those papers it becomes the new Canaan."

Alan leafed through the papers, then squared them up evenly. "Have you ever heard the saying about a man not being able to serve two masters at the same time?"

Joshua searched his companion's face, seeing nothing in the fading evening light. "Yes," he said then, "or else he'll love one and hate the other, or something like that."

"I see you've been reading your Bible."

Joshua got up to flip on the outdoor light switch. "Some," he said after a moment, "but not much in the past week or so," and he paused behind his chair, staring across the ranch, on up to the nearby mountains which were now a solid black under the diminishing orange sky. Alan got up also, as if he might be uncomfortable with Joshua looking down at him. He moved a few steps away to pull himself up on the pool's coping.

"You had better sit down, my friend," Alan told him, "because I've got something to tell you before I sign any papers."

Joshua obliged without comment.

"You know I'm on the Halley payroll," Alan began.

"Yes; we all are, in a way," Joshua pointed out.

"I work for her, personally."

Joshua didn't move or say a word, but inside he was suddenly alert, on his guard. Now feeling on the defensive himself, he thought he should get up and turn the patio lights off. Better they both be in the dark.

"What it amounts to," Alan was saying, "is that I was hired two years ago by Morgan Halley, a few months before he died. You may also recall that you once asked me what I did before I came to work here."

"I remember," Joshua admitted. "You said you worked at the Japanese Deer Park in Anaheim."

"That's true. I was employed in a martial-arts act, and it wasn't a bad job, believe me."

Martial arts, Joshua said to himself. So that explained the man's quickness and discipline.

"One night, late," Alan went on, "Mrs. Halley was at the park, squiring a group of VIP's. Some cat who had too much Asahi started giving her a bad time. Grabbed at her or something. Anyway, I stepped in and solved the problem. Well, old man Halley found out about it the next day and had Gus Holliman call me to offer me a job. Man, like the pay was good, so I took it."

"What job?"

"Bodyguard to Mrs. Halley. I think Morgan Halley knew he was on his way out and was taking certain precautions. She had never had a bodyguard before, and when I met him a few days later he told me it was because of the times, you know, like things getting rough all over."

"Sounds reasonable."

"But a real drag, believe me. But I did it for nearly a year, until you came along."

"So you weren't here before us, after all."

"No; that was a story made up by Britt Halley."

"You mean you were moved in here because of us?"

"Not us, just you," Alan corrected him. "I was assigned here to keep an eye on you, twenty-four hours a day."

"You mean to spy on me?"

Alan dropped his eyes to look down at the concrete deck. "No; I couldn't do that, and I told Mrs. Halley so in the beginning. My understanding was that I was more of a security man; however, the point is admittedly debatable, since I was required to report to her in secret."

Joshua turned the information around slowly in his mind. His first impulse was anger, but the feeling passed in the wake of his understanding that Alan was confessing his role freely and aboveboard. "It's a funny thing," he said then, "but you know, Jerrie mentioned a couple months ago that you just didn't seem to fit in around here."

"She was very perceptive."

"Yeah," Joshua agreed. "But why are you telling me now?"

A full minute passed before Alan finally answered him. "I had to make a decision this week. A rather serious one, I'm afraid," and with that remark he came down from the coping, moved to his original chair where he sat down heavily. He stared at Joshua for a moment. "I'm going to tell you something now, and I'm asking you not to interrupt until I'm finished."

"All right."

Alan settled himself into the chair, brought his hands together under his chin. "On the morning Jerrie died, I was supposed to've followed you to the raceway, but I couldn't get the truck started. I thought at first it was a short in the starter circuit. Like an idiot, I started with the solenoid, then to the dash switch. Finally, where I should've started, I found the cable connector on the battery post was loose. I was just about to wind it up when Jerrie came out of the house with a message from the ETC receiving dock in town. They supposedly had a perishable package there addressed to the ranch. It was a reasonable thing. So I jumped in the truck and took off."

Joshua was tempted to jump in, to ask about the actual time, but he held back per his promise to remain silent.

"As soon as I got to the dock and found out there was no package for us and nobody there had called Jerrie, I naturally got suspicious. And, I guess I made my first mistake. Instead of humping it right back here, I called Mrs. Halley on the truck's mobile phone. I mean, I'd been told to report directly to her any unusual or suspicious incidents." He stopped for a moment, massaging his forehead. "She was in her office, and after hearing what I had to report, she said she'd dispatch Gino Malone immediately to help me. He was downstairs in the ETC motor pool area. She then transferred me to the mobile phone in her Cadillac.

That should've been a break, Joshua thought. The limo was less than five minutes away.

"Gino told me to meet him at the corner up here at 52nd and Jefferson, and that we'd decide what to do then. So, I hot-footed it down Jefferson. Gino was there when I arrived, and we moved right down to the southwest corner of the property line. I got out and climbed on top the truck's cab and could make out a car parked next to the house. I saw that Jerrie's Plymouth was still by the pump house."

Joshua sat stock still now. The Plymouth was still here!

"I guess that was my second mistake," Alan said, his voice lower, as if he were having trouble getting the words out. "We should've crashed right in. But Gino was afraid whoever was in here would have a lookout and they'd all rabbit as soon as we started in the access road. So I cut out down 52 and came in the service road to block off any chance of their getting out that way. Well, Gino allowed me a couple of minutes before he came in. They must've spotted him because they came out the back winding full-bore. They caught me facing the wrong way and by the time I got turned around it was a foot race all the way to Highway 10." He held up his hands in a kind of helpless gesture. "I nearly nailed them once, when they slowed up to make the turn onto 86, and I got close enough to get their plates and a look at the three of them. But that wheel man was good, and he sucked me right up his exhaust once they hit the freeway." He shook his head once. "Once on 10, they were gone."

Joshua picked up the empty manila envelope, pulled the ballpoint pen out of his shirt pocket. He would remain silent, but he would make notes now. A whole lot of questions.

"So I called Gino on the mobile," Alan went on, "and he told me to get back here and to follow the instructions I would find on the kitchen table." Alan Hunt stroked his chin with his left hand. "And, my friend, that brings me to the worst of it."

Joshua closed his eyes.

"When I got back, the limo was gone, and so was your Plymouth. I remember thinking how glad I was that Jerrie was out of it, probably on her way to the airport. I just figured it was thieves, or something. Until I got into the house." He was leaning forward now, toying with his empty cup. "I can only prepare you by saying it was bad. She wasn't here, so I guess Gino took her. But there was blood on the rec' room floor. A lot of blood, Joshua." He leaned back heavily to stare straight up to the now black sky. "And on the wall that was painted over when you came home was a message of some kind sprayed on with black paint." He dropped his head to stare directly into Joshua's eyes. "There was a big word on top, 'WAR,' and underneath, in small letters, the word, 'TRAITOR.' " He continued to stare unflinchingly at Joshua. "I can only hope that might mean something to you."

"Is that it?" Joshua finally asked.

"That's it. Per Gino's instructions, I cleaned up the floor. Found a can of enamel in the barn dark enough to cover the spray paint." He held up his hands. "The rest you know, whatever that is."

"Gino must've wrapped her up in the pool table cover," Joshua said reflectively.

"Looks that way. Although I didn't think of that until you mentioned it last week. I just didn't notice it was missing."

Joshua felt his belly tightening up again. "The question is," he said slowly, "was she alive or dead when he carried her out?"

Alan nodded once, then shrugged. "Only they can tell you."

"They?"

Alan cocked his head, frowned. "Well, can't we presume that Mrs. Halley and Gino were here together?"

"How did she get here? You said Gino was alone in the limo."

"She could've been down in the back seat. And, I was gone for nearly twenty-five minutes. And the Plymouth; who drove it away? Mrs. Halley could've had any one of three or four people drop her off here. I mean, I hoped for a while that maybe Jerrie did drive out, but, believe me, if it was she bleeding like that . . . It was too much. I don't see how she could've been alive."

Joshua jumped off the point, knowing he would come back to it later. Besides, he also suspected that Britt Halley, or someone working for her, was the obvious second party. "I need a whole bunch of answers," he said then.

"You won't have to ask most of them," Alan said, getting up. "I've written out a complete statement. It's got times, descriptions, the whole works. Read it first, then ask me what you want. It's in the upper righthand drawer of the desk in the living room.

Joshua understood now that he wasn't going to get much sleep tonight, after all. "I'm obliged to you," he said gratefully, and the now-familiar knot was back in his throat.

"I'm sorry I waited so long," Alan said.

"It doesn't matter, anyway, because I was out of town."

"Why don't you turn it over to the cops, let them handle it?"

Joshua shook his head slowly, knowing he couldn't tell Alan why he had to play this out on his own. "I'll have to think about it," he said wearily.

"If there's anything I can do."

Joshua studied him carefully, weighing the man. "You know, you're on the spot now," he said gravely, suspecting that Alan Hunt already knew full well the implications of his position. "I assume you haven't told Britt Halley you were coming to me."

"No," Alan assured him.

Joshua abruptly realized there was now even more urgency involved than before. He had unwittingly made their association suspect by proposing to bring in Alan as a partner with him on the Fuller Ranch. He wondered how much Britt Halley might make of such a move. "What are you going to do?" he asked Alan.

Alan grunted in an ironic sort of way. "I almost pulled out last night, after I wrote out the statement for you."

"I'm glad you didn't," said Joshua soberly.

"I got to thinking about the guy who was around about two thousand years ago," Alan said. "And I figured He was up there watching me, patiently, to see what I might do."

Joshua saw that Alan Hunt was really not very subtle in bringing God into the discussion, and he was curious to know whether the cross borne by Alan Hunt had tonight been made lighter or heavier. Joshua suspected he was about to add a pound or two. "So what are you going to do now?" he asked again, the question still as leading as it had been before.

Alan bit on his lower lip, revealing his apparent indecision. "That will largely depend on you."

Joshua felt the weight shift to his back. Alan Hunt was as shrewd as he now looked. "Why don't we maintain the status quo," Joshua said evenly, "for, say, another week?" He was aware of the doubtful security proposed in the plural "we" when in fact he was asking Alan to carry on alone in an exposed position. "I'll promise you I'll not in any way tip the source of any information in your statement. That I can guarantee. And, the fact that you're still here strongly suggests that Britt Halley considers you more valuable looking out after me." He shrugged once. "So keep on reporting, act just as if nothing has changed."

"Fair enough," Alan responded quickly.

"Do you have a handgun?"

Alan looked at him from under the most confident of expressions as he routinely assured him, "I don't need one."

Joshua dropped the ballpoint pen on the redwood table. "Will you please sign the papers."

Alan picked up the pen slowly, turning it in his hand. "In order to maintain the status quo?"

"Oh, ye of little faith."

Showing his first smile of the evening, Alan Hunt started writing.

The therapy spa was attached to the main swimming pool, separated by a ten-foot dam wall, and Britt Halley settled herself on the circular bench, lining up her back for the last time directly in front of the center jet. She alternated between free floating in the swirling water to her present sitting position. As was her habit, she had the water temperature set at 108 degrees, several degrees higher than most people could tolerate.

She looked over her shoulder to the clock mounted on the cabana wall. One minute before nine. She was wondering if Gino would be on time when footsteps on the flagstone deck caused her to look around to see him standing motionless next to the nearby chaise lounge. Gino Malone kept fit, still carrying the same weight he enjoyed as a professional linebacker. He was largely unmarked, considering the battles he had endured, except for the telltale scalpel lines above both his knees, the consequences of which had put him on the bench at the height of his career. Five years on the Halley payroll had not softened him. Britt motioned once with her right hand.

Gino picked up her terrycloth robe, held it for her. She deftly pulled herself out of the hot water, slipped quickly into the comfortable terrycloth. As she settled herself into the chaise lounge, she noticed that he had thoughtfully brought her favorite post-spa drink, Irish coffee. While the air around them was still in the high 80's, she was chilled briefly, coming out of the hot spa water. She reached back, released her hair. He handed her a bath towel.

"Please do it for me," she told him as she reached for her hot coffee.

He obediently sat down on the foot of the lounge chair. She extended her legs, resting her heels on his left thigh. He was dressed in bermuda shorts and a loose weave tank top, and he was obviously embarrassed with the personal encounter.

"You're on the team, tomorrow," she said offhandedly, opening up the subject and the reason for having called him to the meeting.

He nodded once, looking out across the pool.

The alcohol in the coffee began to warm her inside, and she felt herself relaxing further. "What did Gus tell you at the briefing?" she asked.

He shrugged once. "Routine," he replied. He turned to look at her then, a blank expression on his heavy yet almost boyish face. His shoulders rotated in the same motion, as if his heavily muscled and short neck would not permit otherwise. "Gus did mention, though, that he didn't want us to pull any punches," he added.

Britt expected the remark. "I would suggest you do what you have to, Gino," she said, "but I also suggest you do no more than that. Do you understand?"

Looking out again across the pool, he nodded once. "I have a job to do, and I'll do it."

An oblique and non-responsive answer, Britt noted, feeling warmth inside turning cold. Perhaps Gino Malone felt his position had changed, perhaps escalated, because of recent events. She pulled her legs away, covered them with her robe. She had decided it was time to get a message across to Gino Malone. "You never did tell me what happened to that young stable boy, what was his name?"

He turned to look at her, and the blank expression changed to a more complex mode, one which he could not identify. "You mean the Hernandez kid, the one you whipped?"

"Ah, yes," she said lightly. Employee Hernandez had made the grave mistake of making an intimate pass at her while helping her into the saddle one morning. And she had beat him with her crop until he had collapsed. He had stood erect in the beginning, grinning at her out of some macho compulsion, which had only further enraged her. She remembered that she had stopped beating him only because she could no longer lift her arm. "What happened to him?" she repeated.

"What difference does it make?"

"Tell me!" she screamed at him, her voice sharp, cutting across the heavy night air.

"We took him back to Mexico," he said defensively. "As you told me to do."

"I told you I never wanted to see him again."

"You won't."

"Why won't I?"

Gino sighed heavily, looked down to his lap to his clenched fists. "Because he had a bad fall."

"Explain that."

Gino remained silent, and she saw his jaw muscles working furiously. She kicked out savagely with her right foot, hitting his left thigh.

"Explain it!" she shrilled.

"Okay," he exclaimed, and he lurched to his feet, his arms straight at his side. "He went out the helicopter hatch at fifteen hundred feet. And I didn't have to push him because he was already half dead," and his voice ebbed again. "You whipped him to a pulp; it took me two days to get the chopper cleaned out."

"That's all I wanted to know," Britt told him, her voice normal. "Now, about tomorrow morning. The exercise will be on film, so we'll be able to review how well you did your job, won't we?"

His expression was blank again as he nodded once.

That indeed was much better, she thought, and she assumed that Gino Malone was now more surely aware that he, like any other employee, was expendable.

Chapter five

The Jaguar XK-120 looked deceptively stock, from the classic Coventry-designed bubble roof down along the long sloping hood folded between the flared front fenders to the sixteen-inch wire wheels. However, underneath where it counted, from up front with the 327 fuel-injected and totally full-house engine on back through the Corvette four-speed to the positraction rear-end, the power train was purebred Detroit. Having just cleared the Palm Desert intersection of Highway 74, Joshua Bain listened with a critical ear to the tune of the big-bore engine, which was now loaded on the four or five degree incline. Peaking out at forty-eight hundred, he popped into third, loading the engine again, and he checked the tach as the drop-head coupe started to tremble. He grinned a little to himself as he felt the lower-end torque starting to take hold. He was really more interested in the front-end suspension now, which Alan had lashed down with bungee cord to reduce the car's tendency to loft on the uneven desert roads. He held at ninety miles per hour for a few more seconds, until he was satisfied that they had solved the suspension problem.

Backing off to the legal speed limit, he knew he had only a few more minutes before reaching the Fuller ranch turn-off. And they were going to be up there at the ranch, or maybe before on the private road, waiting, and it was supposed to be their advantage because they set it up and he was supposed to blunder right in.

Surprise time for the troops.

Test reaction.

General prowess, physical and mental.

Speed of response.

Reliability under stress.

By his estimate, since Gus Holliman was the wheel on the exercise, they would no doubt include a whole lot of tolerance to pain. And he could feel his body starting to react, gearing itself in anticipation, and Joshua could not help but feel a little foolish. The deeper he got into the situation the more bizarre it became. And he wondered how long he could continue to cope with it, especially to stay out in front.

The desert terrain didn't seem to move by at all; it was just there, placid and deadly sure of itself, endless and all alike, though at that hour in the morning the diminishing shadows lent some suggestion of hospitality. A rank kind of beckoning deception, because in a few hours that same land would become an inferno. Joshua supposed there was some lesson to be learned from the desert, from its own sureness of purpose, and he understood better now why God had put Moses in perhaps such a similar place, a forty-year crucible that could condition a man to take on the Egyptian first team.

Joshua didn't have even forty days.

Maybe forty hours, if he was lucky.

Luck, according to Alan Hunt, was the will of God.

And the turn-off came into view up ahead, and he downshifted savagely, revving the engine, senselessly laying down twenty yards of Dunlop rubber, and he took the turn deliberately at too high a speed, fishtailing in the sand, powering out of the slide and back onto the oiled dirt road. In the exhilaration of speed and maneuvering there was some temporary relief.

But Jerrie was still gone.

And the baby with her.

He streaked along the narrow roadway, recklessly and not caring, and the nearby desert landscape flashed by. And he thought that his was a time of acceleration, of things moving by too quickly for him to comprehend anymore. Tunnel vision. As man's speed increased his field of forward view began to narrow down until finally he could only see directly to his front, and if the Great Jehovah were to rise up on the horizon and ask him what it was he could see, Joshua figured he would have to answer, "Two degrees to the front, sir."

He had topped a rise in the road. Fifty yards ahead, a white pick-up was parked sideways—shoulder to shoulder truck— right smack in the middle of his two degrees. And this has to be it, *my'man.* In second gear, he came off the gas pedal to mash the brakes. Britt had warned him: "They'll come at you at anytime and anyplace tomorrow. They won't kill you, but they are under orders to get you down and out!" And Joshua was raging now, his hundred and eighty-five pounds of bone, muscle and sinew triggered by the latent fury finally released after ten days in a pressure tank, and like the machine under him, he was force-fueled, super tuned, and he didn't care whom he ran over.

The Jag clung to the oiled dirt until at the right moment Joshua forced an angling slide to the right. Out of the corner of his eye he had spotted the grilled nose of Gus Holliman's

Mark V parked behind a nearby sandy rise. In the last second before the Jag ceased to move, Joshua Bain had no plan.

The only weapon he was allowed was a short tire iron tucked in his belt.

The Jag stopped less than a yard away and on an angle from the pick-up. Joshua kept the engine idling, slipped into first gear. As the dust settled, he saw that he was boxed in by two of Holliman's men. The one nearest to his side of the car he recognized. Gino Malone, ex-linebacker and skydiver extraordinaire. An acceptable pilot. And a probable elder. The captain of the first team. A hulking giant who now carried a yard of heavy chain, now grinning from ear to ear, as if he were a linebacker again and it was third down with twenty-three to go. Both men were dressed in company issued white coveralls. Shoulder holsters with the typical heavy automatics, as if they were expecting a grizzly bear in the middle of the desert. The second clown, hunched over like an ape, carried a taped baseball bat. The third man was up now in the cab of the truck, causing Joshua to think that maybe he was the referee, and then he saw the movie camera in the guy's hand and he couldn't believe it.

The heavy chain arched over viciously, virtually destroying the entire front windshield of the Jag. Closing his eyes against the flying glass, Joshua slipped the shift lever into second with his right hand while tripping the door lever with his left. The senseless and stupid act of destroying the irreplaceable windshield did not affect Joshua, who was already at the peak of his fury with Gino Malone.

Malone was still grinning as he leaned over to stare malevolently at Joshua, who now too was grinning in a sardonic way as he coldly measured the distance and angle. He popped the clutch. At the same instant, he jammed the door open, quadrupling the door's inertia as the car jumped forward into a stall.

The leading edge of the top of the door caught Gino at his lower jaw, with the force equivalent to a crowbar being swung by a man of his own size. At its leading point, his mandible was crushed and splintered, along with most of the lower teeth back to the molars. The shock passing through his jaw sockets hit Malone's brain with thunderous impact, dropping him like a sack of sand.

Joshua was already after the other man. With the door

open, he had pushed his feet and legs out, his butt following. In the same motion, he reached up to the overhead jamb with both hands. In a single jack-knife motion he snatched his legs over the top of the coupe.

Unknown to Joshua, Alan Hunt was hidden about two hundred yards to the east, atop a knoll giving him a clear view of the roadbed. Following Britt Halley's specific instructions to protect Joshua at any cost, he was sprawled in the prone position, viewing the action through the ten-power scope mounted on the Winchester 30-06 locked into his shoulder.

He tracked Joshua in the scope's crosshairs, holding his breath as Joshua snatched himself over the coupe's roof. The second man was hunched down, looking through the coupe's side window, apparently trying to figure out what had happened to Joshua Bain, who in the following instant hit him squarely in his back. The big man came erect, pivoting at the same time, bringing the baseball bat around in a vicious but blind swing.

Now crouched at his opponent's feet, Joshua cracked the man's right shin with one elbow-level slash of what looked like a tire iron. It took a second or two for the man's scream to reach Alan, who now relaxed his right index finger on the rifle's trigger. The whole exercise had taken less than a minute.

With his antagonist slumped against the door of the car, Joshua snatched the pistol out from under his arm. The man stared up at him, his face distorted in as much unbelief as in the pain crawling up his leg.

"You'll survive," Joshua said tersely as he turned his attention to the last apparent member of the team, who was still in the cab of the truck and who now was staring at him worriedly over the top of his movie camera. Keeping an eye on him, Joshua walked around the low-slung car to collect Gino Malone's weapon. Putting the two heavy pistols in the car, he moved to the cab of the pick-up, leaning in the open window of the passenger door.

"What's your part in this little scene?" Joshua asked, noticing the huskiness in his own voice. He was still wound up tight, shaking a little.

"Just the camera," the frightened man blurted.

"I see," Joshua observed, and he now recognized him. "You're a gardener at Mrs. Halley's estate, aren't you?"

"Yes sir."

Some gardener, Joshua thought. "All right," he said evenly, "you put that silly camera away and get these two jokers into your truck."

"But, what about Mister Holliman?"

"And after you get them into this truck," Joshua went on, unaffected by the interruption except for a slight hardening of his grey eyes, "then you will take them to the nearest ETC doctor." He turned away toward the Jag, his last order coming over his shoulder. "And you've got just five minutes to clear this road."

He got into the Jag, backed it out, then pulled off the private road in next to the white Mark V. He picked up the two automatics, a Colt .45 and a Browning 9mm, before he climbed out to move around to the rear of the Mark V. Gus Holliman, who was known to be deathly afraid of guns, was hunched down in the back seat. Joshua jacked the first round into the Colt. As a precaution, he put the first shot through the base of the telephone antenna on the trunk.

The heavy, flat muzzle blast of the forty-five BA-ROOMED like a howitzer in the desert stillness, and Joshua was halfway hoping the man in the car would catch the ricochet.

Holliman was screaming hysterically above the residual effect of the first round, but Joshua ignored him, shooting out both the rear radials. He walked to the other end of the expensive car, taking out the front tires, before putting the final two rounds through the radiator. He turned and threw the empty forty-five into the desert. He was satisfied to see the white pick-up scalding down the private road toward the highway.

Beside the rear door on the driver's side, he peered indifferently into the rear seat. Gus Holliman shrank away, burrowing into the hand-rubbed leather.

"Open the door!" Joshua yelled at him.

Holliman shook his head no, staring wildly at him, his lower lip quivering. Joshua pulled the Browning out of his belt, thinking it was going to be some whopping repair bill on the car. He pumped one shot directly through the two rear windows and was not overly surprised to see Holliman frantically releasing the door lock. Joshua hauled the smaller man out of the car, stood him up against the front door.

"Undress," Joshua told him curtly.

"You're insane," Holliman gasped. "You're supposed to be undergoing a test. You're the initiate."

"If you don't do it, I will."

Gus Holliman rubbed his forehead with a thin, bloodless hand. "Please, Joshua," he begged; then, "You know I can't take the sun." But he started anyway, his jacket first, then his tie.

Sure enough, Joshua thought, aware that Holliman hated the sun, staying cooped up all day either in the Sanctuary or in his private quarters on the Halley estate, coming out only when the sun was down, like one of the white, colorless lizards which feed on night abiding bugs. Joshua guessed that Holliman was in his middle forties, a meticulous, careful man, who on this morning's mission was doing his best to prove Joshua Bain inadequate to join the council as an elder.

"That's enough," Joshua said, now that Holliman was stripped to the waist. He roughly turned and faced Holliman into the rising sun. "This is just a sample of what can happen," Joshua warned him. "You see, I can take you back in a little farther, up to where I've been quail hunting a couple times. You know the place because you know everything. Up there, it'd take you all day to walk out, if you could make it."

"All right," Holliman said after a moment, obviously getting the drift of the encounter. "What is it you want?"

Joshua turned him around so they were facing each other nose to nose. "We're going to be busy tomorrow. So, let's say by Sunday night, right here, the same place at ten o'clock, we'll meet again. And, you'll be alone, right?"

Holliman, his head dropping, nodded weakly.

"And you will bring with you specific information regarding the untimely death of Jerrie McKennan." He had to be careful to control his voice at just mentioning her name.

Holliman now looked up, blinking. "What are you talking about? It was an accident," and he began to look a little wide-eyed again.

"There was heroin in her blood, Gus. And the question naturally comes up: where did she get it?"

"What difference does it make?"

"The newspapers," Joshua went on, his voice thickening, "reported that there were a few outsiders in town that weekend."

Holliman frowned, before answering, "Yeah, the Huelga bunch. That was the week the farm workers were demonstrating. You remember, the ruckus at the courthouse."

"I know," said Joshua impatiently, "but I'm referring to

someone from up north, possibly friends of ours from Berkeley, who were down here specifically to look us up."

Holliman was shaking his head. "Come on, Joshua, that was nearly two weeks ago."

Joshua turned a quarter turn to his left, pitched the Browning as far as he could. "I want names, addresses, here Sunday night," and with that final statement he turned away from Gus Holliman.

Back in the Jag and on his way to Highway 74, Joshua assumed he had correctly carried out his expected role in the game sponsored by the ETC. His real accomplishment for the morning was that he had at least made his first contact with Britt Halley on the subject of Jerrie McKennan, something he could not afford to do with her face to face, yet. He no more expected Gus Holliman to show up Sunday night than he would the King of Saudi Arabia. And while he didn't know how or when, he still expected the gambit to pay off.

As he turned onto the highway, he noticed the ETC helicopter veering in from the valley floor on a heading directly toward Gus Holliman's car. He frowned thoughtfully to himself, thinking the chopper got up there pretty quickly, considering that the pick-up back on the road didn't have a mobile phone.

He let the Jag loaf as he started back down the incline to Palm Desert, checking closely in the left fender-mounted rear view mirror. Winding down now, he noticed that in the wake of this morning's incident, he was neither satisfied nor fulfilled. His anger and frustration had been temporarily vented, but in their place was the great emptiness now. Breathing deeply of the air rushing in through the open windshield, he accepted that he would live with it for now. He was not surprised then to see the white GMC pick-up behind him, trailing at a safe distance. You cut it a little close, my friend, he thought curiously.

Alan Hunt backed off the accelerator as soon as he verified that the car ahead was the Jaguar. Keeping up with Joshua Bain now was more of a challenge, and he figured he had an excuse to do some work on the truck's stock engine. Behind him, the Winchester was back in its rack above the rear window. Alan Hunt supposed that he, like Gino Malone, knew a little more about Joshua Bain, who on this occasion had displayed a bent for the unorthodox. For crude, brutal men like Gino, it was illogical for a badly outnumbered prey to boldly press the fight. Remembering he had a chore yet to perform, he quickly picked up the phone, asked for the mobile operator. A few seconds later, he was on Britt Halley's private line.

"He is all right, ma'am," he responded to her first question.

"Where is he going now?" she asked him curtly and without emotion.

"I'm not sure, but he mentioned last night he was going to the Palm Springs Airport sometime today."

"Stay with him, and let me know."

The line went dead.

He allowed his thinning grey hair to grow long, pulling it back over his head so that it hung nattily down the nape of his neck, making him look as if he always needed a haircut. But Calvin Price, still called "Senator" by his close friends, liked his hair that way, so it stayed, looking like the belly hair on a wet collie, because whatever Senator Price liked was usually the way things were. He supposed he could get up some morning, paint himself purple, and go through the whole day without arousing a single comment to his face. When he had been younger, in his forties and fifties, he used to wonder whether it was his millions or the fact that he was one tough hombre that had evoked such fear and respect from his associates. Now, at age seventy-six, and in the wisdom of his declining years, he didn't care. He was stuck with being rich; he doubted that he could even give it all away now. As for his toughness, that was more and more within him now, in his spirit and in his mind.

Watching Britt Halley hang up her phone, he realized that most men of his age and in his present position would probably be wishing they were twenty or thirty years younger. Knowing this woman as he did, Calvin Price was thankful he was not a younger man.

Now, he could hardly detect the slight flush in her cheeks as she showed him once more an example of her extraordinary self-control. Despite her young age, she had somehow already learned to deal with the fact that the body reacted to emotion. It was his notion that the best poker players were older men, those whose emotions had been blunted, and maybe the Orientals, because they started early in life learning to control themselves. During the past few years, he had wondered often what had been responsible for the early demise of her emotions. Her only apparent weakness was her tendency to slip quickly in and out of violent fits of temper, which she didn't bother to conceal, and maybe that was a part of her *modus operandi* too, that she turned it on and off deliberately, for special effect.

He shifted his long, angular body in the leather-covered chair, feeling uncomfortably cooped up. Abruptly, he wished he were sitting opposite a wounded rhino; at least he would know how to cope with that simple an adversary.

"I hope that is the last of the phone calls," he said. His drawl was formidable, like a slow-moving freight train.

Britt was smiling, putting him on immediate alert. "I'm sorry," she said hoarsely, "but it was important."

"It was about Bain, wasn't it?"

She wasn't smiling anymore, but she didn't look put out either.

"Yes," she answered. "Today is the day for field testing. And you know how rough Holliman's men can get."

"How'd he make out?"

"We should check into revising that part of the program."

"I said, how'd he make out?"

"Well, of the four who went out, he put three in the hospital, including Gus Holliman."

Calvin Price laughed uproariously, his voice booming and rattling in the closed-in, soundproofed room. Britt stared at him, expressionless, waiting for him to finish. Her dark brown, almost black hair was cut medium length, coming down smoothly to below her ears where it curled out subtly, carefully styled, like her clothes. Absently then, she reached up to pull an imaginary hair away from the right side of her face. "It isn't funny, Senator," she finally said.

Price was pleased with the report, more than he was amused, and as he settled himself back into his chair, he was still chuckling. "How come," he said breathlessly, "how come he let one get away?" and he was having trouble getting control of himself, for he could not imagine a squirt like Gus Holliman getting tangled up in a fight.

"He let the camera man go," she said indifferently. "Apparently to bring the others back to the dispensary."

Price was thinking he would've paid a thousand bucks for a ringside seat. "Is Gus all right?" he asked then.

Britt shrugged. "Just shaken up, I think."

Senator Price levelled a probing look at her then, out from under his weathered brow. "I told you he was gonna be a good one."

Britt nodded that she remembered. "But he's all uptight now."

"Because of the girl, what's her name?"

"Jerrie McKennan."

He had been studying her carefully during the exchange, and his eyes narrowed down even more as he came at her broadside, "You want him, don't you, little lady?" He deliberately avoided saying she was in love with Bain, because he doubted she knew what the word love meant. To her, Joshua Bain was probably more of a challenge, or maybe even a trinket, a toy she obviously hadn't yet been able to purchase.

She didn't answer him right away, and he went on, "It doesn't matter what you say, honey, because I already know the answer."

She was looking puzzled; her brow turned down into the provocative vee which must have turned Morgan Halley every way but up.

"I had it figured about three months ago," Price said, "but I have to bring it up now because it looks like we're gonna have to use him."

"So," she offered after a moment. "We're all being used, in one way or another."

"Why do you think I'm in so early today?" He had not gotten to the point of the meeting yet, but normally he and the rest of the ex-com didn't arrive until late on the night before the scheduled session, which, in this instance, was tomorrow.

"I think you're about to tell me," she said then, and he saw that she was back to normal. Her face was calm, the full mouth was firm, the eyes clear. She had the confident look of the gambler who on her fourth card up had the board locked.

"Hal Fleming called me yesterday morning," he went on. "He's got hard info that the FBI has got something going against us." He pivoted his head around, trying to relax his neck muscles, thinking that maybe he would play some golf tomorrow morning. "Unfortunately," he continued, "the source doesn't know what it is they've got, only that the ETC is the subject of a classified inquiry."

"They've poked around before," she pointed out.

"I know," he said. "But we're a lot further along now. Gus told me last week that we've actually turned the corner."

"We're about half finished," she told him. "But they can't possibly be onto Omega. Our last analysis indicates we're still in the green by a wide margin."

He had brought his hands under his chin, staring at her thoughtfully. "We might assume that, and I think you're right. But, you know, little lady, we're not playing stud poker. We can never look at the cards and say we've got the board locked."

"I don't look at what we're doing as a game," she said, and there was the shadow of her feelings again darkening her cheeks. "This operation is the product of five years' detailed and careful planning," she insisted.

"Whoa, honey," he said gently, holding up his right hand. "You don't have to sell me." He straightened up to lean forward in his chair. "But we're obliged to do what we can to protect ourselves, to keep ourselves in the green belt. And, that's where Joshua comes in right now."

Britt sighed heavily, shook her head. "So what's with Joshua?"

"He's a natural to move in as a double agent in the Bureau."

Britt frowned slightly, then lifted an inquiring eyebrow. "I don't know," she said softly, almost in a whisper. "I see what you're driving at, but the timing seems a little awkward. I mean, if they are on to something, won't it strike them a bit strange that a contact just falls into their lap?"

She was sharp, he thought admiringly. He had only thought about that angle on the plane coming in this morning. He shrugged once, leaned back again into the soft leather folds of the chair. "We roll the dice on everything we do, honey. A couple weeks ago I nearly killed myself on a throw rug, can you imagine, on my way to the john in the middle of the night. Besides, if they're really after us, they'll be happy to find a source."

"So what do we do?"

"It's fairly simple," he said. "You're familiar with what happened to Joshua a couple years ago up north. The Courtland kidnap case?"

"Yes."

"The FBI man on the case was an agent named Cleveland Lambert, a crusty old dog who's about ready to retire. He's now a wheel of some kind in the local L.A. office. Anyway, we can point Joshua in that direction, let him use Lambert as his contact."

"How will we do it?"

Maybe she was really hooked this time, he thought. Since

Morgan Halley died, Britt Halley had indulged herself with a batch of brief one-shot affairs. But apparently she's got it bad this time. With any other person in the organization, she would already have dismissed the details, turning them over to Gus Holliman to handle. "He uses the telephone," he said matter-of-factly.

"You're not my father," she reminded him curtly. "So stop talking to me as if I'm your teenage daughter."

He laughed appreciatively. "All right, honey. We prep' Joshua with a story of some kind. We throw 'em a fish, something to justify his coming to them."

"And?"

Senator Calvin Price stared hard at her then, and the look around his eyes was colder, sterner, the threatening visage of a man whose emotions had definitely been blunted. "And he will find out quickly what it is the FBI is after, what it is they have."

"He can do it," she said confidently, "if it can be done."

He didn't like the qualification, but he let it pass. "We'll discuss it tomorrow night, after we vote. I can tell you that Hal is already for it."

"Marshall will go along," she suggested. "Have you thought about when Joshua should start?"

"Monday."

"That's a little soon. Shouldn't we have some preparation?"

"Huh-uh," he said. "Let him go in cold turkey; he'll be more natural that way. The Bureau boys are clever, especially a pro like Lambert, and they'd spot him in a minute if he tried to play it heavy."

"I suppose you're right."

"Why don't we set you and him up for Sunday. Have him over to the house. By then we'll have the details ready for you to pass on. All he has to do is play it straight and let the cards fall."

"Okay," she agreed, "then Sunday it is."

Calvin Price could hardly keep himself from smiling now, because he knew that if you push against the reed with the wind you need far less force to bend it.

The pieces of the Avion were scattered around at the rear of the hangar, arranged within the roped-off area guarded by two free-standing signs. The two signs were identical and succinctly warned passers-by that the area was restricted and under the control of the FAA.

Joshua Bain was waiting impatiently at the open entrance to the hangar. Two men, both dressed in white coveralls, were working on the wreckage, like two drones under the harsh overhead light. For fifteen minutes Joshua had been watching them stooping and squatting, making some kind of notations on clipboards, moving lethargically, deliberately, apparently able to make some kind of order out of what to most people was a hopeless, mangled, charred mess.

Joshua was immensely relieved to see one of the men, a Mister Herlihy, finally detach himself from the wreckage to step over the rope. Joshua moved forward to meet him at the middle of the hangar.

"I'm sorry to keep you waiting," Mister Herlihy apologized, "but you weren't supposed to be by until later this afternoon," and he moved on officially without giving Joshua the chance to respond to his apology. "As you know, Mister Bain, all synthetics used in the plane's construction, including cockpit accessories, have to be made of self-extinguishing material. Both we and the ATA are pretty sticky on enforcing this requirement."

Joshua nodded that he understood. Such plastic items as switch buttons could burn at high enough temperatures, but they were supposed to extinguish themselves if removed from the ambient heat source.

"Just before you came by," Herlihy went on, "we were able to isolate a portion of the instrument panel," and he checked his clipboard. "From the panel openings, I'd say it's midframe. Not totally charred. And we have definite evidence of a polyvinyl residue." He held up a small clear plastic envelope. "I scraped this piece off while you were waiting."

Joshua took the envelope, backlighted it against the open hangar door. "Could it be green?" he murmured. He couldn't tell the color; it looked nearly black.

"Could be. It's been scorched, but I'd say if I had to pick a color that green would be my guess."

"Got any guess what it might be from?"

Herlihy shrugged, smiled a little. "Who knows. Obviously it was something that was brought aboard. My guess would be that it is from one of those cheap plastic raincoats. You know, the kind you can fold up and put in your pocket. Some pilots keep them on board in case they hit bad weather at the other end."

Joshua handed him the envelope. "Have you got enough to figure what caused the crash?"

"At this point," Herlihy said thoughtfully, "we'd have to say pilot error. The plane's trim appears normal. Engine functioning at full power. No evidence of fire or explosion prior to impact. But, we're still a few days away from finalizing the investigation."

Joshua extended his right hand. "Thank you, Mister Herlihy. You've been more of a help than you realize."

"Don't mention it. Jeff Capstan is an old buddy of mine."

Joshua turned to head out of the hangar.

"By the way, Mister Bain," Herlihy called after him. "Is there anything about this accident you know that maybe we should?"

Joshua pulled up, turned to face him angularly. "No, sir," he said. "Only that I authorized the flight, and the pilot, well, she was a friend of mine."

On his way back to his car, he detoured by the administration building to use a pay phone, placing a collect call to his attorney in Riverside. Bill Olson wasn't in his office, so Joshua waited impatiently while his secretary transferred to another outside line to find him. Joshua's mind tumbled out of order as he tried to sort it all out. He had stopped by the ranch, exchanging the damaged Jaguar for the Ford wagon. Two down and two to go for today's schedule. He heard clicking noises in his ear then, followed by the resonant voice of Bill Olson. Joshua identified himself to the man he'd never met face to face.

"I'm at the courthouse now," Olson told him. "And I've got the answers you want. First off, your wife was definitely killed by the accident."

"There's no doubt?"

"None whatsoever. These people are required by law to pin down the cause of death. And in this case, it's fairly simple to detect." And he paused for a second or two. "Are you sure you want these details? I mean, Mister Bain, it can get kind of messy."

"I need to know," Joshua insisted.

"Well, after death, certain changes occur in the body's cell structure, and if the body is torn or dismembered, it's fairly simple to determine, and in this instance, since the body was so thoroughly broken up, the autopsy people literally had dozens of specimens for comparison."

"I get the picture," Joshua said, interrupting him. "What about the heroin saturation?"

"Her blood solution suggests anywhere from a low of five minutes to a high of twenty minutes."

"Okay," said Joshua. "I get the feeling we should back off from these people."

"You're right," Bill Olson agreed. "While you have the privilege of requesting the formal autopsy, if you keep pushing, the police are going to start wanting some answers themselves."

"All I need is some time," Joshua told him, and he hesitated, trying to think. "Get a copy of everything you can. Especially the pathologist's report and the autopsy report, and take them to a doctor you can trust and have him give us a more detailed estimate on how long before the accident she was injected with the heroin. And tell him to use at least three respiration rates. The lowest at, say, an unconscious and badly wounded level. The highest at a conscious, probably excited level. The other in between." He paused for a moment. "You understand what I need?"

"Yes, I understand. What about the remains, Mister Bain? We're over the deadline now, especially since the autopsy is finished."

"Try to get to the doctor today," Joshua suggested. "If he has enough, then have the remains cremated."

"We can use the doctor's report at the inquest."

"Negative!" Joshua said sharply. "Let the official version stand as it is."

"That the drug was self-administered, a routine accident?" Bill Olson asked skeptically. "I mean, if you're trying to turn some kind of incriminatory evidence—"

"We're doing it on our own, at my request," Joshua insisted. "It's for my own satisfaction." There was a following pause.

"I get the feeling, Mister Bain," Olson said then, "that you might be interested in administering your own justice in this matter."

"Not at all," Joshua assured him. "And please allow me to point out that what I've asked you to do is perfectly legal and ethical. Is that correct?"

"Yes, so far it is."

"Will you kindly let me know, then," he said cordially, "when you find out anything?"

"Can I pass it to Mister Hunt if I can't reach you?"

"No," said Joshua after a moment. "Please reserve this for me, personally."

With the closing amenities out of the way, Joshua promptly hung up the phone. He checked his watch, noticing that his hands were shaking. He had less than thirty minutes to make his next appointment. He headed for the Ford wagon, hoping he had time to grab a quick hamburger.

Jeff Capstan was waiting for him in his office at the Bermuda Dunes Airport. Before he sat down in front of the desk, Joshua pulled a fifth of twelve-year old Scotch from under his arm, sat it on the desk in front of the airport manager.

"A token of my appreciation," he said warmly.

"Not a bribe, of course," Jeff said good-naturedly, and he took the heavy, squat bottle, started to put it away in a desk drawer. "Should we crack it now?" he asked suggestively.

Joshua held up his hands. "Not for me; I can't stand the stuff," and they both laughed.

"So how'd it go?" Jeff asked as he closed the drawer.

Joshua shrugged indifferently. "Fairly routine. Herlihy is convinced it was pilot error, and I'm inclined to agree with him." Joshua was doing his best to sound conversational, even uninterested at this point.

"She made a mistake, Joshua," said Jeff Capstan soberly.

So that was it, Joshua thought, and he took a deep breath in an effort to keep control of himself. It was obvious by Jeff's tone that the word was out, that Jerrie McKennan had been higher than a kite when the Avion went in. That nice pat answer made it easy for Jeff Capstan, for Herlihy, for the whole interested pack. Joshua pushed himself to his feet. "You're probably right," he said evenly, "and I want to thank you for your help."

"Glad to do it, Josh."

Beside the more obvious fact, Joshua thought cynically, that the ETC account was the largest single source of revenue for the airport. "There is one more and final thing," Joshua said then.

"Just name it."

"You tape all the tower transmissions, don't you?"

"Yes; in fact, all the operation's traffic is recorded."

"It would be a big favor," Joshua said, still offhandedly, "if I could listen to the tape of her take-off exchange. I mean, you know it was the last thing she probably said to anyone."

"No problem," said Jeff. "I can get it recorded and have it for you by Monday."

Joshua shook his head. "I don't need it on a recording. Can I just listen to it once?"

"Right now?"

"If it's not too inconvenient."

"Not at all," Jeff said as he reached for his phone. "You go on over to operations, and I'll tell them you're coming."

Joshua was smiling genuinely as he turned to leave. This could do it, he thought, feeling his own pulse quicken. This could nail the lid down once and for all, and he wondered why it had taken him nearly ten days to think of it.

And immediately I was in the spirit: and, behold, a throne was set in heaven, and one sat on the throne.

And he that sat was to look upon like a jasper and a sardine stone: and there was a rainbow round about the throne, in sight like unto an emerald.

And round about the throne were four and twenty seats: and upon the seats I saw four and twenty elders sitting, clothed in white raiment; and they had on their heads crowns of gold.

And out of the throne proceeded lightnings and thunderings and voices: and there were seven lamps of fire burning before the throne, which are the seven Spirits of God.

And before the throne there was a sea of glass like unto crystal: and in the midst of the throne, and round about the throne, were four beasts full of eyes before and behind.

And the first beast was like a lion, and the second beast like a calf, and the third beast had a face as a man, and the fourth beast was like a flying eagle.—according to the author of The Revelation

Chapter six

The first two floors of the ETC headquarters were rectangularly shaped. The long axis of the first and lower floor measured three hundred and eighty-five feet. Above and offset back, the second floor measured an even two hundred feet. The third floor, called the Sanctuary, was an exact half circle. The straight, front wall of the Sanctuary overlapped the second floor by ten feet for its full one-hundred foot length. Behind, the rear supporting wall of the Sanctuary curled in a circle, fitting snugly in and anchored to the massive recess carved out of the ascending slope, which reached on up toward Indio Mountain. The roof of the Sanctuary had been entirely fill covered after its construction, the earth and granite replaced to match the original incline. The three-foot thick, steel-reinforced concrete walls and roof of the Sanctuary were laced with miles of electrical wiring to detect immediately any tunneling effort. The wiring matrix was so dense that a quarter-inch carbon-tipped drill could not penetrate more than six inches without interrupting a circuit and tripping an automatic alarm.

The only normal entry to the Sanctuary was through two elevators, access to one through Britt Halley's private office, the other through Gus Holliman's office. The elevators could be activated only by the proper sequencing of nine lighted push buttons located at chest level just to the right of the elevators' doors. There were no guards in the Sanctuary; its security was provided entirely by electronic and mechanical means. The two elevators opened at opposite ends of the long hallway running the length of the front of the Sanctuary. A few feet from the elevator on Britt Halley's end, a single door gave access to the private lounges reserved for the executive committee.

At the opposite end of the hallway, a few feet from the elevator lifting from Gus Holliman's office, was another single, matching door. Inside, there was a foyer-like room, with a second, heavier and more formidable door, which gave access to the most elaborately protected room of all, the Documents Room. The room was deceptively small, only 9 x 12 feet. Here were stored the working records for the secret echelon of the ETC. The more mundane but still highly classified records, such as computer tab runs, accounting and fiscal documents, individual project plans with supporting files, closed studies and historical files, were on microfiche, filed in 4 x 6 containers on 105mm film cards. The microfiche file was in a small wooden cabinet, measuring 2 x 3 feet, atop a hip-level bench-type shelf running the length of the room on the right. The only other item on the heavy shelf was a microfiche viewer. A single four-drawer filing cabinet, also made of wood, stood alone against the wall directly opposite the door. To the left, a small wooden work desk, with one chair, was against the wall. There was a single black telephone on the desk.

To gain entry to the outer foyer, one had to properly sequence a nine-button board in the hallway. The foyer was automatically lighted when entered and fully scanned by two closed-circuit TV cameras which reported to the security station on the second floor.

To enter the Documents Room itself required the sequencing of what appeared to be a more complex multi-station switch assembly located near the door. Instead of nine buttons, this assembly had sixteen, four rows of four. To activate the heavy steel sliding door, one had to sequence the proper order of numbers on the last three stations. The first station, comprised of four buttons in a vertical row, was a protective device, and had nothing to do with releasing the door. Devised by Morgan Halley, the floor of the Documents Room was free-floating, and the total weight on the floor was constantly monitored by a solid-state sensor. When one entered the room, he or she had to have pushed the correct button of the four on the first station, within a margin of safety, or else within exactly sixty seconds the room's igniter system would automatically fire. The first button allowed extra weight on the floor up to two hundred pounds, the second up to three hundred, the third up to four hundred, and the fourth button permitted a total weight of five hundred pounds. There was no provision for override.

The walls and ceilings of the Documents Room were composed of alternating layers of magnesium and compressed oxygen. The igniting surface was a mixture of thermite and magnesium, interlaced with a fine network of ignition wiring, not unlike the matrix in the self-defrosting windshield of a car. Within two seconds after ignition, the room would become a crucible of the sun, reaching a temperature of over three thousand degrees Fahrenheit.

In the middle of the hallway, a large, double door entered

the largest and only other room left in the Sanctuary, the Throne Room. Used only by the executive committee when in formal session, the Throne Room aptly fitted its name. Ninety feet away and opposite the door, an enormous elevated throne rose nearly to the fifteen-foot-high ceiling. The huge dark chair was starkly plain, carved out of solid mahogany. From the front of the room the side walls ran straight for twenty feet. The back wall curved symetrically behind the massive throne. The entire surface of the curved back wall was covered by a single mosaic, the inlaid scene on the left showing a tranquil sky, graced by a full rainbow. To the right of the throne chair, the mosaic developed into an angry, tumultuous scene of lightning and storm clouds. The remainder of the huge room was entirely carpeted, including ceiling and side walls, with a velour-like wine-red carpet.

With their backs to the throne, the four pews for the executive committee were in a semicircle, facing inward. Each of the four compartments was equipped with a microphone, a built-in desk, an electronic keyboard for voting, and a multi-station telephone. A display board above the entrance reported the committee's voting score. The 4 x 6 front of each pew was sculptured in bas-relief. From left to right, the first was the maned head of a lion, the second a calf, the third the face of a man with strong aquiline features, and the fourth of an eagle in flight.

A semicircle of seven gas lamps burned continuously around the base of the throne chair. On the seat of the throne was a large, leather-bound book sealed with seven unbroken seals. All this, the permanent fixtures in the ceremonial room, were lighted indirectly, so that one standing near the entrance could not see the light's source. The heavy symbolism was deliberate and, to a student of the Holy Bible, had obviously been drawn from the fourth chapter of The Revelation. For the late Morgan Halley, the designer and decorator, the Throne Room had been necessary to remind the executive committee of the gravity and seriousness of their affairs.

At present, two items of temporary furniture were placed in the open space before the committee. To the left, near the doorway leading to the lounge area, was a large black desk, occupied by Gus Holliman. Twenty feet to his front, a single straight-backed chair faced the committee. From left to right, the four committee members were all present. First, Marshall Higgins, out of Chicago. His enormous personal wealth ran from steel to ship-building to vast holdings in midwestern farm and livestock properties. The least talkative of the four, he was, at age sixty-two, a large, florid-faced man. Impatient with details, he usually spent his time at these meetings doodling, seldom talking, as if his silence might hurry the proceedings along. Next was Harold Fleming, New York City. Fifty-six years old, he was a near genius with a lawyer-like capacity to probe and deal with the details shunned by his companion on his right. Slender, poised, always impeccably well-groomed, he was the dandy of the group. His personal wealth was also enormous, though it had been largely inherited from a family fortune rivaling the Rockefellers. Third in line was Calvin Price, the admitted maverick. He was the catalyst to get the group moving from talking about something to doing it. The rough-and-tumble Senator enjoyed the meetings immensely. Lastly, and to his left, was Britt Halley, occupying the pew formerly used by her late husband, Morgan Halley. Cool, always calm at the meetings, she was the moderator. Resented at first by one or two of the committee members, she had in the last two years gained the respect of them all. The five persons present in the room were dressed in identical white toga-like robes.

The committee had been in session now for nearly two hours, and the afternoon's agenda had so far gone smoothly under the guidance of Britt Halley and Gus Holliman. The last subject just introduced by Gus Holliman was the matter of the current FBI investigation being conducted against the ETC. Calvin Price sat forward in his chair, scrawling notes while he listened attentively to Hal Fleming finish his brief estimate of the situation.

"We can therefore conclude," Fleming argued, "that at least one specialist in the Special Litigation Section has been assigned to the project. Our informant also reports that the section chief, Dick Martinson, is unhappy with the arrangement, angry in fact, which naturally suggests the director himself is behind the project, probably actively involved. So, even though our input to date is sketchy, there is enough to suggest more than a routine look-see." Fleming paused for a moment while he arranged his papers. "My recommendation is that we go first priority, starting right now."

Seeing Hal Fleming was finished, Calvin Price addressed himself to Gus Holliman, "What's in your library on this Special Litigation Section?"

Gus pulled a folder out of the rack in front of him, opened it up. "We have an up-to-date file, which we started last year. There are currently seventeen persons, excluding the section chief." He paused, his thin nose elevated as he read through his bifocals. "According to our majority decision on ex-com session of January 18, this year, we suspended detailed background check on section members, for the reason that since we had received a clean report, any further digging might arouse the Bureau's suspicion."

Price was nodding slowly, grunting to himself. He remembered the majority vote very well, since he had been the lone dissenter. When you have a wolf pack on your back, you didn't put out the camp fires just because you think the wolves have given up. "All right," he said then, "do we agree that we need to get on this immediately?"

Four green lights appeared on the display board above the entrance.

"I say we work both ends," he said evenly. "Hal, our next two objectives on Condition Y are in your area, right?"

Hal Fleming nodded. "We should have them stabilized by the end of August."

"Can you spare four of your six people?" Price asked him, refering to the Eastern council of elders operating under Fleming.

Hal Fleming assumed a studied expression. "Three for now, and I can probably break out the fourth by next weekend."

"Good enough," Price said. "Each of the three of us will assign to you two of our people on a temporary-duty basis. Gus, you work out the travel plans and set up the transfer. Hal can arrange the NYC end, where to stay, and so on." He paused for a moment. "We'll concentrate first on finding a weak link in that special section, with emphasis on the known man working against us. Why don't we assign an open chit of, say, a million without committee approval, so Hal can move quickly if he has to. We don't want to get balled up, Gus, in accounting procedure."

"Why not two million?" Marshall Higgins suggested. "We might bag a pair of canaries."

"Let's vote on it," Britt said impatiently.

Four green lights appeared on the board.

"Is that one million per man?" Gus asked.

"An open number, regardless, right?" Price answered,

looking around to the other three.

Four green lights again appeared on the board.

Senator Price moved on, satisfied that with two million bucks in his pocket, Hal Fleming could buy the cooperation of at least one FBI lawyer. "For this end," he went on quickly, "Britt and I have agreed to develop a double agent."

"Why not just fund another million?" Higgins suggested laconically.

"What we've got," Britt said, "money can't buy."

Price smiled to himself involuntarily. "Why don't we wait until we vote on Mister Bain?"

Britt nodded her agreement.

"All right, Gus," Price said then, "unless you've got something further on the general agenda."

Gus was shaking his head no. He proceeded then in a dull, flat monotone. "This initiate is Joshua Bain, no middle name or initial. Please refer to background sheet, appendix F, attached to agenda." And he waited for a moment, allowing the committee members to find the appendix. "Joshua Bain was sponsored by Calvin Price and jointly nominated by him and Mrs. Britt Halley. Background investigation has been carried out over one-year period per bylaws. Initiate Bain was born in Warsaw, Poland, exact date unknown. Both Jewish parents were killed in Auschwitz concentration camp."

His hand on his brow, Calvin Price watched both Marshall Higgins and Hal Fleming, seeking their reaction to the fact that Joshua Bain was a Jew. As he hoped and expected, neither man showed any outward sign.

"He survived the Nazi occupation," Gus was saying, "in the friendly custody of a native Polish family. After the war, his only known surviving relative, an invalid aunt, took him into brief custody. She soon thereafter died of natural causes in a detention camp on Cyprus. Bain was subsequently adopted by an American Red Cross worker and her husband, a military attache, from whom he obtained not only his surname but his U.S. citizenship as well. At the time of the adoption, the Bains were both in their middle fifties. They returned to the continental U.S. in 1949, residing in Washington, D.C. for four years. In 1953, the elder Bain retired from the civil service and moved his family to San Jose, California. He passed away in 1961, natural causes. His wife survived him by six years, dying in 1967. By then, as you can see in the record, Joshua Bain had completed two years at San Jose State College. When his adoptive mother died, he enlisted in the Army. He served a hitch in Vietnam as an infantryman and as a special-weapons advisor. Usual medals, including the Bronze Star. Copy of citation attached to appendix." Gus stopped to take a drink from the glass on his desk.

"Shortly after returning to the U.S.," Gus went on, still in the same monotone, "he was accepted on an inter-service application as a Naval Aviation cadet. Completing that training, he was assigned to his second tour in Vietnam, where he flew an attack-bomber, carrier based. He was shot down over North Vietnam three months later. He was captured after thirty-three days of evading the enemy, held for eighteen months and three days. He obtained his release at the termination of hostilities between the U.S. Government and the Democratic Republic of Vietnam. After his rehabilitation and release, he enrolled in the University of California at Berkeley, where he obtained his bachelor's degree in Communications Skills, a specialized major involving both English and speech." Gus Holliman closed the folder in front of him.

"As you can see by the record, Mister Bain was involved in breaking the Mayberry Courtland kidnap case, and that two-year-old incident gave us our first contact with him. For the past year, he has been the resident manager of a grape ranch near La Quinta. That property is privately held by a subsidiary wholly owned by Mrs. Halley. The only correction to the record is that Mister Bain has asked for a transfer to another ranch property," and he looked inquiringly to Britt Halley.

"That's correct," she told him. "He has a buy-out agreement on the present property. I'm making arrangements to have it transferred to the Fuller ranch."

"Why don't we take a break," Calvin Price suggested, "for fifteen minutes before we interview him. Give us a chance to go over his record a little more closely."

Four green lights appeared on the board.

Fifteen minutes later, Joshua Bain was ushered into the Throne Room by Gus Holliman. As he sat down in the exposed straight-backed chair, Joshua felt like he was a slave going up for auction. He was dressed only in a light-weight linen toga, belted at the waist, and a pair of flimsy leather sandals. Gus Holliman introduced him, briefly explained why he was there.

Joshua did not recognize two of the committee members,

who apparently were to remain anonymous. He had surveyed the room when he entered, and he was still a little shaken by the splendor. The symbolism meant nothing to him, but he filed it all away, item by item. He was careful to note that there were only two visible entrances. If there were any records stored in the Sanctuary, he had yet to turn a clue to where they might be. He noticed that Calvin Price was smiling warmly at him. Joshua remained expressionless, avoiding looking at Britt Halley.

"It is my task, Mister Bain," Gus Holliman was now saying, "to question you first on particulars which for the record need clarification. And, as I reminded you before you came in, you will be subjected to a polygraph test immediately after the interview."

Go ahead, Gus, Joshua thought confidently, because he knew the truth wouldn't hurt him as much as his protagonist might hope, at least to that point.

"Regarding your motives for assisting the FBI in the Courtland case," Gus began. "May we assume you came forward on your own first? I mean, you were not contacted first, offered money or immunity?"

Joshua: That's correct.

Holliman: Well then, why did you come forward?

Joshua: I knew Miss McKennan was involved in the kidnapping. It was her action group which master-minded the operation.

Holliman: Action group? Please explain.

Joshua: Jerrie McKennan was an active member of the Weathermen for Action and Revolution. It was part of her thing at the time. The WAR people, like most radical underground groups, are divided up into small, sometimes-called combat-teams. Action groups. Firing groups.

Holliman: Even though she was addicted to hard drugs?

Joshua: That's not unusual with these people. Some of the purer strains forbid it, but most tolerate it while discouraging it.

Holliman: And you knew about her role in the kidnapping?

Joshua: Yes. I had lived with her for nearly two years by that time. And, well, when she was really under, she would talk to me. You see, she didn't really like what was happening. The kidnapping was something she hadn't bargained for. As far as she was concerned, it had gotten out of hand. And, I agreed with her. I figured it was only a matter of time before the FBI nailed the whole bunch, including her.

Holliman: So your motive was to protect her.

Joshua: Of course. I wanted her out of the Weathermen and off the drugs.

Calvin Price wondered if Joshua Bain could see through Gus Holliman's line of questioning, that what Gus was really striking for was Joshua's attitude toward the law of the land. Had Joshua reacted because he was an accessory to a crime, out of conscience against the criminal act itself, or had he reacted out of more self-serving interests?

Holliman: All right, Mister Bain. On to another subject. Have you ever killed someone?

Joshua: Yes, in the war.

Holliman: Did you enjoy it?

Joshua: Absolutely not.

Holliman: You were then, shall we say, a reluctant soldier?

Joshua: Not exactly. I should add to the answer by saying that thinking about it now I enjoy it considerably less than I did at the time.

Holliman: Since you've had time to reflect?

Joshua: To an extent, yes. The ones I'd really enjoy killing would be those who start the wars. War, in general, is heavy with irony, but perhaps the most ironic note of all is that those who start the wars seldom spend any time on the front lines. If they had to, I guarantee you we'd have far fewer wars.

Holliman: You seem bitter.

Joshua: You better believe I am.

Holliman: Because of your friends lost in Vietnam, your imprisonment?

Joshua: Partly, yes. But more against the whole scenario, the up-front gamesmanship, that allowed the fiasco to take place.

Holliman: I see your point. Now, since you've admitted that you'd enjoy killing those who start the wars, we may infer that you've consented to a precedent, specifically, that under the proper circumstances you would in fact willingly take another person's life, or, at least, be willing to be part of a plan to take another person's life.

Calvin Price studied Joshua even more closely now, for Gus Holliman was applying the heat. The Senator moved his arms back and forth across the sides of his chest cavity to interrupt the sweat trickling down his sides, and he had the same feeling now that he enjoyed in the middle of an all-night poker marathon.

Britt Halley watched with a cool, calculating detachment. She was concerned more about the ego of Gus Holliman, who in fact, as she knew, was a weak and easily controlled individual. Now, he was at his supposed best, playing out his role as the advocate, and she was concerned that he might take the opportunity to bolster his own image, especially at the expense of Joshua Bain, whom he obviously detested.

Joshua: Before you too firmly define that precedent, Mister Holliman, let me give you a specific qualifying example. Going back to Nazi Germany, I would have been in full sympathy with and willingly participated in the staff plot to murder Adolph Hitler.

Bravo! Senator Price exclaimed to himself. A neat, side-stepping maneuver, and he looked curiously to Gus Holliman, who was now right back to his original question.

Don't go for the kill, Britt thought, looking straight into Gus Holliman's eyes. There would be time, later.

Holliman: I doubt seriously, Mister Bain, that a Jew would've been allowed on Hitler's general staff, and—

"Mister Holliman," Hal Fleming cut in, "you're not only out of order, you're also on the verge of seriously impugning the integrity of this committee. For the record, we can correctly deduce that Joshua Bain would support regicide under certain circumstances. And, I'm sure as time progresses we will have ample chance to further qualify his feelings on this so-called precedent. I now offer to you, Mister Bain, my own personal apology. And, I'm sure we are all sorry, sir, if you have been offended.

"Hear, hear," Senator Price added.

Holliman: I apologize, Mister Bain, officially and personally.

Joshua: No offense taken.

I wouldn't want to bet on that, Senator Price said to himself, thinking then that the polygraph tape on that answer would make interesting reading.

Holliman: Thank you, sir. Now, in view of your apparent sympathies, why did you select the University of California at Berkeley when you returned from Vietnam: The choice seems incongruous.

Joshua: Not really. I was totally cut off for eighteen

months, and, when I returned, I was staggered by the changed attitude of the country toward the war. I was, you might say, pretty well confused. I wanted to return to school, anyway, so I picked Berkeley, figuring that there I could get to the heart of the anti-war movement. If they had a valid point, I felt obliged to expose myself to it. You know, find out the motivations, their side, so to speak. I was also interested in the draft-evaders issue as well.

Holliman: So you were in the opposition camp, then.

Joshua: Well, I didn't look at it that way. If you want to find out what makes a watch tick, the best place to start is at the watch factory.

Holliman: Perhaps the committee might be interested in your findings.

Joshua: They're not very conclusive, I'm afraid. The briefest and most descriptive report I can offer is that many of the hardcore organizers, the gut level of the real leaders, are essentially after power. I lived with them for nearly three years, and after a while I noticed how easily many of them could switch causes, to move to any popular front so long as they could establish or maintain a base. If it wasn't the war, it was the women's liberation movement, the marijuana issue, whatever. To me, there seemed to be a relationship between the degree of radicalism and the individual's quest for control or power. As they began to peak out at the top, content took more and more a secondary position.

Holliman: Were you able to resolve your confusion?

Joshua: Substantially so, yes. It was at Berkeley that I came face to face with the really professional radicals. It was frightening, really, to see how good they were at their work, how much they could influence public opinion. They were incredible manipulators, especially when they went to work on the news media. Only having seen them on TV, I started out thinking the radicals were naive, but as time went by, I found out it was the news reporters who were short on wisdom and being taken to the cleaners.

Holliman: All right, Mister Bain. To the last question I have. And I want you to know, beforehand, that each of us in this room is in full sympathy with you; we understand your grief. And, while I regret having to bring it up, I must do so in order to fulfill my commitment to these proceedings. I'm referring to the untimely and tragic death of Jerrie McKennan.

Joshua: That's all right, and I understand.

Holliman: Thank you, sir. Are you satisfied in your mind with the inquest's probable decision? Specifically, that her death was an accident?

Joshua: No, I don't think so.

Holliman: For the record, then, it is your suspicion that the WAR people were somehow or other involved?

Joshua: Someone from Berkeley; perhaps the WAR people. Someone had to give her the heroin.

Holliman: Would you accept our help in this matter?

Joshua: I've already asked you once.

Calvin Price was frowning, wondering why Gus or Britt hadn't yet briefed him on this development. He knew he would have to pursue this further in private, because they couldn't afford to push Joshua into an undercover role with the FBI if the man was mentally handcuffed with this kind of nonsense.

Holliman: That's all I have for the moment. The floor is now open for general questioning.

Hal Fleming leaned forward to address his microphone. "Mister Bain, are you aware of what this corporation is involved in? What we do?"

"I've read your annual report," said Joshua.

Hal Fleming smiled a little. "That's our public image. What I'm talking about is the real, more secret, function of the ETC Corporation."

"I guess I don't really know."

"That's one of the reasons why we're here now." Fleming fussed with something on his desk while he arranged his thoughts. "Our motives, like yours, are based on certain facts, and of course we'd like to have you share in our agreement. You might say it's essential."

Joshua nodded once, slowly, thinking that right now he might agree to just about anything.

"You may be surprised to learn that we, too, have our own think-tank downstairs. Our data processing center on the first floor, which we proudly show off to visitors, is simply a cover. We actually use only a fraction of the full system's capability to process our routine day-to-day work. The bulk of the system is to back up our top secret operations department on the second floor. As Gus explained to you before coming in here, we employ a special council staff, reporting directly to us, of twenty-four elders. Pound for pound, this council represents the most efficient intelligence gathering group on the face of the earth. We gather facts, statistics; we measure trends, with heavy emphasis on human factors. Our operations department is comprised of perhaps the finest minds available within their fields, ranging from social psychology to quantum physics. We thus deal in facts, and the computer interprets for us." He paused then for a moment, searching through his papers. "It might please you to know that we've named our computer system 'Daniel,' a man of some prophetic reputation."

Joshua noticed that the heavy-set man on the end looked like he was about to go to sleep.

"I will give you one small example in detail," Fleming was saying. "Five years ago we began a study on the future of the traditional family unit, a program which we update annually. At the end of the first year's study, Daniel informed us the family unit had a healthy eighty-three years to go. Such a projection, of course, is considered indefinite, primarily because of the expected interim variables of influence about which we know nothing. However, the projection began to decline sharply. Down to fifty-four, three years ago. Then to thirty-two, two years ago. Last year, it was at twenty-two. Two months ago, our last update, the expected life span of the traditional American family was projected by Daniel to be fourteen years." Fleming took a deep, relaxing breath. "And we're not talking about how long a man and wife stay together," he went on then; "we're discussing how long the basic family concept itself is going to survive. Now, what does this projection suggest to you?"

Joshua frowned thoughtfully. "A lot of things. Mostly, what is going to take its place?"

"So what we're talking about is change, what we might call radical change."

"Yes, sir."

"And that forms the basis for our being. Radical change. Specifically, the changes that have occurred in this country during the past twenty to thirty years. And this example I just gave you is a miniscule part of the whole design. Nearly ten years ago, all of us here, and especially the late Morgan Halley, began to recognize these trends. We met and talked, and soon thereafter we joined together to study the phenomenon. We certainly had the bucks to put the program together. And as we progressed, we began to see that while there was no conscious conspiracy as such, there was certainly a common scheme of influence at work. Believe me, Mister Bain, we are caught up in an era of change for the sake of change, without regard for the consequences."

Senator Price gestured with his right hand, asking for permission to take the floor. "Assuming you were a student, Joshua, what notes would you have taken by now?"

Joshua pondered the question briefly before answering. "Three things. Scheme of influence, change, and consequences."

The Senator nodded approvingly before relaxing back into his chair.

"Remember especially the consequences," Hal Fleming went on. "As you so correctly pointed out, what is going to take the place of the family unit?" and he leaned forward on the rhetorical question. "Many of our studies have been released through front organizations in the hope of revealing the manipulators, the prime movers in furthering the scheme of influence. We exposed the national news media, TV in particular, for its blatantly slanted editorializing. We forced the exposure on the harmful effects of marijuana and cocaine. And all of these studies have been conducted under strict empirical conditions. We have classified programs underway now which you will be made privy to in time. All I can say is that they are on the subjects of our national security, our basic food production, and so on." Fleming paused again, turning a sheet of paper on his desk.

"If you don't mind my saying so," Joshua said then, "why don't you ask Daniel for a projection on how long the country's going to last?"

Hal Fleming stared at Joshua, as if he might be measuring him.

"Tell him," Calvin Price growled.

"We've got less than five years to go," said Fleming.

The Ford wagon moved slowly past the house, and Alan Hunt waved for Joshua to park it behind the pick-up. He waited in the open doorway of the barn while Joshua got out of the car. It was about six o-clock, still early evening, and it was still light outside, though the sun was about to slip behind the high mountains to the west. As Joshua walked up to him, Alan noticed how gaunt he looked.

"You look beat," Alan observed, squinting against the sun.

"I've had it," Joshua admitted, and he sighed heavily as he pulled up beside him.

"Come on in," Alan urged, and he moved into the barn. He walked up to the Jaguar, laid his hand on the new windshield. "Not factory, but it sure keeps the wind out."

"Well, what do you know," Joshua said admiringly, and he leaned down to inspect the windshield.

"Tinted to boot," said Alan.

"Some purist you are," said Joshua kiddingly as he straightened up.

"In this heat, you'll learn to appreciate the shade."

"Amen to that, brother," agreed Joshua, and he tapped the glass with his knuckles. "You know, I forgot the glass was flat. I thought it was curved some, and I didn't see any way we'd ever get it replaced."

"You've been conditioned."

"No; I'm punchy," Joshua insisted wearily. "But that's a fine job, and I want you to know I appreciate it."

"Forget it."

They both turned to leave the barn.

"How'd it go?" asked Alan as they both pushed the two heavy doors closed, and he hoped he didn't sound like he was snooping. All he knew was that Joshua was supposed to have been interviewed at the ETC office.

"All right, I guess," said Joshua.

"How about a steak?" Alan asked him as they both started toward the house.

"Can you believe I'm getting tired of steak."

Alan chuckled understandingly. "I not only believe it, I'm kind of glad to hear it. How about TV dinners for two?"

"After a swim."

"You're on."

Alan Hunt sensed that Joshua was strung out even worse than he looked and acted. And, for the better part of the next hour, Alan tried over and over again to piece together what he could say and do to help. It occurred to him that God in His wisdom and mercy had provided a way for every man. It was not in His will that anyone should do without, should lack, or even perish, and Alan Hunt struggled with his seeming impotence to speak out, to translate what he felt inside into the language that Joshua could understand and respond to. He wanted to talk about God's love, that He really cared, was really interested. But he couldn't even put together an opening remark. How palpably absurd, he thought angrily, that children could understand and cherish love, yet when they grew older and became men, the words sat awkwardly in their minds and was so difficult to even discuss.

By the time they finished eating, he realized he was no nearer an answer than before. But he knew that he now had to say something, somehow or other trusting that the right words would come out. Sitting on the patio, relaxed and drinking iced black coffee, Joshua's face was slack and expressionless as he finished reporting what he had put together regarding Jerrie's accident. "And there's still one item hanging loose," Joshua added. "The forest-service lookout who spotted the fire."

Waiting, Alan turned the cold glass in his hand and looked up to see Joshua staring at him.

"I'm sorry to put you on the spot like this," Joshua said.

"I wouldn't be here if I didn't want to."

"All right, then, take off Monday morning early. The directions are on a piece of paper on the desk. Get up there and talk to the guy. He must've had his glasses on the general scene. We don't want a deposition, but get him to tell you everything he can remember."

"You sound as if you're after something specific."

"I am, but I can't tell you what it is. We don't want to put any thoughts in his mind that aren't already there. Okay?"

Alan nodded that he understood. "Should I report this to Mrs. Halley?"

"Not unless you feel it's necessary. I really don't want her to know, if you can avoid it."

Alan Hunt felt the struggle inside himself again, and he couldn't help but ask, "What are you going to do when you find out who did it?"

Joshua didn't answer, staring past Alan, his expression was vacant, empty.

So that's the way it was, thought Alan, and he wasn't surprised. Joshua Bain had made a covenant with himself.

"You've not the right sex, you know," Alan said.

Joshua looked at him blankly.

"Nemesis was a woman. The goddess of retributive justice."

"So," Joshua said after a moment. "All that proves is that the Greeks probably had a better insight into human nature than we do."

Frustrated and unable to answer, Alan bit down on his lower lip. *Vengeance is mine, saith the Lord. Do not fight evil with evil. Do not think it strange concerning the fiery trial which is to try you . . .*

No, he thought then, there has to be another beginning.

"Do you really feel that is the right way?" Alan asked, probing now.

"The *right* way," said Joshua contemptuously. "What's right anymore? Or, better yet, what makes sense anymore?"

Alan spotted an opening. Joshua Bain was looking for answers. That was it! he thought jubilantly. "You strike me as being confused," he suggested quietly.

Joshua laughed once, shook his head. "Would you believe two degrees to the front, sir."

Alan frowned, not understanding. "What does that mean?"

Joshua reached over his shoulder to scratch his back, his face again relaxed. "It means I don't have much of a handle on anything, anymore," and he settled himself back into the lawn chair. "It means things are going by me blurred."

Alan drew his hands under his chin, deciding at the same moment that he was compelled to speak out. "You said you were sorry you were putting me on the spot," he said softly. "So now I'm going to return the favor, with your permission."

"Fair enough."

"The Bible says that all men experience the sure knowledge that there is a God," he began, and he was now sure of himself. "The Bible also says that all men are given grace as well. So, the Lord not only gives each of us the chance to believe in Him, but he also gives us a push. The Holy Spirit is that part of God most active in the process. For those who accept the invitation and go all the way, He provides an insight, an understanding, an awareness into the truth of things. What was once foolishness becomes wise. We also experience peace, or, at least, we have the means to. We certainly have the means to end the confusion."

Joshua was looking straight ahead now, staring moodily at the darkening landscape of the Coachella Valley.

"And you must understand that you've been led," Alan went on soberly, "to your present point of confusion for a reason. The Holy Spirit has done His work well. You see, my friend, we are built to experience frustration but not to endure it indefinitely. We demand resolution. Which, also is part of the plan." He paused for effect. "For you are required to make a decision."

Joshua Bain was now studying him guardedly.

"Can you see," Alan insisted, "you've been jammed! And it doesn't make any sense. You lie in your rack at night saying, why, why? How many people go through the same bit. The tragedies are usually always of our own making, yet we cannot come to grips with the explanations, which also seem to elude us. A man loses his business, another, maybe, his whole family. And, all for no apparent reason." He shook his head, a gesture of sorrow. "Believe me, you've got the chance right now to pick up your soul."

Joshua's face was locked now in a defensive expression, the kind of apologetic yet determined mask of rejection.

"Like it or not, Joshua Bain," said Alan levelly, "you're in the process right up to your ears. And, you're not equipped to deal with it alone. Isn't that obvious? You just admitted it. You're really under the gun, my friend. Because you *know now*. You can't plead ignorance any longer. You've been exposed. Decision-making time is at hand."

Joshua's face seemed to relax some then. "Believe it or not," he said, "I've always believed in God, and, well, I can even accept that Jesus Christ did exist." He drew a deep breath, sighed heavily, as if he was having trouble getting the words out. "Maybe even intellectually, in my mind, I've been exposed to enough to even consider that perhaps Christ was really the living Son of God."

Alan Hunt had closed his eyes, and he was praying inside now.

"But," Joshua went on, obviously trying to sound sincere, "something inside keeps telling me I'm not ready for a commitment I might not be able to live up to," and he hesitated then.

And Hunt was listening to yet another verse of the old familiar tune lamenting man's oldest and most basic error: that *he*, man, had the responsible role to play, that by *his* conduct he would qualify, that *he*, Joshua Bain, had to measure up. "You're right to a certain extent," Alan suggested, trying to disarm him momentarily. "Because without Jesus Christ you had to live up to a commitment yourself. This is what we refer to when we talk about the old law and what it imposed. And, you're right also when you admit being afraid that you can't live up to it, because no man or women on this earth could then or now ever hope to obey the law perfectly."

Joshua shrugged. "I'm sorry," he said softly, "but I'm not ready."

Alan appreciated that one could not be argued into accepting the Lord. "All right," he said. "But it seems important for you to realize that Christ wasn't sacrificed just for kicks, that He didn't come onto the scene just to verify God's existence. He came for a specific reason. To reconcile us to the Father. His commitment is all you need. Take the first step! Believe in Him, Joshua. Accept Him. Then take what follows," and he looked beckoningly at Joshua. "The rest will come to you, for it's been promised to you." And he was pleading now. "I can't believe you don't feel it in your very bones."

"Do you know I'm a Jew?" said Joshua abruptly.

"Yes," said Alan just as quickly. "So was Jesus Christ, so was Peter, so was Paul, so was James, and what a line-up to have behind you."

"It seems," said Joshua as he pushed himself up out of the chair, "that you've made your point," and he moved away toward the kitchen door. "I've got to call Mrs. Halley," and he looked back over his shoulder, smiling. "Got to find out if they accepted me."

Watching him go into the house, Alan fought off his sense of loss. Yet, he felt much better now than he had an hour ago. When one began to believe, as Joshua Bain obviously had, then the Holy Spirit would certainly keep the pressure on. Joshua Bain was at least starting to find out that he couldn't hack it alone, and Alan Hunt expected that the frustrations were going to continue building.

Chapter seven

By eleven o'clock, Sunday morning, Britt Halley was in her office. The other three members of the executive committee had gone their separate ways for another three months, barring emergency. Prior to adjournment, late yesterday afternoon, the committee had made two important votes, both yes. One was to admit Joshua Bain into the Western council as a stand-by elder, the other was to assign him immediately as a double agent against the Federal Bureau of Investigation. Per Calvin Price's recommendation, she would personally issue the final orders to Joshua Bain. According to Calvin Price also, the time for the move was excellent, and they should expect concrete results within a week. Not convinced herself, she was concerned that what Price really meant was that the pot was boiling and along with the opportunity was an increased danger factor.

Checking her watch, she heard a knock on her private door leading to the main hallway. She got up, walked briskly across the room to open the door. Gus Holliman was outside, Joshua Bain behind him. Britt told them both to come in.

"Do you have it all?" she asked Gus as she returned to her desk.

"Yes, ma'am," Gus answered. Following her, he carefully placed a heavy manila envelope on her desk.

Britt suggested they both sit down while she opened the envelope. Checking over the contents of the envelope, she was pleased to notice that Joshua looked much better. The haggard look of yesterday had been replaced with the more relaxed and confident expression she was used to.

"You must've had a good night's rest," she remarked casually.

"Yes, ma'am," said Joshua, and there was a touch of a smile around his mouth.

Britt almost told him to stop calling her "ma'am," but deferred it because of Gus Holliman.

"Well, Gus," she said then, "unless you have something further, you can go ahead and run along." She looked at Joshua. "Even on Sunday, you have to pry Gus out of the office. I sometimes think that Morgan should've built him an apartment in here."

Gus Holliman smiled, obviously embarrassed. He stood up, as if the movement would ease the situation. "No, ma'am," he said. "Except that we must be very careful with the eight-hundred series phone number. It's to be memorized and not given out under any circumstances." He moved around the chair, excusing himself as he left.

Britt followed him, securing the door's lock. Like Joshua, she too was dressed casually on this Sunday morning. As she returned to her desk, she noticed that Joshua, as usual, looked just like he had stepped out of a band box, despite the fact he was dressed in slacks and an open-necked, white short-sleeved shirt. Even his hair, usually in an interesting state of disorder, seemed to be groomed for some reason.

"Okay," she said cheerfully as she sat back down at her

desk. "As I told you on the phone last night, we'll take a few minutes here to get you acquainted, then over to the house for lunch." She felt awkward, alone with him in the room, and she caught herself nervously wetting her lips. Britt Halley understood that she was now playing a dual role with the man before her.

"Sounds good," Joshua was saying.

"How about a drink?" she asked.

"If you'll join me."

She got up, moved across the room to the bar. "You take tequila, right?"

"Negative," said Joshua, and he got up. "Plain tonic on the rocks will be fine."

That's interesting, she thought then. Perhaps it was too early in the day for him. She decided to take the same, quickly putting the two drinks together. She turned around when she finished, handing him his glass.

"To a good future," she said, holding her glass up.

"To a good day," he countered, and he was grinning now in a provocative way.

She moved away from him, thinking it had better turn out to be a good day, since she had spent the entire morning planning it. At the desk, she picked up the envelope. "Let's see," she said as she turned around to face him. "You've already been upstairs."

"Is that all there is to it?" he asked offhandedly.

"Just about. You were in the lounge, right, to change your clothes?"

He nodded yes.

"And the Throne Room?"

"How could I forget that."

"That's about it up there," she said thoughtfully.

"I noticed a door next to Holliman's elevator when I came in."

"Oh, that," she said lightly. "I forgot about the storage room. We call it Holliman's library, a dull, lackluster little room which wouldn't interest either of us."

"I'm sure it wouldn't," Joshua agreed. "So what's next down here?" he asked, as if he might be getting impatient to get moving.

"First, I should explain the Throne Room to you," she said. "Our corporate initials, for example, are derived from it, and the meaning is known only to the members of the ex-com and the elders. Altogether, we are known as the Eternal Throne Council, hence ETC."

"So," Joshua observed, "the elders and the executive committee comprise the Council."

"That's correct," Britt went on. "But don't get carried away with the symbolism. My husband was a deeply religious person. It was his belief that we were nearing the end of the world, and that the scheme of influence we discussed yesterday was actually worldwide, preparing the way for the Antichrist. And, the Throne Room was originally a haven for him, a place where he could pray and meditate. He also allowed the ex-com to use it for its quarterly meetings. After his death, we on the executive committee decided to continue using the room, primarily because of its sobriety, its obvious solemn effect."

"It's part of the glue holding you together," Joshua suggested.

"Not really. But it helps in the discipline, and it is an appropriate backdrop, so to speak."

"Yes, it is impressive," Joshua admitted.

"But don't let it get to you," Britt again cautioned him. "We are a pragmatic, highly professional, and very much down-to-earth group."

"So I've noticed."

"Yes," she said, smiling now. "And in time, you'll become an integral part of the Council." She turned the corner of her desk, reached out to take his hand. "For now, follow me, sir," and she led him toward the inner door leading to her secretary's office. In the hall, she started to explain, "All the executive offices are along here on the left. Mine and Holliman's at either end. VIP spaces in between, including a one-man security station." They were at the center of the long hall now, abreast of another connecting hallway.

"Along this hall," Britt went on as they stopped briefly, "are the offices and working areas of the planning and operations departments. This is the work area for the people you were told about yesterday. The entire second floor is a restricted area and is heavily guarded." And she turned to face the guard station, which was fully glass enclosed. A single guard was in the enclosure, dressed in typical ETC security garb. They moved on down to the other end of the hall. "This is Gus Holliman's office," she told him.

"I'm about to get oriented," Joshua said. "When I came in yesterday, before the interview, Gus and I used a private elevator in his office to get to the Sanctuary floor. It's the same floor plan as your office, then."

"That's right," she confirmed, not at all surprised at his perception. She then pushed through a door across the hall from Holliman's office door. With Joshua behind her, she walked quickly into the long room, which was divided into separate, private cubicles.

"This is the restricted area for the elders," she told him. "and here is your private office," she said, opening a door. Joshua followed her into the small room. "As you see, you have a desk, a four-drawer filing cabinet, typewriter, a multistation phone with an outside line. There's a copy machine out the door and to your right." She sat down behind the small metal desk, where she opened the manila envelope to dump its contents. Joshua pulled the only other chair in the room up next to the desk, sat down.

"Here's your ID package," Britt told him. "Card for wallet, one to hang on your pocket. These give you access to the executive area. Also company credit cards, Hertz, American Express, and so on. You have an unlimited credit line."

Joshua took the cards, shuffled through them. "Blue Branch, Incorporated," he said inquiringly.

"It's a front subsidiary."

"What do I tell people I do?"

"You're an operations executive, if you're ever asked. You do field survey work for your employer. No matter where you are, you are checking out local properties for prospective purchase. It's simple."

"How often do I use this office?"

"Very seldom and only when you need to. You can make private calls, do the kind of homework or whatever you don't want exposed. That trash can is a burn chute. Use it. Take no written material out of here unless it is approved by Gus or me."

"Okay," said Joshua. "You've told me what my cover job is. What do I really do now?"

Britt Halley brushed her hair away from the right side of her face as she looked down to the desk top. "For the time being, you'll continue on at the ranch. And, as soon as possible, we want you to call a Mister Cleveland Lambert." She looked up to see him staring at her, his face expressionless. "You don't know him?" she asked then.

Joshua was frowning now, obviously trying to remember.

"The only Lambert I can remember is an agent with the FBI in San Francisco. That was over two years ago, and I don't think I ever knew his first name."

"That's the man," Britt told him. "He's now in L.A., the local agent in charge."

"Why should I call him?" said Joshua, and he looked perplexed.

"We want you to set up an appointment, preferably for tomorrow morning if you can arrange it." She hesitated for a moment, giving him time to absorb what she was saying. "This is important, Joshua," she went on. "Very important and urgent. You will tell Lambert when you meet him that you've been associated with the ETC for a year now, and that during the past two months you've been employed by the operations department as a courier. You're a pilot, and you fly a lot, so the assignment makes sense in case they want to check. Tell him that we've checked you out thoroughly and that you have classified access in the executive area. And, on a couple of occasions when you were in here, you've seen some things that make you suspect we are involved in something irregular."

Joshua was studying her now, and she could see the wheels turning.

"Specifically," she said then, "tell him that you have seen a blueprint bearing the code number ABM 62.6."

Joshua repeated the number out loud. "And what does that do? I mean, does Mister Lambert turn green at the magic number?"

She smiled broadly. "All right, Joshua. You've been assigned to operate as a double agent. You will pretend to want to work for them to spy on us, when in fact what you're really after is to get them to divulge information to us."

"Now we're getting to it," Joshua said appreciatively. "What am I after?"

"Therein lies the problem," Britt admitted. "All we can tell you is that the FBI has quietly opened up an investigation against us. We want to know what it is they have, if anything, plus what they might be after."

Joshua shook his head. "I may not be a pro at this, but something tells me they're not just going to sit down and lay it out."

"We don't need that," she assured him. "We're banking on them to tell you what to look for, which should point us in the right direction."

Joshua was nodding that he understood. "We play a little game, a guessing game of sorts."

"In a way," Britt agreed. "If they're investigating apples, they're not going to send you back here looking for oranges."

"We hope," said Joshua. "Aren't they smart enough to suppose I might just be a double agent?"

"Normally, yes," she said. "But in this instance, the odds are loaded in our favor. Number one, you're not a pro, as you said. Secondly, you've already helped them out once before. You're clean, honest."

"Not anymore," he said placidly.

Britt got up. "I've got to get back to the house, get things ready for our lunch. You make your call to Lambert from here. The number is on the outside of the envelope, and make it good, Joshua." She moved to the door, opened it. "This is urgent, and we're banking on you to come through." She frowned then, thinking that he looked a little pale. "Are you all right?" she asked concernedly.

"I'm fine," he assured her, and he smiled. "You just run along and let me get on with my business. I tend to work better alone."

"Good luck," she told him, and with that parting comment, she left.

Joshua sat without moving a muscle. Still stunned, his mind raced with the implications. How was Lambert going to react to this twist? And, worst of all, was the phone call. He looked apprehensively around the small, stark room, and he had the suspicion that he was being watched. He had to assume the room was at least bugged. And the telephone itself had to be at least tape monitored. Or maybe Gus Holliman was sitting in his office, waiting impatiently. Joshua's mind scampered for any reason not to make the call from here, but it came up empty.

What a lousy fluke!

And for a passing moment he thought back to last night, to Alan and his solemn and certainly correct assumption that Joshua Bain had been jammed. Man, oh man, he thought dejectedly, if you only knew. He pulled the envelope around to see the area code 213-number. And he could hear Cleve Lambert on the other end, chewing him out before he could get a word in edgewise, "What's the matter with you, Joshua, calling me on this number?" or words to that effect, and he could imagine Gus Holliman coming unglued. Joshua figured he'd just about make it to the first security station, at a dead run, before catching a half dozen thirty-eight caliber slugs.

Maybe the phone wasn't really monitored.

Sure, and maybe dogs don't bite.

He once more considered the option of just getting up and walking out.

And blow it all, totally.

He picked up the phone.

A two-card draw to a flush.

He dialed the number. He remembered then that it was Sunday, so Lambert shouldn't be in his office. He felt a slight glimmer of hope. If he could skate by with leaving a message, he could catch Lambert from a pay phone. A pleasant female voice answered.

"Mister Lambert, please," said Joshua.

He was advised that Mister Lambert was not in, but if it was important he could be reached.

Joshua swallowed hard. To leave a message now would be as bad as not calling at all. "It is extremely urgent," he said sternly. "and please tell him it is Mister Joshua Bain, from Berkeley."

He waited, feeling his heart thumping in his chest, and he assumed he had at least one chance, to start talking first and fast.

It took an interminably long two or three minutes for the telltale transfer sounds to come on the line. He heard Cleve Lambert's voice then, clear and distinct, like he might be sitting in the next cubicle, "Hello, this is Lambert speaking."

"Ah, Mister Lambert," Joshua said quickly. "This is Joshua Bain, and I don't know whether you remember me or not." Joshua's eyelids were clamped down so tight he was hurting his eyeballs. He caught himself uttering one short, silent prayer.

"I'm not sure," Lambert said hesitantly.

Joshua felt the relief flooding his body. He jumped to his feet, almost pulling the phone off the desk. "From Berkeley," he said then, realizing in his excitement that he was about to blow it anyway. "The Courtland kidnapping case."

"Oh, yes, Mister Bain. Now I remember," Lambert said cordially. "How have you been?"

"Just fine, sir," said Joshua, and he couldn't really put enough meaning into the statement.

When he got in from church, Alan Hunt went directly to his room to change his clothes. Sunday had always been a day for taking it easy on Rancho Canaan, and he decided he might tinker with the tune on the engine of the Jaguar. He came out of the tack room dressed in a pair of weathered jeans and a tee-shirt. The old barn was still reasonably cool, and he guessed that he had at least an hour before the heat became unbearable. He had just walked up to the work bench next to the Jag when the barn door came open.

Joshua Bain stood silhouetted against the harsh outside light.

Surprised, Alan looked at him for a passing second before asking, "What's happening? I thought you were going to the Halley place."

Looking preoccupied, Joshua walked up to the other side of the car. "I don't have to be there until one o'clock," he offered slowly.

Alan didn't have a watch, but he figured it was about a quarter to one now. "The lunch bit, with Mrs. Halley?"

Joshua nodded once.

"Having second thoughts?" Alan guessed.

"Yeah," said Joshua listlessly. "I know I have to go through with it, but the closer I get the less I like the idea."

Alan sympathized with his friend, knowing what Joshua had to be going through now. The deception itself was out of Joshua's character, but, even worse, had to be the still fresh memory of Jerrie McKennan. For some reason or another, he caught himself feeling glad that Joshua had the problem. "Do you really have to go?" he asked then. "I mean, once you get over there, alone with her, you're going to have to make a choice, probably—"

"That's what is bothering me," said Joshua.

"You mean you could wind up hurting your cause more than helping it?"

"Something like that."

"So, call her up and cancel."

Joshua shook his head slowly, before suggesting, "I thought about that too, driving over here. But, there's too much at stake. She might get suspicious, or something."

"How far are you prepared to go?" Alan asked flatly.

Joshua was smiling then. "No farther than I have to. I need to get next to her today, because it's on my schedule, but that's all, nothing more. You might say that contact, brief and simple, is what I'm after."

"Then you have a problem," said Alan, "if she has planned for you and her to be alone over there all afternoon."

Joshua turned the front of the Jaguar to walk up to the work bench. He reached up to the tools hanging behind the bench, selected an eighteen-inch crowbar. "So it's time to resolve the problem," he said then.

Alan Hunt followed him out of the barn. In a few seconds they pulled up next to the pump house, where Joshua turned to face him. "I know how you feel about lying to people, so I'm going to make it easy," Joshua told him. "We have to irrigate tonight, right?"

Alan nodded once.

Joshua opened the door to the aluminum shed, stepped inside. He opened the lid on the pump timer, threw on the manual switch. The well pump spun into operation. Before Alan could say or do anything, Joshua turned to the electric pump, jammed the crowbar into the vent around the cooling vanes. The pump screamed in protest before grinding to a halt. The electrical conduit shorted, started to smoke. The circuit breaker popped. Joshua jammed the crowbar between the contacts at the pump. Letting go of the bar, he then reached up to the circuit breaker box next to the timer, pushed the 220 volt breaker back to reset, holding it closed. The pump connection was now a dead short, and it took only a few seconds for the end of the wiring to jump into flame. Joshua released the circuit breaker, and the small fire went out.

"There," he said with a defined note of satisfaction. "The pump is out, and there's been a small fire," and he looked at Alan with a broad smile.

"You didn't have to do that," Alan said.

"Yes, I did," Joshua told him. "It's a crazy business we're mixed up in, and this may actually be one of the more sane things we're both going to have to do." He turned up his watch. "I'm heading for the Halley place. At exactly one-fifteen, you call me there. Remember, it's an emergency."

Alan took the crowbar from him, thinking that the emergency wasn't only going to be here at the ranch.

It was uncommonly humid outside, and Britt Halley knew that the moisture in the air was a seasonal thing, brought on, according to Morgan Halley, by the valley's agricultural expansion. She checked the temperature gauge on the cabana wall. It was ninety-six in the shade. The heat didn't bother her at all, and she hoped that it didn't bother Joshua, because she felt inclined to take a swim. She moved slowly and thoughtfully across the flagstone between the huge pool and the glass-enclosed patio, where they would have lunch. The 20 x 40 patio was enclosed during the harsher summer months, when it was air conditioned along with the rest of the twenty-three-room house. She was informally dressed in shorts and midriff, and she felt the afternoon's heat on her back before she stepped through the sliding glass door.

The small table was correctly set. Not too pretentious, she thought, because he wasn't that way. She removed her wristwatch, placed it behind the bar counter. Rubbing her wrist, she thought that Joshua's assignment, after all, was a better one than she had first imagined. There was actually little risk involved; it was all rather a matter of how well Joshua could play his role.

Movement from across the pool caught her eye, and she saw Joshua's wagon coming in the driveway. She moved slowly through the house to the front door. Except for the outside security guards, all the hired help were off and gone for the day.

After letting Joshua in, she took his arm to steer him into the enclosed patio. "The first order of business," she said lightly, "is what would you like to drink?"

He stood next to the bar, looking out across the swimming pool. "How about a Coke, if you have one."

"Certainly," she said, and she reached into the bar refrigerator. "But if you don't mind my asking, why not something stronger?"

"Got to keep a clear head," Joshua said lightly, a small kind of smile around his mouth.

"So I'll join you in the same, and for the same reason," she said, and she was smiling also.

He took the glass, and it appeared that Joshua Bain was a little nervous. She figured to remedy that in a hurry. "Why don't you head for the cabana," she suggested. "I personally checked your peg, and your bathing suit is still there."

He extended his right hand to take hers, looking at her more gravely than she figured he should. "I want to thank you for the invitation," he said softly, and he leaned forward to kiss her cheek.

She felt herself reacting, and she held on to his hand, not wanting to let it go. "I know it's kind of soon," she heard herself saying, "but I want you to know—"

"It's all right," he assured her, and he put his glass on the bar counter. "And it's thoughtful of you to be aware of it, because it's going to take me a while to get used to things the way they are now. And, especially, to the way things might come to be."

So that was why he was so nervous, she was thinking, and she was satisfied that her probe had yielded the desired result. "So why don't we take a swim?" she offered then.

"All right," he said, and he kissed the back of her hand before letting it go.

Watching him move out through the sliding glass door to start across the flagstone patio, she was thinking that it was about time to rid both their minds of the ghosts of times past. Thus absorbed, she hardly noticed the ringing of the house telephone, until the insistent and rhythmic sound finally reminded her that she was alone in the house. Annoyed with the interruption, she reached out to take the call on the patio extension.

Chapter eight

Trail Lakes was one of the many popular tourist attractions in the Los Angeles area. Located near the International Airport, just off the San Diego Freeway, the sprawling facility was an enormous garden of rich, lush foliage graced by winding paths and waterways. The Lakes was a bird lover's paradise, where one could view in as natural habitat as possible hundreds of feathered species collected from around the world. Cleve Lambert was neither impressed by, nor interested in, birds as he made his way to the enclosed food stand Joshua had designated as their meeting place. Irritably waiting his turn in the short line leading to the service counter, he tried to appear like a normal tourist as he searched the large, glass-enclosed room for Joshua Bain. He fingered his right ear, which always started to throb when he walked too much. As he took his soft drink, he finally spotted Joshua sitting by himself at one of the small tables near the glass fronting the adjacent lake. As he pulled up next to the table, Joshua looked up.

"Hello, Cleve," Joshua said.

"Stand up, you idiot!" Lambert hissed under his breath.

Joshua did so immediately, a look of surprise on his face, and he took Lambert's extended right hand.

"How do you do, Mister Bain," Lambert said, a little loudly.

"Just fine, sir," Joshua said then, having composed himself.

"That's better," Lambert said curtly, again under his breath. "You know we haven't seen each other in two years. So act like it, please," and he was smiling in a forced way, hoping he had conveyed the message as he sat down. He put his briefcase on the floor next to his right leg.

Joshua was grinning now obediently, and Lambert figured that he just might be enjoying this Monday morning's tete-a-tete.

"How did you know, yesterday?" Joshua asked.

"You mean the phone call?"

"Uh-huh," Joshua murmured. "I thought we'd had it. I was in the ETC office and had to make the call."

"A couple of obvious things," Lambert said. "First, you called on the regular bureau number, which you'd been told never to do. Secondly, the formal message, especially the Berkeley bit. I just played it straight as a normal kind of precaution."

"It could've all gone up in smoke," Joshua said. "It's kind of scary, how easily things can get messed up."

"That's right," Lambert confirmed. "One simple little slip. The wrong word. Especially the closer you get. Your problems multiply at a geometric ratio."

"Like two degrees to the front."

"What does that mean?"

Joshua looked out across the nearby lake, toying with his empty paper cup. "Nothing really," he said then.

"Okay, Joshua, what's going on?"

Joshua looked down to his cup. "I'm supposed to approach you with an offer to spy on the ETC, while at the same time trying to get information out of you."

So they're working him in as a double agent, Lambert

thought. He figured he already knew the answer to his next question, "Why?"

"They know you're investigating them."

"They give you any details?" Lambert asked quickly, and he felt their available time suddenly draining away, like water through a sieve. The question now was how much did they know? Could they possibly have penetrated to find the code name "Anzio"?

"Very few," Joshua said. "Except that I'm convinced they don't know exactly what the subject is you're working on. In fact, that's what I'm supposed to find out. They're banking on your sending me after the kind of information that will lead them to the subject."

Lambert grunted once, showing his doubt. "They could be using you, Joshua. Setting us both up."

"What do you mean?"

"It's a ploy of a similar cut," Lambert explained. "If they are in fact on to you, they could be using you for their own purpose, instead of simply doing away with you outright."

Joshua shook his head confidently. "I'm positive they're not on to me, yet," and he put heavy emphasis on the "yet."

Lambert was nodding his head. Thank heavens, he was thinking. "Have you got any leads to where the records might be?"

"Oh, yeah," Joshua said offhandedly. "I know where they are."

Lambert was briefly taken aback by the abrupt good news.

"There is a room in the Sanctuary," Joshua went on, "where I'm sure your evidence is located."

"Have you seen it?" Lambert asked skeptically.

Joshua Bain didn't answer right away. He pulled on his right ear, suggesting he might be problem solving, but when he looked straight at Lambert, there was a kind of serene, distant expression around his hard, grey eyes, as if, unbelievably enough, he was bored.

"Mister Lambert," Joshua said then, "I'm going to make you a deal. You want the evidence, and I'll have it for you before this weekend. In exchange for that evidence, you're going to turn this over to me, lock, stock, and barrel."

"Come on, Joshua, you can't—"

"Shut up!" Joshua snarled at him.

Cleve Lambert felt the blood running out of his face. His mouth was hanging open, and he closed it, licking his upper lip. Caught flat-footed, he could only cough to help clear his throat.

"I'm up to my ears," Joshua went on vehemently, "with all this cloak-and-dagger jazz." Joshua had come part way out of his chair, leaning forward, his palms flat on the table. "So get out your pencil and paper and start writing."

Content to remain silent, Lambert pulled a notebook out of his jacket pocket, followed by a ballpoint pen. He opened the small book to a blank page.

"Item," Joshua said as he settled back into his chair. "They gave me a drawing number, probably something to do with national defense hardware, number ABM 62.6, which I'm supposed to give to you to authenticate me as a reliable source. Item, you get a warrant tomorrow that will do it for you between then and Friday. Also, fifty pounds of plastic explosives, with five automatic detonators. Divide the plastic into five equal satchel charges. You'll need yourself and four men on ten minutes' call starting Wednesday at midnight. Suggest you use motel row in Palm Desert. Have an emergency vehicle, van type, from the local gas company, including field work clothes and working equipment. And, you'd better come well armed and equipped for an all-out assault. Flak vests. Smoke grenades and frag types. Automatic weapons. If you can borrow one, include a four-point-two bazooka that works, and make sure that whoever is carrying it knows how to use it quickly," and he paused for a moment. "In fact, we have to have the bazooka. I'll be in touch with you after Wednesday night and give you the details." There was another pause as Joshua reached up to scratch his hairline. "Do you want that Coke?" he asked then, his voice returning to normal.

Writing furiously, Lambert shook his head no.

Joshua downed the cup's contents in one motion. "Item," he went on, "tell your boss to freeze everything back there. I don't know what you've got going in Washington, but it's got a big hole. So get it stopped, cold. Lock it up tight. And if by Wednesday night I hear the least rumor from anyone, especially Britt Halley, that the investigation is still going on, I'm walking. And don't waltz me, Lambert, I'm warning you."

For the first time, Lambert had to fully agree with Joshua Bain.

"Now," Joshua went on. "They've replaced the Avion with a bigger aircraft, a second-hand Rockwell Commander 690. And I'm going to fly it back early tomorrow morning out of

L.A. International, so I'll be staying near the airport tonight. So, between now and, say, two o'clock this afternoon, you're going to dig up the following for me. First, here's the license number and the description of a car," and he handed Lambert a small piece of scratch paper. "Get me the ownership. I'm sure it's a rental job, and get me the name of the party renting it on the day Jerrie was killed. Next, I want the phone number and address of the local WAR wheel."

Lambert swallowed hard, feeling something creeping up the back of his neck. His first impulse was to object, but he held back.

"And you stay out of this," Joshua warned him, as if he might be reading his thoughts. "I want to hit this guy cold turkey. Do we understand each other?"

"Yes, I guess so."

"Okay, so now it's your turn. What have you got on Alan Hunt?"

Lambert quickly finished his note taking. Putting the ballpoint pen down, he reached into his briefcase, pulled out a file folder. "You've got yourself quite a boy, here," he said soberly, and he opened the folder. "Born in San Diego County, September ninth, nineteen forty-nine. He actually started out as a reservation Indian. Funky record since. Arrested several times in the Riverside area while in late teens. Mostly gang-oriented activity. One assault conviction. Formal education grade school only. Served in the Marine Corps for two years. Given undesirable discharge because of repeated offenses, mostly minor, like AWOL eight times." Lambert read on before continuing. "Seems to have settled down after his discharge. Let's see, worked as a Karate instructor. Clean record since. Employment includes Las Vegas, where he tended bar, also did a part-time act, martial-arts stuff. Then three years ago, he started at the Japanese Deer Park, doing the same kind of act. Was well-thought-of there. Good worker, no trouble. Picked up his high school diploma, some college, night school."

"Anything else?"

"A couple statements here," Lambert went on. "He was mixed up with a girl in Vegas, engaged, according to one of his friends there. But they were involved in a high-speed car accident, and she was killed." He turned to the last statement. "I get the impression you like this guy."

"Yes, I do," said Joshua firmly. "He's as straight as they come."

"Well," Lambert said then, "here's an interesting item. According to one of the guys he worked with in Anaheim, about two years ago Alan Hunt got religion."

"What does that mean?" Joshua said sharply.

"Let's see," Lambert went on more cautiously, "he was running with a motorcycle gang during his spare time. Kind of grubby bunch. It seems there was a religious crusade going on, and a few of the gang got together to take it in just for kicks." Lambert put his hand to his mouth, having to control himself to keep from laughing. "How about that," he said then. "Three of them got converted, including Alan Hunt." He looked up to see that Joshua Bain apparently had also found the report amusing, for he too was grinning broadly.

"How about that," Joshua was saying amiably, but then his manner shifted into reverse. "And no more smart remarks about him getting religion," Joshua warned him. "Or I'll stuff that report down your throat."

"All right," Lambert said placatingly. "You've got the upper hand for the moment."

"How about the info on Jerrie?"

Lambert was glancing around the room apprehensively. The crowd was increasing, and he figured they had worn out their welcome. He had already noticed one of the park attendants eyeing them. "Let's move outside," he suggested before answering the question. Joshua followed him out the stand's side exit. It was warm in the open air, and Lambert loosened his tie. "Over here," he suggested, pointing to one of the paths leading away from the crowd, and they moved up the walkway slowly. "You know, Joshua," Lambert began carefully, "since we're really putting our cards on the table, it's my official opinion that you've been off base in putting so much time in chasing shadows."

"You mean Jerrie's killers?"

"I mean we're up to our ears in this ETC business," Lambert said persuasively, "and we can't afford to jeopardize that now," and he had his hand extended, waggling his finger like a school teacher. "You're emotionally involved with that; you're following your heart instead of your head, and it's going to kill you if you're not careful."

"What have you got on Jerrie?"

Lambert sighed heavily, unable to put anything else together. They were near one of the turn-outs leading to some special item of interest, and Lambert turned in, wanting more privacy. They both pulled up at the fence line. A small, quickly moving stream ran below them, emptying into a small pond. The immediate area was deserted, and Lambert reached into his jacket. "All right," he said. "Here are two photographs, both taken in Indio at the weekend you asked about."

"Only two?"

"Those are the only two which have people from up north. The rest are strictly locals. The names are on the back." He waited for a moment while Joshua inspected the two pictures. "Mean anything to you?"

Joshua shook his head. "Not right now, but I'll go over them later," and he pushed the pictures in his shirt pocket.

Lambert sat down on the nearby bench, opened his brief-case. He looked around carefully, making sure they were alone. He then pulled a small automatic pistol out of his case, handed it to Joshua, butt first.

"What's this?" asked Joshua as he turned the weapon in his hand. "Very exotic," he offered then. "Never seen one like it before. What is it, twenty-two caliber?"

"That's right. Notice its weight."

"Joshua weighed the weapon in his hand. "Super light."

"Developed by the ordnance people at China Lake a few years back. Primarily as an assassin's weapon. They call it a Viper. Go ahead, shoot it."

Joshua looked at him sideways, doubt on his face.

"Go ahead," Lambert urged him. "Into the pond."

Joshua laid his wrist on the top rail of the fence, barrel-sighted the weapon. Even though Lambert knew what to expect, he was still impressed with the Viper as Joshua squeezed off the round. There was zero recoil action in Joshua's hand. Absolutely no sound. No telltale smoke. Only a quick *zuunk* in the water as the metal slug ripped the tranquil surface. Joshua turned to look at him, turning the pistol slowly in his hand, both his eyebrows raised appreciatively.

"All the moving parts are teflon coated," Lambert explained. "The silencing is in the specially fluted barrel itself. And the barrel is titanium, never needs cleaning."

"Very deadly," Joshua mused.

"More than you think," Lambert went on. "The ammo is just as special. Subsonic load, which is the main reason why it's so quiet. The slugs are a special hollow-point design, which explode on impact. And, the reason they call it the Viper is that each slug carries enough pure crystalline cyanide to put three or four men down."

Joshua whistled. "Makes handling the ammo kind of risky."

"Not at all," Lambert assured him. "The poison is fully encapsulated, sealed. You could carry one of the bullets around in your mouth for a week and not be affected." He took the weapon, put it back in the briefcase. He then handed the case to Joshua. "It's yours," he said. "There's five hundred rounds of ammo in there and a special thigh holster, which I suggest you use. It keeps the little devil up near your crotch, where it's hard to find."

"That's nice," said Joshua. "What if it accidentally goes off?"

"No chance. It has three safety features. The normal side lock. The butt safety, like the issue forty-five. And, a trigger pull of six pounds."

"All right," said Joshua, "but I don't think I will need it."

"You've got three or four days left, at least," Lambert said, "during which time it is important you survive. And, the Viper might just do it for you."

"Okay, so I'll carry it," said Joshua, "for the next three or four days. For now, though, let's get out of here. You can brief me on the way out as to what you want me to say to Britt Halley."

Well, well, thought Cleve Lambert. So Joshua Bain didn't know everything, after all. He got up, feeling the weight of his years, yet alert and thinking rapidly, because Joshua Bain was going to need a good story to take back to Britt Halley.

A little after 2:15, Joshua was in his motel near the International Airport. He had just finished talking to Cleve Lambert on the phone, and he was staring coldly at the list of answers Lambert had provided. The second name on the list was that of the local WAR chieftain, Huey Orville.

Joshua felt his gut turning over.

Huey Orville, former all-pro safety, who had hit the skids because of his weakness for hard drugs. Spent a couple years at Soledad. Then on to Berkeley, where he had registered moderate success at hitting the top again; only then it had been as an activist in the black liberation movement.

So he was still at it, Joshua thought. General Pao-min.

Weathermen wheel. And probably as ruthless as ever.

He backed up to the first name. Anthony Seastrom. Tony Seastrom, another less but familiar name out of his Berkeley past. The car used by the WAR team visiting the ranch the day Jerrie was killed had been indeed a rental from a budget type operation near L.A. International. Out for four days, registered over four hundred miles. And Tony Seastrom had rented it. The Weathermen were good at that and could almost be depended upon to use their real names. Especially in this instance, since it left no doubt as to who had carried out the verdict of the people's court. A public lesson for the troops. It was also an arrogant trademark: defying the police.

He checked his watch, seeing that he still had fifteen minutes before he had to report in to get checked out on the Commander 690. He leaned back on the double bed, closed his eyes, thinking again about yesterday afternoon, trying to assess the harm that might have been done by his not being able to finish out lunch with Britt Halley. Their relationship was critical now and would continue to be so until his final plan went into motion. Britt Halley might not be his only ticket, but she was by far the most available. However, she had not seemed overly upset yesterday, especially after he had reassured her that they had ample time to be together in the future. Still, Joshua now sensed that he was walking a thin line by not indulging her to the extent she obviously wanted, and he knew he had to be careful for at least the next few days.

He could work that short a time in his favor.

At any rate, he figured he was now over that hump and on the downhill grade.

Unable to relax, he got up to sit on the edge of the bed, looking down at the scrap of paper bearing the name of Huey Orville. The telephone number for Huey was a local one. He reached for the telephone. Might as well get with it, he thought wryly, dialing the number giving him an outside line.

The Compton Avenue address was in the Watts community of south Los Angeles, and for Joshua, driving through the black area reminded him of their old apartment in Oakland. It was nearly 7:00, and he was thankful it was still daylight. If Watts was anything like black Oakland, then a strange white man alone was just itching for trouble after dark. Coming up to Compton Avenue, he turned to his right, now poking along as he watched the street numbers starting to get close.

A few minutes later, he had curbed the rental car in front of the address. The single-floor store was deserted, a crumbling, decaying stucco structure which showed the signs of being victimized by the riots. Joshua got out, and, following his telephone instructions, moved around to the south side of the building. At the corner, he stopped briefly to survey the area, which he found clean. He put his hand in the right front pocket of his slacks, slipping his fingers through the rip in the lining to touch the comforting butt of the Viper. He then walked along the side of the building to the door he was supposed to find. The door was unlocked, and he opened it gingerly. Seeing it was dark inside, he stepped back, closing his eyes for a few moments.

With his eyes adjusted, he then stepped inside and to his right, pulling the door closed behind him. He was in a small office partition, empty except for piles of rotting wallboard and various other debris. The enclosed room smelled of old chicken fat and rats' litter. Joshua breathed through his nose, fearing that he might get infected with something. He stepped across the littered floor to the opposite door, kicked it open.

Huey Orville, alias General Pao-min, was standing a few feet inside the door. The light filtering in from the street through the front windows showed enough of the side of his face for Joshua to recognize him. He hadn't changed much in the past two years, except for the Fu Manchu mustache and goatee. Shoulders slack, feet apart, bent slightly forward at the hips, looking relaxed in his leather togs, but Joshua knew better.

His hands alongside his hips, Joshua was reluctant to move through the door, for he knew from experience that a WAR general was never without his troops.

Huey Orville was grinning at him, his even white teeth looking cosmetic against the more natural golden ebony of his face and neck.

"Brother Joshua," Huey was saying, and Joshua noticed that his manner had not changed much either; Huey was still a con man, a mechanic really, in his suave capabilities. "What a pure pleasure," Huey added, with all the pleasantry of a cobra enticing a bewildered muskrat.

"A pure pleasure," Joshua repeated in the same patronizing tone, but he had not moved. He stood tensed, ready to jump in any direction.

"Come on in, my'man," Huey said cordially, beckoning with his long right arm.

"Let's go for a walk," Joshua countered. "It stinks in here."

"Oh, Joshua," said Huey Orville, showing he had been hurt, cut to the bone. "You don't trust your brother Huey. Like we go way back."

"I trust you, Huey," Joshua said evenly. "It's your soldiers. Like we don't know each other at all."

"Why should I even talk to you?" Huey asked, and his voice was its more normal, calculating self.

"Like we go way back, and what other reason do we need?"

Huey Orville digested the comment, then shrugged his shoulders indifferently. "That is a pure good point, brother." He looked aside, snapped his fingers.

Joshua stood poised. There were twelve rounds in the clip of the Viper, and unless they got him with a sawed-off shotgun. . . . He heard another door opening farther down the building, toward the rear, and he relaxed some.

"You don't mind giving up your hardware, brother," Huey was saying.

"I'm unarmed."

"You don't mind if we check to make sure?"

Joshua moved backwards a step, spread his legs slightly, raised his arms. He heard a car start up behind the building. A short heavy black man slipped around the door jamb, moved up to Joshua. He patted Joshua down, then turned back to disappear into the deeper shadows of the other room. Huey Orville stepped forward, grinning again, his right hand extended palm up.

After the amenities, they got into the back seat of the Lincoln limousine now parked just outside the door.

Telling the driver to head for the freeway, Huey moved the glass divider up, giving them privacy. "How'd you get the private number?" Huey asked as he settled back into the white leather upholstery.

"I'm still in touch," said Joshua, and he noticed that Huey was a little jumpy, his eyes moving furtively around the passing scenery. He was probably still on the stuff, Joshua thought. But he was still slick.

"So what's on your mind?" Huey asked him.

"Need some help."

Huey Orville grunted derisively. "Yeah, brother, like those kids out there," and he gestured with the flat of his left hand, and Joshua was reminded that Huey Orville at one time had the surest hands around.

"Tony Seastrom," said Joshua flatly.

Huey looked back from the street, his face solemn under the black headband. His hair was short, but perfectly trimmed, providing a good balance to his thin, finely clipped features. "Been a long time for Tony, too," he said casually.

Joshua almost smiled, but he knew that Huey was now measuring his reaction too. What a stupid, though necessary, game, he thought. "Tony is still active," he said evenly. "And you've got the contacts."

"Why?"

"You heard about Jerrie?"

"Yeah; it was in the news, and we all sympathize with you, Joshua. She was a loyal, supporting sister to the cause." He looked again out through the side window. "She was a righteous one, that redhead."

"She went down full of snow."

Huey turned to look at him slowly, his thin brow turned into a small, inquiring frown. "I thought she had kicked it," he said.

"She had; and that's where Tony comes in, because he was down there that weekend."

"So what can I do—"

"I want to see him, face to face."

General Pao-min was frowning again. "Man, you got to know that by now that dude is probably twenty miles into Big Sur. Like he's retreating, if he had anything to do with it."

Joshua reached carefully into his shirt pocket. "Here's five one hundred dollar bills," he said, handing Huey the folded money. "This'll cover his plane fare and the long distance calls, with a little left over for the righteous cause. Have him down here Wednesday night, same time. But, do me a favor and arrange the meet at a place that smells a little better."

Taking the money, Huey was shaking his head doubtfully. "You must think I've got some kind of heavy pull."

"You're a general, aren't you?"

Huey Orville was smiling back at him, and they both laughed then, as if they were both party to some special inside joke.

Chapter nine

It fell to Gus Holliman to arrange the conference call, and he did so in his office. Britt Halley's instructions of a few minutes ago had been simple and specific: get Calvin Price on the line and report the results of Joshua Bain's first meeting with Cleveland Lambert. Waiting on the operator to make the Dallas connection, he quickly ran over the events leading to the call. Joshua Bain had made his meeting with Lambert yesterday morning, right on schedule, and, along with Britt Halley, Gus was satisfied to this point. Joshua Bain apparently had thus far played out his role according to their wishes, including his initial contact on Sunday. Gus was unable to flaw the performance.

The drawling voice of Calvin Price came onto the line, clear and distinct.

"This is a conference call, sir," Gus advised him. "Mrs. Halley will be on in a second." Britt Halley almost immediately announced that she too was on the line.

Deferring amenities, Gus opened the conversation. Though the line was assumed clear, he introduced what he considered necessary security procedures. "We will refer to our representative as alpha," he said, "the other as bravo. Per plan, alpha made contact Sunday morning, successfully arranging rendezvous with bravo mid-morning, yesterday. Meeting was without surveillance on our part, also per agreement."

"Gus," Price butted in, "aren't we both on the garble phones, or whatever you call 'em?"

"Yes, sir."

"We blew a quarter million bucks on this equipment," Price said, "and you told us it was foolproof."

"Yes, sir, it is."

"Well, Gus, I've punched the right buttons."

"Talk in the open, Gus," Britt told him impatiently.

"Yes, ma'am," Gus said obediently. "The meeting yesterday morning was rather uneventful, I'm afraid. Alpha, I mean Joshua Bain, conveyed the information we gave him, just as ordered. Lambert apparently listened but was otherwise largely unresponsive."

"What do you mean, uneventful?" Price drawled, a tone of exasperation in his voice. "A smart fish smells the bait first, nibbles a little maybe, before he makes up his mind."

"Yes, sir," Gus replied. "And I expect the analogy is appropriate, because Lambert has asked for a return meeting tomorrow."

"There you go," said Price confidently.

"We'd like your advice, Senator," Britt said then, "as to what Joshua should report to Lambert tomorrow. You may recall, we left that option open pending results of the first meeting."

"No problem," Price told her. "Lambert needs some time to check out the drawing number. He'll be in touch with his boss, and they'll be laying out their little plans. If we're lucky, they might begin to tip their hand as early as tomorrow."

"Is there some way we can stimulate that?" Gus asked.

"Sure," said Price. "Have Joshua come right out and ask Lambert what it is he should be doing or looking for. You might say, Gus, we need to get the seed corn in the ground."

Calvin Price's suggestion rankled Gus Holliman, for the Senator had not too long ago taken him to task for being too devious, too careful, with the Texas observation that one didn't wait until the weather was perfect to plant corn. A typical Calvin Price over-simplification. He was now of the mind to remind the Senator that their present predicament, if indeed they were in one, might have been shaded differently if they had looked for a little better weather somewhere along the line.

"That sounds reasonable," Britt was saying, her voice studied.

"Okay, then, let's get to it," Price said cheerfully. "Did we hear anything from Hal?" he asked then.

"Yes, sir," Gus answered. "Early this morning. But, all they have so far is the name of the Special Litigation man assigned to the investigation."

"That's enough," said Price, and he suddenly wasn't his usual devil-may-care self. "Call Hal and Marshall today for sure," Price went on. "Alert them to be on call for an emergency committee meeting. If Joshua comes up with the right answers tomorrow night, we might have to vote on contingency, whatever it is."

"Phase-two acceleration," Gus supplied.

"Have a copy ready for each of the four of us," Britt told him.

"And a briefing on phase three," Price growled, "in case they're on to Omega."

They can't be, Gus thought concernedly.

"You've got your work cut out, Gus," Price was saying.

"I understand, sir."

"End of conference," said Britt.

"Check," replied Price.

Gus shut down the conference line, released his line from the scrambler. After a moment of reflection, he closed the folder on his detailed notes. First things first. Right now he needed to think, to find resolution. After which he was going to have to spend the rest of the day in the library. He picked up the folder, stood up, restoring his desk to its normal order before he moved across the office to the private elevator leading to the Sanctuary.

In the long Sanctuary hallway, he paused briefly by the entry to the Documents Room before moving on determinedly to the massive center doorway to the Throne Room. He stood before the door, unable to reach out for the ornate brass handle. It had been over two years since he had been in the room alone. In the beginning, his feelings of guilt had ebbed and flowed, until recently they had grown stronger, surfacing more often, a dark spectre more and more pervading his inner being. His hand shaking, he reached out, turned the heavy handle. He pulled up inside to stare out across the huge room.

Gus Holliman did not believe in the supernatural, yet he was inclined to accept that in a man's work there might remain some of his spirit, so that perhaps around him now there was a remnant of Morgan Halley's inner being. There was so much of the man physically present that it was reasonable to assume the presence of the more abstract, spiritual portion.

Which was why Gus Holliman had steadfastly avoided being in the room alone—until now, because he sensed that there had to be resolution.

He walked slowly to the pew used by Hal Fleming, where he swiveled the executive chair around to face the throne itself. Putting the folder on the desk, he settled himself carefully into the chair. The only illumination in the room now was from the eternal flames of the seven gas lamps surrounding the huge wooden throne chair. The small flames were steady, rising up to six or seven inches, and Gus was conscious of their hypnotic effect.

"Omega is in jeopardy," he heard himself saying, and he

compressed his eyes tightly closed, fearful of what his comment might bring down on him.

Morgan Halley had conceived the basic idea himself, when he in his genius had foreseen what it had taken an army of experts and a third-generation computer system three more years to verify. Omega. The End. That in x-number of years the United States of America would become so vulnerable that any one of two or three projected powers could easily render the country helpless.

It had been Morgan Halley's thesis that the power would be the United States of Europe, or some such similar confederation, under the one-man dictatorship he had called the Antichrist.

Or, perhaps Russia.

It hadn't really mattered, one way or the other. Omega was Omega.

Daniel, the computer system, had brought the matter to a head by proposing that the only practical answer for the United States was a coup, military of course, after it had verified the projection of Morgan Halley. The old man had rejected the coup option, because he had been for reversing the trend via peaceful and non-violent means, if at all possible. Via the people, via the ballot box, by exposing the facts, and by prayer, by appealing to his God for help.

Morgan Halley, too, had shown himself to be defeatist to the extent he had suggested that the developing events perhaps ought not be dealt with, since they might be the natural consequence of his God's own plan.

Daniel had coolly and with precision reported otherwise. A different, more sophisticated proposal, refined, and offering specific marching orders. The computer projected three minimum conditions which had to be met, which it identified as X, Y, and Z. Condition X was that the opposition leadership to the coup had to be eliminated ahead of time, systematically and undetected, avoiding post-coup martyrs. Condition Y required the enlistment and stabilization of key leadership necessary to support the coup. Condition Z, the more complex and requiring the most time to implement, required that the national mood be receptive to a radical change in government leadership.

Daniel had also confidently confirmed that the ETC had the long-range capability to implement and realize success in all three critical conditions.

128

"Condition X is now fifty percent satisfied," Gus reported dully, hearing his voice flat and emotionless in the empty cavernous room. "And minimum norms on Y and Z are being realized on schedule."

But Morgan Halley had balked, objecting first to his wife, then to his most trusted confidante, Gustave Holliman.

And Morgan Halley's name had gone directly to the top of the opposition leadership.

And his death had been attributed to natural causes, a lie known only to his wife and Gus Holliman.

Gus Holliman let his head drop, his chin touching his chest. Resolved then, he lifted his head, began speaking, his voice no more than a whisper, "It was pathetic, the way she used me. There was the importance of Omega, which I rationalized as the primary reason. You have to understand, sir, that Daniel is really our god, and I believed the computer. But the real reason, as you must have guessed, was because she promised me she would come to me, that she would give herself to me, if I would help," and he lowered his head, closed his eyes. "For eight years I wanted her; surely you can understand," and he finally broke down, sobbing. The room and its elaborate furnishings seemed unresponsive, providing him with no relief or solace.

Several minutes later, Gus Holliman lifted his head to stare at the nearest of the seven flames. There was then the first light of revelation in his own eyes. What a blind, stupid fool I have been, he said bitterly to himself. The truth had been spoken in this very room. Joshua Bain, the initiate, had hit it squarely on the head. The radicals at Berkeley. What had they been really after?

Power.

What they were really after had been POWER!

Pushing himself up out of the chair, he turned to retrieve the folder. With determination and a sense of inner purpose, he walked to the half-opened door. He turned in the doorway to look back into the room.

"I promise you," he said evenly, "that I'll do what I can," and with that parting remark, he marched off toward the library with more than a hint of authority in his gait.

The call was expected, so when Cleve Lambert was told by his secretary that a Mister Huey Orville was on the outside line, he took up the receiver already prepared.

"It's about time," he snapped into the mouthpiece, not in the least concerned that he might be offending Huey Orville, whom he hated without any qualification. Orville was a thug, a criminal by-product of the legitimate, struggling black population he so deceptively claimed to represent.

"Be cool, my'man," said Huey Orville, his voice serene, distant, causing Lambert to suspect he was higher than a kite.

"What happened?" Lambert demanded rudely.

"We had a classic reunion," Orville said then. "Like an experience, you know."

"Get to it, Huey."

"He's looking for Tony Seastrom; like he wants to see Tony bad."

"That's all?" Lambert asked cautiously.

"Yeah, that's all, and I tell you the truth," Huey assured him. "He thinks Tony slipped Jerrie the stuff, you know, and I ain't about to debate him. Like you said, I got to play it cool."

"You put him off, didn't you?"

"Tried the best I could, like you told me," Huey said. "But have you tried to put that Joshua cat off? I mean, like he's the king of the stubborns."

Lambert realized that he should've known better. "So what does that mean?"

"That means I've got Tony comin' in. Be here tomorrow morning. And I say we let 'em talk."

Lambert was thinking furiously. He now had two choices. One, he could hold up Seastrom and try to stall Joshua for a few days, the really critical days. Or, let the meeting take place and play it out, hoping to put an end to it. In his present frame of mind, stalling Joshua Bain was a little like trying to hold back an avalanche.

"All right," said Lambert, and he now put all the threat and authority he could muster into his voice. "Go ahead and let them meet. Brief Seastrom to deny everything and make sure he holds to his story. But I'm warning you, Huey Orville, that if you birds so much as touch one hair on his head, I'll personally get on your tail with every resource available to this Bureau. And, I'll not only put you out of business for good, I'll also chase you back to Zamboanga where you'll wind up chucking spears for the rest of your natural life!" And he paused for a second, measuring his own words. "Do you dig that, General?"

"You're out of date," Huey said after a moment. "We're

using AK forty-sevens over there now."

"You got anything else, Huey?"

"Yeah, man, like you could've stepped around this by not giving him my name and number."

"With his Berkeley contacts, he would've been on you in another hour." And he hung up the phone.

Cleve Lambert had already resolved that he had no other choice but to go as he was going. Once Joshua had turned over that license plate number, they both really had no other way to fly. Joshua on his own could have obtained the registration via any one of a half dozen ways. Lambert could have used a fictitious name in place of Tony Seastrom, but if Joshua had bothered to routinely cross check, then Lambert would suddenly become suspect. Besides, who would ever expect the finger man in a potential murder situation to use his correct name, anyway. By playing along and playing it straight, Lambert figured he not only could continue to orchestrate the proceedings, but he could also keep him and the Bureau out of Joshua's suspicions. So far, so good.

The one unknown that really intrigued him was who was in fact responsible for flying Jerrie McKennan into that mountain. The only logical answer, assuming it wasn't an accident, had to lie in the ETC Corporation, somewhere. Going in yesterday, he was going to push Joshua into revealing his plan for getting the records out. But he backed down in the face of Joshua's obvious temper and mood, and he now suspected that Joshua's plan somehow involved the two separate and unrelated subjects.

The Ford wagon moved heavily along the access road, burdened down by the 4 x 10 enclosed trailer. Joshua Bain and Alan Hunt were in the front seat of the loaded wagon, with Joshua behind the wheel. The oiled road turned slightly around a sandy rise, and Joshua backed off the gas.

"There's the gate," he said as he started braking the wagon. "I don't know which key it is," he said then.

Alan had a ring of keys in his hand, some of which were tagged. As the wagon stopped a few feet short of the metal gate, he held up one of the tagged keys. "This is it," he said, and he got out.

Joshua surveyed what he could see of the main grounds to the ranch they now call Canaan. The main house was about fifty yards beyond the gate, a stately, Spanish-style ranch home. Two-story, thick-walled, probably adobe, with a heavy tiled roof. A covered veranda ran the entire second floor, protected by an ornate wrought iron fence. A number of trees were about the house and grounds, providing plenty of shade and atmosphere. They had swapped houses today, with the former caretaker family from here moving to the grape ranch earlier in the day. The gate was now open, and Alan waved him on through. Joshua pulled through, stopped on the other side to let Alan get back in.

"Welcome to Rancho Canaan," Joshua said.

"And it's really ours," Alan said, not able to entirely hide his skepticism.

"So long as we make the payments."

"We're going to have to work that out, you know."

"We will, next week," said Joshua, thinking to himself that they would work it out provided he was still around. Or, for that matter, provided they both were still around. He had a hunch that in the next couple of days, both he and Alan Hunt were going to earn their right to Rancho Canaan. He pulled into the long, curving cement driveway, stopping in front of the entryway landing. They both got out and unhitched the trailer. It was early afternoon, and they had plenty of time to unload and return the trailer.

Now, they had a more serious matter to attend to.

Behind the front seat, tucked in carefully and protected by one of Joshua's bath towels, was a small brass urn holding the cremated remains of all that the rescue team could find of the once living Jerrie McKennan.

Joshua pushed the lightened wagon around the main house, back through a cluster of individual cottages. In a few minutes he had cleared the main grounds, following a seldom-used dirt road. The two men were quiet as the wagon climbed steadily for another five minutes, until they finally ran out of road. They both got out then, and Joshua opened the rear door to get the brass urn.

"Up there," he said, pointing with his free hand. "Just above that sheer line, there's a flat spot." And he started walking, the urn under his left arm.

Alan Hunt followed behind. It was cooler at the higher elevation, but the landscape was still harsh. The rapier-branched ocotillo bush was thick on the ascending slope, which was spotted with an occasional barrelhead cactus and random yucca plants. A steeply draining washbed to their left was choked with the delicate smoke tree, so called because at a distance the shrub's mantle of tiny, brownish-grey flowers suggested a low-lying cloud of smoke.

Alan paused near the gully for just a moment, studying the stand of smoke trees, knowing that this variety of shrub was unique in all of the desert flora because of the way it managed to survive. Its small seeds had an outer shell of such hardness that neither moisture nor even the stomach acid of birds and animals could break it down. Left alone in the desert soil, the seeds could not germinate in the way all other seeds managed to spring to life. It was only when the brief rains came to the upper mountains, when the first water from above crashed down the cuts and streambeds, that the smoke tree found its way to new, regenerative life. For it was in the brief flash floods that the rocks and boulders were tumbled and smashed against each other, and in that random conflict the hard shells of the smoke tree seeds were shattered, enabling the embryo seed to escape and thus to grow.

Alan turned away from the gully, hurrying to catch up with Joshua, and he was impressed with the irony that the destructive cataclysm of a flash flood could also yield new life.

The footing was good, and the two men worked upward at a steady pace, so that it took them only a little over five minutes to scale the top of the cliff. As Joshua had said, there was a sizable flattened area above the edge of the falling-away cliff.

The view across the Coachella Valley was breathtaking. "We had a picnic up here once," Joshua said as he labored to catch his breath. He rubbed the back of his free hand across his mouth, and there was a faraway look in his eyes, as if he might be considering something remote, distant. "Good quail hunting up here," he said then.

"Wonder how high it is," Alan said.

Joshua chuckled once. "We wanted to know too," he said, his voice now carefully controlled. "So she talked me into buzzing it." He shook his head then, a small smile coming briefly to his mouth. "The thermals are something else around here, but we got an altimeter reading. It's thirty-two hundred feet, exactly."

Joshua felt himself losing control. He handed the urn to Alan.

"You better get on with it," he said, and he swallowed hard.

"Are you sure you want me to do it?"

"Yes."

Alan nodded slowly, turned away to face the cliff. Though Alan's back was to him, Joshua could tell by the motion of his right elbow that he was unscrewing the flat metal top. Sooner than he expected then, Alan's right arm swung up and out.

The effect in the insistent wind was hardly discernible. A small bloom of substance giving brief essence to the air, then even that swirling away into a nothingness.

His vision blurred as he said good-bye for the last time.

As the next few seconds passed, he was aware that Alan was saying something, though he could not make the words out because his friend's back was still to him. When Alan finally did turn around, Joshua asked him, "What was that all about?"

Without hesitation, Alan answered, "I said that our hearts go out for the precious soul of Jerrie McKennan, that we loved her, and she loved us in return. That she should have peace now," and he then hesitated before going on, "and I asked that we, the living, find both peace and understanding."

Listening, Joshua had closed his eyes. A few seconds after Alan finished, he opened them to see that he had been left alone on the promontory. Yes, he thought then, give us, the living, the understanding. He turned away, moved toward the lower elevation, on down toward the car and what he had left to do.

The main floor of the ranch house was largely occupied by the dining room, whose cathedral ceiling reached to the second-story roof. At the rear was a kitchen facility capable of serving a hundred people. To the right of the entrance was a registration and switchboard area, an office, a laundry storage room. To the right of the dining room and behind the office were two long rectangular rooms, one behind the other. The first was a recreation room, the other a library. The second floor, balcony fronted around the dining room, was given to the private quarters for the ranch management personnel.

Finished unloading the trailer and having temporarily stored their belongs, Joshua and Alan made a quick inspection of the main house. Alan was pleased to see that the furnishings were not only complete but still in good condition. While Joshua inspected the office and desk area, he toured the rear of the house. He found a 9 x 12 walk-in cold storage locker off the kitchen. The kitchen's equipment was clean, apparently all in good operating condition. A fairly new cash register was at the food-checker's stand. In the dining room, he estimated they could feed seventy-five to a hundred people at one time.

As he started toward the library, he spotted another door, which he opened curiously. He was in a small office, probably the maitre d's. He went on through to a second door inside, finding himself looking down a flight of stairs to a small underground wine cellar. He estimated there were probably a couple hundred bottles of wine in the racks.

He met Joshua in the recreation room, where he settled down in a leather-covered, overstuffed chair while Joshua looked over the bar running along the far end of the room. Alan did not really know what he ought to say. He was simply overwhelmed, and when Joshua asked him what he thought, all he could do was to shake his head in bewilderment.

"It's going to take me a week," he said, "just to find my way around this place."

"It's not really that big," Joshua suggested as he poured them each a glass of tonic water. "We can only accommodate a hundred and ten people, maximum."

Only a hundred and ten, Alan thought.

"And we can figure each customer will average from thirty to fifty bucks per day," said Joshua as he walked toward him, passing the two pool tables, "which comes out to between three to five grand gross per day."

"But the Fullers couldn't make it go."

"They went about it in the wrong way," said Joshua. "Old man Halley had it figured to cater to the tournament crowd exclusively instead of the typical dude-ranch trade." He handed Alan his glass, and he sat down in a nearby chair. "We've already got the landing strip, don't forget." He shrugged then, smiling. "If nothing else, we can always run dope in from Mexico."

"That tournament idea just might do it," Alan was saying, and he had ignored Joshua's last comment. "We've got the room for a nine-hole practice course right around the main area. How about water?"

"Two operating wells."

Alan was shaking his head. "I don't know."

"Let's let it ride for a couple weeks," Joshua suggested. "Right now, it's time for some serious talk about something else."

When was it all going to end? Alan thought wearily, and he

was silent, content to listen because he didn't have the slightest idea what he could say.

"You know I'm involved in trying to clear up Jerrie's death," Joshua said, his voice low and deliberate. He looked around the room then, as if he might be listening for something. Alan couldn't hear a thing.

"Let's go outside," Joshua said abruptly, and he got up.

Alan followed him out through the rear of the house. They eventually wound up near the pool, now empty, in a pair of tree-shaded lawn chairs.

"As I was saying," Joshua went on, putting his glass down between his feet. "I've just about got it figured out who was responsible with maybe one or two loose ends to go." And he paused, gathering his thoughts. "You're sure that lookout didn't see anything before the crash?"

"It was too far away. And, he wasn't looking exactly at it; the fireball caught his attention."

"Eight miles away," Joshua mused under his breath.

"A shade over," Alan said. "We ran an azimuth check and plotted it on the map."

"But he couldn't say that something wasn't there?"

Alan shrugged. "No; as I said, he was too far away, that's all."

"Okay; it isn't that important, anyway."

"You were hoping for a parachute sighting, weren't you?" Alan began hesitantly. He had so far kept his peace, but he now felt it was time to start opening up.

"Yes," Joshua said, showing little reaction. "There was in fact a parachute; I've been able to put that much together for certain. I was hoping for a witness, though. But it doesn't matter."

The witness would be important to the police, Alan was thinking.

"It looks like we're going to have to trust one another," Joshua continued.

"Why not?"

"Yeah," said Joshua offhandedly. "Why not." And he finished off his tonic before settling back into the chair. "I'm going to tell you these things not only because I'm tired of having to hide them from you, but also because I'm going to need your help, provided, of course, that you want to help."

Alan Hunt listened for the better part of an hour. In capsule form, Joshua traced the action from his initial involvement in the Courtland kidnapping case right on up through the screening interview last Saturday, including his ETC assignment as the result of his meeting with Cleve Lambert yesterday.

As Joshua finished describing his meeting with Huey Orville, Alan was acutely aware that he was now privy to a most extraordinary set of circumstances. And, too, that Joshua Bain had extended his already vulnerable neck even further. There was silence then, and as Alan tried to contemplate the whole remarkable montage, he was wondering how he might fit into the scheme of things.

"How did you get onto them?" he asked. "I mean about Senator Turner."

"Strictly an accident," Joshua told him. "It was at one of the pool parties at the Halley estate, about a month ago. You remember, the one where you put on the diving exhibition."

Alan nodded, recalling the night.

"Jerrie and I were in the rumpus room," Joshua went on, "listening to Britt's stereo. We were on the floor, taking it easy and out of sight. The patio door was open—you know, where the bar is. Gino was serving drinks for the guests. Well, I guess the patio was empty at the time, because most of the people were out by the pool watching you show off."

"Mrs. Halley asked me to do it," Alan said defensively.

"Sure," said Joshua good-naturedly. "Anyway, Gus Holliman came in to get a replacement drink for one of the guests. I vaguely remember him ordering a grasshopper. He'd been in the water and was dripping wet. Gino must've dumped the mixings into the blender, and it wouldn't work. He was swearing and carrying on, and that's when I looked around and started paying close attention. Apparently the cord to the blender was unplugged, and Gus picked it up to plug it in. Well, man, Gino crawled all over him. You know, the shock hazard, wet feet and all, and just at that moment he said something like, that's what got Senator Turner, or something like that."

"A lousy slip of the lip," said Alan.

"It had to happen sooner or later," Joshua suggested. "I'd been looking and listening for over twelve months, you know."

"Most people wouldn't have noticed it," Alan observed.

"When you work for Cleve Lambert, you notice everything."

"Is that why we're out here instead of in the house?"

"You know Mrs. Halley as well as I do."

"Not really, but I understand, anyway, that it may be bugged."

"The telephone people will be in tomorrow," Joshua said. "Be sure to have multi-station phones installed in both our rooms upstairs. If they can, have them tie a direct line into the switchboard. We don't want any busy signals up here for the next three days."

"What do you want me to do?" Alan asked.

"First off, I'll not involve you in anything connected with Jerrie's situation. That's all mine." He paused then, as if making sure of his words. "If something happens to me between now and Thursday, then you're going to have to help Lambert as best as you can."

"What if something doesn't happen to you, as I fully expect?"

"Thanks for your confidence; but in such a case, then you'll have plenty to do. I'm putting down the detailed plan for Lambert tonight, and you can sit in on it. You're going to guide him and his boys in Thursday."

"What's up for tomorrow?"

"Phones in early. I've got to make a run to Riverside to settle up with Bill Olson. Then I'm taking the 690 to L.A. in the early afternoon to meet first with Lambert, then on to Huey Orville, and, hopefully, a face-to-face meeting with Tony Seastrom."

"The driver?"

"And the finger man," said Joshua, and his voice was heavily laden now.

"I suppose there's no talking you out of it."

"Haven't you tried enough already?"

"Apparently not," said Alan. "No matter how you try to rationalize it, you're going to lose if you wind up killing someone. You're allowing them to suck you down to their level. In a way, you've given them a double victory."

"They're going to be punished," said Joshua. "I owe her that much. I mean, can't you imagine the pain she had to endure in those last few moments? And I mean the inner pain. Knowing about her child, knowing about what she had. Can you really imagine that special kind of terrible grief?" Joshua looked aside, his face screwed into an agonized mask.

"And you hold yourself responsible, I suppose."

"Of course; I was the one who brought her down here."

Alan waited for a few seconds, allowing the conversation to cool, because he didn't want to drive Joshua away now. "You're carrying more of a load than you deserve," he finally said. "Jerrie McKennan was tough, and you know it. She was about as far from being a quitter as you can get. And, you know that too. So, don't sit there and tell me that she gave up at any time. Not only was she tough, she was smart as well. Those people who were after her at the ranch had plenty of time to finish the job, and quickly. But they didn't. Why? Haven't you ever asked yourself why? My guess is that she played them off somehow." Feeling more confident of himself, Alan pushed a little harder. "So don't give me that stuff that she was all broken up inside. I say my answer is more reasonable than yours."

"Perhaps," Joshua conceded, but all too reluctantly.

Okay, thought Alan, it was time to go all out, because he suspected that this was the last chance he would have. "How is what you're trying to do any different from what the ETC executive committee is doing? I mean, isn't it a bit ironic that you, the one-man avenger of the year, is at the same time about to put some people away for doing the same thing as you are? Come on, Joshua, fair is fair."

For the second time in the past few days, Alan saw the mask of rejection appear on Joshua's face, and he thought that Joshua would again get up and walk away from the conversation.

"It's not that simple," said Joshua, and he stayed put in his chair. "Theirs is a deliberate conspiracy, involving murder as a means to an end."

"They're simply being pre-emptive," Alan argued. "And you're after the fact, but, after all, killing is still killing."

"Kindly address that argument to the killer of Jerrie McKennan," said Joshua harshly.

"Joshua," Alan began then in his most persuasive manner, "the bright spot of this afternoon has been for me to see that you are against senseless killing, because of some compelling reason within you. You could never fit comfortably on the ETC executive committee, no more than I could."

"Look, my friend," Joshua said, interrupting him. "You're wasting your time by trying to talk me out of something I've already made up my mind to do. Unless, Alan, you can make me understand why Jerrie had to take the rap she did. I mean, that's all you have to do."

"That's unfair."

"You're reneging."

"No, because you know I cannot give you an adequate explanation, simply enough, because I don't have one. So you're being unfair. The whole fact of the matter, really, is that there is an explanation available but you refuse to even consider it, let alone accept it."

"In religion, I suppose."

"No, in the Bible. You see, there's a distinction between the two. One is entirely God's work, the other, unfortunately in many cases, is largely the work of man."

"Tell me, Alan," said Joshua evenly; "you say you loved Jerrie, too."

"I certainly did."

"And you don't care that the people who cut her and flew her into that mountain are still walking around, enjoying life?"

"I tell you true, if I had gotten back sooner and caught them at it, there would've been some busted heads."

"That's comforting, but it's not the answer to my question."

"You better believe I care," Alan insisted. "But you've got to believe that the Lord will resolve the issue *if you'll just let Him help you.*"

"He can help me all He wants to; I can use it."

"No, you've got to ask Him."

"He's funny that way," Joshua said grimly.

Alan sensed his frustration again.

"I'm sorry," said Joshua. "That was crude and uncalled for."

"No; it's all right," Alan assured him. "It's just that I'm not very good at trying to explain what I feel inside."

"Don't sell yourself short; maybe it's that I'm very pigheaded."

Alan Hunt stood up, walked up to the edge of the empty pool, and when he spoke his voice was low, reflective. "What I'm really talking about is faith, I guess. Even though I don't have a plan, as you probably do, I still *know* that things are going to be resolved. You know, becoming a Christian doesn't mean you roll over and play dead. For example, Jesus Christ never once proposed that we stand idly by and watch someone being beaten to death. But when we do intervene, we've got to believe that we're not alone. You see, it all hinges on believing. I don't understand why Jerrie died either, but I have the faith that we will all endure it, as tragic as it was, and somehow or other the Lord in His incredible wisdom will lead us through it. You have to have that faith first."

The late afternoon was closing in around them, and Alan watched with detached interest as the animals started cautiously coming out of their mid-day hibernation to begin their nightly search for food on the deserted ranch. He had already seen two big jack rabbits in the past few minutes. A more brazen ground squirrel was scampering around now near the pool's filter. And a big bluejay arguing vociferously, probably with himself.

"Then you'll be asking me to forgive them," Joshua was saying, "and to love them, even. Isn't that right, my friend?"

Alan had turned around slowly to face Joshua. So that was what was really bugging him. "First things first," he suggested. "You don't build the house before you pour the foundation." Or, maybe a better analogy, he thought, was to suggest that you crawled before you walked, since it would take a man of considerable dimension to forgive as grievous a hurt as Joshua Bain had endured.

Chapter ten

It was hot in Los Angeles, one of those inversion days, and the smog by mid-afternoon had built to its peak in the still, listless air hanging over the basin. Waiting at a stoplight near the airport, Cleve Lambert squinted to check the calendar on his wristwatch band. Wiping his eyes, he reminded himself that he now had less than six months until he retired. Maybe he would stay in Baja for a full year. There was a secluded cove below Ensenada that he had stumbled on last year, so far off the beaten path he could probably go for weeks without seeing another living soul. And zero smog. *Langusta* up to three and four pounds right in the shallows. Let his beard grow down to his knees.

The driver in the car behind him sounded his horn, snapping Lambert out of his reverie. He stamped on the gas pedal irritably, and the car lurched forward. A few minutes later he pulled into the motel, parked in front of the room next to the one registered in the name of Joshua Bain. As was his habit, he delayed for a minute, gathering his thoughts. He picked up his jacket then, checked the inside pockets. Getting out, he put the jacket on with the door still open. That too, was habit, a necessary one to conceal the thirty-eight on his right hip.

Joshua let him in, and Lambert immediately shed his coat, savoring the refrigerated coolness in the air. He saw an open bottle of tonic water on the coffee table.

"Got another one of those?" he inquired, gesturing toward the bottle.

"In the bathroom sink," Joshua replied.

Loosening his tie and rolling up his sleeves, Lambert went into the bathroom, where he found four bottles of tonic water in the sink, immersed in ice cubes. He pulled one out, unscrewed the cap. He had downed half the bottle by the time he got back to sit down across from Joshua, who was on the bed. He enviously noted that Bain was barefoot, dressed in a cotton pullover, bermuda shorts.

"We still on the same schedule?" Lambert inquired idly.

"Why don't we first work on the reason why I'm here," Joshua suggested.

Sure, Lambert thought, why not. "How did they react?"

Joshua shrugged. "Normally, I guess. I told them that it appeared you wanted to check out the drawing number, that you wanted another meeting today. So, here I am. What do I tell them this time?"

Lambert settled himself deeper in the chair, crossed his legs. "Because of the critical time we're in right now, it's best we take every precaution to guarantee your protection. They've got to figure they've made a mistake somewhere or that there is a leak, an informer. From what you've reported so far, it looks like they're pretty much in the dark. That's why they moved you in so quickly. They want answers. And, finding out what we have will go a long way toward telling them how they made their mistake, or, where the leak may be. I've discussed this with Washington, and we agree that we should give them something solid to make it appear we're reacting normally. And, what we give them should also work to protect you."

"I'm glad you worry about me, Cleve."

Lambert chuckled under his breath. "Per your request, we've frozen the investigation back there. But we made pretty good headway before yesterday. For example, it appears that a Harold Fleming, out of New York, is the owner of registry on one of the three Lear jets parked near the ETC hangar last weekend. We suspected Fleming, of course, of being a member of the executive committee for the past year. Anyway, one of Fleming's pet projects is an institute on Long Island which specializes in grant-supported studies of various sorts. Two months ago, the institute held a three-day seminar reviewing the long-range consequences of the current arms control agreement being negotiated with the Russians. Among those present were three wheels from the Pentagon, one of whom is on the Joint Chiefs of Staff, Admiral J. S. Foxworth. Also a specialist on tactical nuclear deployment, General Alvin Petersen."

"Sounds kind of heavy," Joshua observed.

"Heavy enough," Lambert agreed. "Anyway, it is interesting that both of these officers not only had a closed dinner at Fleming's estate the final night of the seminar, but they also spent the entire night there as Fleming's house guests." He pulled a piece of paper out of his jacket pocket. "Give them these two names, and tell them you have been instructed to obtain and report to us any information relating thereto."

He then reached into his right front pocket of his slacks, pulled out a small, rectangular metal object. "We're even throwing in a 16mm camera, with which you're supposed to photograph any documents bearing these two names," and he put the small camera on the end table near Joshua.

Joshua took the piece of paper, inspected it briefly before putting it on the same table. "What's the connection between them and the ETC?"

"All we can say is that we're positive of a link with Foxworth. The general's name is just smoke." He finished off the rest of his tonic water, returning the empty bottle carefully to the table. "What this does, Joshua, is give them grist for their mill. And, more importantly, it points the finger of suspicion back to the east coast, taking any possible heat off you. Okay?"

"Looks good to me."

Lambert leaned forward, putting his elbows on his knees, and asked, "What about the schedule?"

"You've got everything lined up?"

"We're ready to move tonight. The only thing I couldn't get is the rocket launcher. How about rifle grenades?"

Joshua contemplated the proposed substitution. "No problem if they're anti-tank."

"They will be."

"They'd better be," Joshua told him gravely. "In fact, I want to inspect the equipment myself, and it all had better be fresh. One dud and we've had it."

"It's so important?"

"Without the grenade launcher you probably won't get your records," said Joshua. "As to the schedule, you can be at the motel whatever time you like, provided you're ready for my briefing at eight o'clock tomorrow morning." He stretched out then to reach his left front pocket to extract a piece of scratch paper. "Here's the new phone number where I can be reached in case of an emergency. Remember, the line may be tapped."

"Shouldn't have to call you," said Lambert. "I've had an advance man down there since last night. We're going to be at the Yucca Canyon Inn, room 112."

"Good," said Joshua, obviously pleased. "I don't have to tell you to keep a low profile. That area is ETC country, wall to wall. If you accidentally show a handgun, Gus Holliman would probably know about it before you could get it back into your pocket."

"We'll be careful," said Lambert, and he then glanced around the room. "Why the motel room this time? Aren't you heading right back?"

"Got an important appointment," said Joshua.

"Mind telling me about it? I mean, it seems to me that we both ought to be a little careful now."

"It's none of your business," said Joshua evenly, and his face reflected the same slight warning. "And if I spot anyone following me, I'll just head on out to Vegas for a few days rest and relaxation while you do the same in Palm Desert."

"All right," said Lambert. "Like I said yesterday, you've got the upper hand." He got up then, retrieved his coat. "How about a dry run with the van?"

"No need. You'll have a guide to get you in."

"Impromptu, huh?"

"From start to finish. But don't feel badly, it'll be the same for all of us, including me."

Lambert let himself out, walked stiffly to his car. As he closed the door behind him, he was furious, knowing that Joshua Bain was going to jeopardize the entire mission of breaking the ETC just to get some stinking information out of a low-grade rat like Tony Seastrom. He had coppered that bet for Joshua by giving him the Viper, just in case Huey Orville somehow lost control of the situation.

After making sure Lambert's car was gone, Joshua hurried to the pay phone located at the front of the motel. Using his new credit-card number, he placed a station-to-station call to Britt Halley's private number. She answered after one ring.

"It's Joshua," he reported, trying his best to sound affectionate.

"I'm glad it's you," she said, obviously pleased, even relieved.

"Hope I'm not interrupting."

"This is the kind of break," she said quickly, "that I can live with two or three times a day," and her voice was an octave lower, going from being pleased to a kind of intimate tone implying he should reciprocate.

"Now you've made me glad," he said, and he was laying it on now, not caring what he might have to do.

"What's on your mind?" she asked suggestively.

"Officially or otherwise?"

"Let's get the official out of the way first."

"I'm in L.A. now," he said, "at the airport. I just finished up with Mister Lambert." He pulled the folded paper out of his pocket, gave her the names, spelling them out at her request. "Does that do us any good?" he asked then.

"Maybe more than you think," she said. "Looks like we're going to be busy around here tomorrow, but that's all I can tell you on the phone."

Joshua translated her remark to mean the executive committee was going to be called in for an emergency meeting. The ex-com meeting was not necessary to his plan, but the extra activity could help tip the odds a little more in his favor.

"So back to us," she was saying, "and how about having dinner with me tonight?"

"Oh, nuts!" he exclaimed. "It'll be eight or nine tonight before I can get away. They're still checking out the 690, and the instrument check won't be finished until then." He was lying now, but he sensed he was enjoying it. "How about tomorrow night?" he said then. "Just the two of us, and we can make up for lost time."

"Good idea," she agreed. "Provided the boys are all gone by then."

"I hate to wait until tomorrow night," he offered. "Why don't we squeeze lunch tomorrow in between," and he knew just asking for the critical luncheon meeting was not enough, for she might decline, so he tied it down with, "I've got something urgent to talk to you about, anyway."

She agreed without hesitation, and Joshua told her he would pick her up at the office at eleven-thirty tomorrow morning."

"I miss you terribly," she told him then.

The deception was coming easier now. "I miss you, too, much more than you think."

She hung up, and as he returned the receiver to its catch, he felt inside a renewed firmness of purpose.

Back in his room, he quickly changed into street clothes. He checked the Viper in its thigh holster, practicing a number of times to make sure he could get it out quickly. He had removed the entire right pocket lining of the slacks, not wanting anything to interfere with the quick removal of the pistol. He deferred a coat this time, content with the open-necked, short-sleeve shirt.

Turning out of the motel to head east on Century Boulevard, he was aware that the next act of this week's drama was going to be almost entirely extemporaneous, unlike the carefully prepared script for the rest of the show. The car he was driving had been rented from the same agency that handled Tony Seastrom's car before. Some insistent and well-financed questions to two of the agency's employees produced the disappointing fact that Tony Seastrom had been alone both when he picked up the car and when he returned it. However, and more interestingly, Tony Seastrom, again using his real name, had rented another car just this morning. So out of a bad break came a good one. Maybe.

He was now heading toward the meeting with Tony Seastrom, and, very likely, with Huey Orville as well. Joshua did not have the slightest idea what he was going to do, except to get out of it alive. That Tony Seastrom was here somewhat surprised him. While five bills might draw a favorable response out of Huey Orville; that it could bring a finger man back to the scene of his crime hardly made sense. Although it was not above the WAR style, like Seastrom using his real name, to brazenly accept responsibility for what they did. Recognition was part of their reward, he supposed. If all else failed, he had the option to scat back to the car agency and wait for Tony Seastrom to show, where he could get him alone. He wondered if Tony Seastrom might not tend to be loose-lipped while he was standing in the open hatch of a Commander 690 at eight thousand feet above the blue Pacific.

It took him only about twenty minutes to reach the same Compton Avenue address. Per his instructions, he pulled in to park in front of the same dilapidated building. There was no one on the street near him, so he cut the engine to wait.

He noticed then that there was a man in the car parked about twenty yards in front of him. Only a few seconds passed before the man got out, started along the curb toward him. Staring at him in the strong afternoon light, Joshua sensed he recognized the man, who was big, over six feet, weighing probably two-fifty. His face was heavy, his eyes widely set, piggish, but far apart. The dark blonde hair was what jangled Joshua's memory. Curly and long, almost heavy afro proportion. The stranger was beside the car then, near his elbow.

"You looking for Huey Orville," the man said, his soprano voice thin, almost childish.

"Yeah," said Joshua, "my name is Bain."

"Follow me, and stick close, you hear."

Joshua nodded he understood. The big man moved away heavily, back toward his car. Watching him, Joshua's eyes narrowed, and he felt the blood starting to pound behind his eyes as he realized that he was looking at a man exactly matching Alan's description of the second man in the getaway car. For a fleeting moment, Joshua figured he could take him right now, but before he could move, he saw the car starting up, moving away from the curb. Joshua hit the starter, accelerated from the curb to move right up on the other's rear bumper.

The car ahead turned left off Compton and they moved slowly for the next few blocks through a residential neighborhood of old and weathered stucco and wood-frame houses. Joshua calmed himself down with the observation that the man in the car ahead of him might not in fact be involved. He was wishing now that he had brought Alan along. The car ahead pulled into the curb then. Seeing the other man getting out, Joshua pulled in behind, got out himself.

The house was a typically small wood-frame on a typically

small lot. The weedy, ill-kept yard looked as neglected as the house. Quiet and grim faced, Joshua followed behind his contact, pulling up behind him on the small porch. Their feet made rasping, echoing sounds on the gritty, worn wooden surface of the landing. The big man pulled the screen door open, knocked twice on the scarred door. The house looked like it might collapse at any minute. Joshua looked over his shoulder to see a number of black kids playing on the narrow street, and he felt even more depressed and let down, as he always did when he was in such a neighborhood.

The door opened. The big man with the fat face stepped inside, turned to gesture for Joshua to enter. The house inside was no better than the outside. They were standing in what appeared to be the front room. Huey Orville was slouched over in a tattered, overstuffed chair in the far corner, next to a mock fireplace. To his right, with his back to the front window, was a man of medium height, on the thin side. He was dressed in hippy style, a black headband holding back his long, stringy hair. Joshua recognized him as Tony Seastrom. Joshua figured conservatively there were two or three others out of sight elsewhere in the small house. The front room was wallpapered, a yellowish-blue, indistinguishable design. Huey Orville didn't get up; unmoving, he stared at Joshua for a few seconds. He showed his teeth then, gesturing with his right hand. "Hands on the head."

"Come on, Huey," Joshua complained, raising his arms. The big man behind him frisked him clumsily.

"Have a seat, Joshua," Orville told him cordially, pointing toward the overstuffed couch turned away from the wall to the right of the fireplace. Joshua obliged, settling down lightly on the arm of the couch nearest the wall. He was careful to put his weight on his left leg, extending his right leg out straight.

"You know Tony," said Orville.

Joshua nodded once. Tony Seastrom, not responding to the introduction, took a step to his right to sit down in a straight-backed chair. Joshua was of the opinion that Tony Seastrom looked a little worried, and suddenly none of it made any sense. It was patently obvious by his expression and manner that Tony Seastrom was there against his will.

"And that's big Fred," Orville said, pointing toward the man who had escorted Joshua in and who now leaned back against the front door, his heavy arms crossed.

"Meet Joshua Bain," Orville said.

"We've met," said Fred.

"Fred who?" Joshua asked.

"Bingston," Fred told him, and Joshua figured the man had to have something wrong with his throat. He was almost willing to bet even money that Huey had deliberately lined him up with the two men who had hit Jerrie. Huey was just twisted enough to pull it off and laugh about it later.

"Like okay, my'man," Huey was saying, still cordial, still showing his beautiful teeth. "So here's Tony, and he's all yours."

"Leave us alone," said Joshua solemnly.

"No way," Huey answered quickly. "Like we don't have any secrets. Ain't that right, Tony?"

Tony Seastrom grinned sardonically, shaking his head.

"Okay, Huey," said Joshua. "Then we'll play it your way." And he levelled a look at Tony Seastrom. "What were you doing with Jerrie?"

"What are you talking about?"

"I'm not here to play games, Tony. You were seen at the ranch house. We got your license number, the car, so start giving with the answers."

"Okay, okay," Seastrom said defensively. "So we were there. We were down there for four days standing up with our brothers and sisters in the fields. And, we stopped by to see Jerrie. You know, like old friends. Nothin' else, I swear."

"Give, Tony," Joshua said threateningly.

"That's it, I swear. She laid a can of brew on us, and we split. That's it, I swear."

Joshua had been standing up slowly, to lean against the mantle over the fake fireplace. He wiped the sweat off his right hand before casually slipping it inside his pocket. "With big Fred, huh," he said then. "And the black broad," and he turned to look at Fred Bingston, who was now staring at him with a shocked, disbelieving expression on his face. "Who is she, fatso, your woman?"

The disbelief turned to immediate rage, and Fred Bingston took a tentative step toward Joshua, his heavy arms hanging loose.

"Cool it!" Huey shouted, and he came out of his chair to shoot the gap. He pulled up before Fred Bingston, whispered something to him. Bingston relaxed against the door, staring hatefully at Joshua.

"What's the matter, Huey," Joshua demanded, and he

didn't care now one way or the other. "You always play nurse-maid to your soldiers?"

On his way back to his chair, Huey Orville stopped briefly in front of Joshua. "Like I don't provoke," he said, his voice under obvious control. "This is like all news is good news, you dig?"

"How'd you find her, Tony?" Joshua asked then, his voice still accusing.

Tony Seastrom, still a little wide-eyed over the confrontation between Joshua and Fred, could only shrug his shoulders. "We picked it up from some dude up north. I can't remember who it was."

"What about the heroin? You on big 'H' now?"

Tony Seastrom frowned. "No man, you know better. That place was crawling with fuzz. We got shook down twice in Indio on Saturday alone."

Now puzzled with their placid, almost indifferent attitude, Joshua looked again to Fred Bingston, figuring the big man's temper was his best hope.

"You, fatso," he said contemptuously, "were you the one who painted the pretty letters all over the wall?"

Fred Bingston was shaking now, and he looked once to Huey Orville.

"Like cool it, big Fred," Huey said in a veiled cautious tone. "And this about wraps it up."

"What's the matter, fatso," Joshua went on, loading his voice with all the acid he could muster, "they take out your guts when they cut you?"

"Like forget the man!" Fred screamed shrilly, his face livid, and he started toward Joshua, a switchblade in his right hand.

Joshua lunged at the same time toward Huey Orville.

Movement in the room now took place in sodden, slow motion.

As Joshua expected, the closed door behind opened a crack, and the ugly snout of a twelve-gauge shotgun appeared.

Tony Seastrom fell flat on the floor, his arms over his head.

Huey Orville was screaming something, an inarticulate, animal sound, like a warning.

The Viper was out, in Joshua's right hand, and he figured he might have to drop Bingston, but then the shotgun went off, and Fred Bingston suddenly began to veer to his right, his mouth wide open, and he slammed into the fireplace.

The muzzle blast of the shotgun, confined to the small room, staggered Joshua. Deafened and dazed by the blast, he realized then that he had Huey around the waist with his left arm, using him as a shield, with the nose of the Viper jammed in Huey's right ear.

He vaguely noticed that Tony Seastrom was up on his feet and running out the front door, and Joshua thought dazedly that Seastrom was getting away and he'd never see him again. Huey had been struggling, but he now ceased to move. Joshua realized that two other men were now in the room, both bending over the slumped form of Fred Bingston. One of them turned to look impassively at Huey Orville, shaking his head negatively.

It dawned on Joshua Bain that they must've accidentally shot one of their own men! Baffled by the turn of events, he continued to hold Huey Orville in the death grip. Feeling his own head clearing then, he understood that Huey was telling the other two men something, and the next thing he knew they were picking up Fred Bingston, one at either end, to drag him out the rear of the house.

Joshua shook his head, yawning to clear his ears, and he was aware then that Huey was trying to say something to him. Since they had been left alone in the room, Joshua let him go. Huey turned to face him, straightening out his rumpled clothes.

"It's all over!" Huey yelled at him.

The smell of cordite was heavy in the air, and Joshua coughed once.

"The cops will be here in a couple of minutes," Huey warned him.

"What happened?" Joshua asked him, his ears still ringing.

"An accident," Huey said. "Big Fred killed himself cleaning his gun."

"Get off it," Joshua snapped.

Huey Orville, alias General Pao-min, was already turning toward the front door. "You can stay here and explain it, if you want to," he said, and he was gone.

Joshua stared stupidly around the empty room, and it took a few seconds for him to realize he had been left alone in the house. He stumbled out the front door, across the narrow porch. Huey had started the car used by Fred Bingston, and he left the curb with a screech, careening off down the street. Joshua's hearing had improved enough for him to make out the distant but closing sound of police sirens. He loped along the uneven walkway toward his car, thinking numbly that maybe he was dreaming, or, worse yet, maybe the strain was getting to him and he was starting to crack. In the car, he tossed the Viper on the seat beside him, started the engine. He punched the gas, screeching away from the curb.

It was his opinion that the police were moving awfully quick, but, then, it began to dawn on him that the quick response, too, was probably a part of it.

Twenty minutes later, Joshua pulled slowly into the motel entrance to park in front of his own room. It was still hot in the fading late-afternoon light, and he sat unmoving behind the wheel of the car. He neither heard nor felt the noise and heat of the city coming at him through the open window. He leaned his head back, closed his eyes, afraid to get out for fear he might fall flat on his face, or, maybe, just wander off aimlessly, a new option he had not considered before. There was still the residual ringing in his mind.

In the past few minutes, he had had to accept the probable conclusion of who had been responsible for setting in motion the chain of events leading to the murder of Jerrie McKennan. In his rage and with his last breath, Fred Bingston had given him the answer, one which had been right under his nose all along. The answer, too, made all the rest of it fall into place. But probable was not enough, he supposed, so he had to find a way to nail it down. He realized then that his stomach was finally reacting. He abruptly got out of the car, lurched to the door of his room.

In the bathroom, he leaned unsteadily over the open toilet, retching uncontrollably. A few minutes later, he was standing before the wash basin, his face smothered in a wet towel. His mind was blank as he dropped the towel into the sink, and it took him a few seconds to realize the face peering back at him in the mirror was his own. He was looking at a stranger, a pathetic, beaten caricature of a man who didn't look at all angry anymore, certainly not sure of himself. Looking aside, he sighed heavily, coughed once to clear his throat. Joshua, my'man, he thought dejectedly, you are in desperate need of some help. Sleep maybe. Or booze. How about a little of both, one to help the other?

He moved slowly and carefully into the main room, heading for the stand holding the telephone. He would have to get someone from the motel to bring him a fifth of vodka. Room service. The number for room service. He pulled open the small drawer under the phone.

He stared into the drawer for a passing moment, uncomprehending.

A Gideon Bible.

Still startled by the totally unexpected revelation, he realized he was sitting down on the bed. His hand reached out, as if with a mind of its own, and took the Book from the drawer.

Chapter eleven

8:00 a.m., Thursday morning. The weather over the Coachella Valley had leveled off. Although the predictions were it could continue hot during the day, it would be a few degrees cooler than the day before. Cleve Lambert felt little comfort with today's 102 degrees versus yesterday's 108 degrees. Considering a high layer of thin cirrus forming overhead, he moodily predicted another ten points on the humidity scale.

Dressed in field working clothes, including a light windbreaker, he hurried along the motel walkway. With a full ice bucket in his hand, he entered his room, quickly closing the heavy door behind him. His four men were assembled in the small, cramped room. They were the best, personally selected by him, and, like him, they were all on edge now. No matter how many years you were at it, he thought, it was still the same. The acid dumping into the stomach. The butterflies. And it seemed as if you had to go to the bathroom every fifteen minutes.

He handed the ice bucket to Burt Ingstrom.

The room's cold air drew up the skin on his face.

Ingstrom jerked a thumb over his shoulder toward the bathroom. Cleve Lambert checked his watch. It was one minute past eight.

Joshua Bain came out of the bathroom, rubbing his hands.

"How'd you get here?" Lambert asked curiously.

"The back way; Alan dropped me off."

Joshua was using the old noggin, Lambert thought approvingly.

Joshua had moved to the small table near the front of the room. He reached into his shirt, pulled out a large piece of what looked like heavy sketch paper, folded once. Gesturing for Lambert, he unfolded the paper, placing it flat on the table.

"Gather round, boys," Lambert said.

"This is the layout of the ETC floorplan that you'll need," Joshua started to explain. "Alan will take you in to this point, here, the executive entrance on the second parking level." He used his finger for a pointer.

"It's all underground," Lambert pointed out.

"That's right," Joshua confirmed. "And you've got plenty of clearance for the truck. Now, Alan Hunt will break away from your group as soon as he puts you on the first security station."

"Why can't he go all the way in?" Lambert asked.

"In the first place, you don't need him beyond the first station. Secondly, and the main reason, is that Alan is going to use Britt's limo to drive directly to the Halley estate."

Lambert frowned puzzledly.

"He's going to round up the executive committee."

Lambert shook his head. "Man, why didn't you—"

"I only found out about it myself last night," Joshua told him. "And it's strictly a long-shot, anyway, since I can't say for sure they'll all be here by noon. But, I'm banking on it, okay?"

"He should have some help."

"Negative," said Joshua, and he was smiling a little now for the first time. "Alan is known by the estate security people, and he can get in, with any luck at all, without a fight. Some stranger along would only complicate things for him."

"If you say so," Lambert conceded reluctantly.

"Now it's fairly clean up to this point," Joshua went on. "From the first security station you run straight down this hall for exactly ninety-eight feet, where you'll hit a hallway to your left." He paused for a moment, and when he began again his voice was intense. "When you look down that hallway to your left, you'll see another security station at the far end, facing you. It's fully enclosed. Metal base up to about hip level. Glass from there on, heavy stuff, and we have to assume it's bullet-proof. That station is exactly eighty feet from where you'll be standing when you turn the corner." He looked around the four men gathered near the table. "Who's got the rifle grenade assignment?"

One of the four men held up his hand. He was tall, a tough looking young man with a crew cut.

"You know how to use the gear?"

"George has used it," Lambert said confidently.

"How high is the ceiling of the hall?" George asked, his voice sure and calm.

Joshua was now smiling for the second time. "Excellent," he said then, and he leaned forward. "When you come to the corner, prone out next to the wall and bring the weapon around the corner on your belly."

Lambert was shaking his head. "That anti-tank grenade is heavy, falls like a rock," and he looked at the young agent concernedly. "Can you get it to the security station without bouncing it off the floor?"

"It will make it," he said. "By launching it from a low point, as the man says. That'll give us an improved trajectory."

"Why don't you let him dash down the hall for, say, twenty or thirty feet?" Lambert asked.

"That leads us to the most pressing precaution of all," Joshua said gravely. "The records are stored in a room in the Sanctuary, and we don't know what their destruct plan might involve. I'll be in the Sanctuary when you start in. Hopefully, by then, I'll have the records room open. Now, Gus Holliman is the key, because if he is alerted to a break in, you know he'll blow those records immediately. So, we've got to keep him in the dark until I can first get the room open and then disable Holliman to prevent him from probably blowing us all to kingdom come."

Lambert took a deep breath, exhaled heavily. "Man, I don't know; I get your point and it all looks too squeaky to me. What you're saying is that we've got to get that second security guard before he can alert Holliman."

"That's right," Joshua told him. "Not only him but the first guard as well."

"Can't you get Holliman out of the building on some pretext?"

"Negative," Joshua said irritably. "In the first place, that might arouse his suspicions, and secondly, if he's out, then the guard has got to have stand-by provision to destruct or at least to hard seal the room himself. I can deal with the situation better if Holliman is in the building."

"All right," said Lambert resignedly. "What's next?"

"It's all downhill after you blow that second station," said Joshua. "You hot-foot it down this hallway to Gus Holliman's office, where I'll meet you and take you to the Sanctuary."

"By myself?"

"You alone. The two of us can handle it."

"What about Mrs. Halley?"

"Leave her to me," said Joshua, a note of finality in his voice. "The rest of you place your satchel charges where I've indicated. Set times for twenty minutes and clear the building fast. The rest of your instructions are here, building evac', where to meet afterwards, and so on." He got up stiffly, stretched, a little too casually by Lambert's estimate.

"All you have to do, really," Joshua said, "is to stick to the schedule to the half-minute. I'll be allowing you a thirty second margin at my end."

Cleve Lambert didn't honestly know what to think of the thirty-second tolerance. He had been on tight margins before, and he supposed they could put it together. "What about our watches?" he asked then.

"Synchronize at the first security station," Joshua told him. "There are clocks all over the place, and they've all got exactly the same time."

Probably another one of Gus Holliman's idiosyncrasies, Lambert thought worriedly. And he wondered then if Holliman's urge for detail and exactness would work to their advantage or disadvantage. He realized then that Joshua Bain was the one who had to deal with the question, because his life was on the line.

9:15 a.m. The Throne Room was dark, save for the seven flickering lamps, and Gus Holliman sat reverentially quiet, his head bowed so that his chin was nearly on his chest. Seated again in Hal Fleming's pew, he was taking a moment to verify his own plans. He was also seeking the courage to go through with what he figured he must do.

He had gone through several options.

One, and the most tempting, was to simply disappear. Morgan Halley had arranged that a full set of escape documents were to be kept up to date and ready for all the committee members in case they would have to flee the country. Now, Gus deferred that contingency plan.

He had considered eliminating Britt Halley himself.

He knew he lacked the guts to pull it off alone.

The best tack was to try to convince the rest of the committee, Price, Fleming, and Higgins. Tell them the truth. But he had to catch them alone, because with Britt Halley present he wouldn't stand a chance.

He had discreetly checked her appointment calendar earlier that morning; she was scheduled to have lunch with Joshua Bain at noon.

The three other committee members would be at the Halley estate no later than twelve-thirty. Gus had elected to drive to the estate about that time, confront them there.

It was a good plan, he told himself.

He thought again about the passport, and the money, stored in the Documents Room, and he knew it was going to be a rough morning.

9:45 a.m. In his own personal chair forward in the passenger compartment, Calvin Price looked disinterestedly out the port window of the Lear jet. By his estimate, they were over the Colorado River now and should start descending any minute. While he didn't know the full gist of the report bringing him west, he knew that Joshua Bain had obtained the name Foxworth. That choice piece of information interested him more than he had let on to Gus Holliman on the telephone.

Calvin Price trusted his intuition, and an inner voice kept telling him that the FBI did not set up a separate task force just to chase a probable conspiracy lead. With their recent budget cuts, the Bureau didn't have the manpower to go around squashing ants with sledgehammers. Gus Holliman's optimistic attitude disturbed him. And a totally-out-of-character performance by Britt Halley, too. Maybe they were selling each other. Gus Holliman's recalcitrance he could understand, but he had always relied upon Britt to check and balance that situation.

Feeling the plane's power slackening off, he sat more upright in his chair, thinking then that the only recent influence having a bearing on the situation was Joshua Bain. He ran a thoughtful hand through his unruly hair.

10:00 a.m. Coming down the balcony stairway to the dining room level, Alan Hunt was fully dressed for the first time since he couldn't remember when—a cool, lightweight seersucker jacket over a darker blue cotton pullover, white double-knit slacks, and a pair of two-tone black and white loafers he reserved for special occasions. He found Joshua near the pool, the open place they now called "the office." Joshua was bent over the rickety card table, and as Alan got close enough he saw Joshua was reviewing their own rough copy of the plan.

"We all set?" Alan asked as he bent over the table. It was already hot outside, and he could feel himself starting to perspire.

"Not quite," said Joshua under his breath. "We've still got a couple items left. You get the clothespins?"

"Oh, yeah," said Alan, and he reached into his pocket to get the wooden pins.

"There are eight sets of cuffs in the Ford," Joshua went on. "The only change is that I'll take three instead of two. That'll still leave you with enough to handle the gang at the estate."

Alan didn't bother to ask why Joshua now needed the extra set of cuffs. "It's time for me to pray now," he said straight out. "Why don't you join me?"

Joshua turned his head to look up at him from under his arm.

"After yesterday afternoon," Alan suggested, "don't you think you should have at least a suspicion that someone is looking after you?"

"Perhaps so," Joshua seemed to agree as he straightened up. "But, for your information, and since I've got the time, I'm going to go up on the hill after we finish here."

That might be a start, a beginning, Alan thought happily. The promontory, after all, was a little closer.

10:15 a.m. Cleve Lambert paced the carpeted floor nervously. They had just finished rehearsing the complete run for the third time. He found the confinement of the small motel room almost too much to bear now, and he wanted to push out the front door and run around the motel grounds until he fell down exhausted. He looked at Burt Ingstrom, a stocky, bull-like kind of a man, who also looked as if he was about to come unglued.

"Let's go through it again," he snapped irritably, and his order was met with a chorus of negative groans. "Come on," he said, "our technique on that first guard is going to be super critical."

The phone rang.

Instant dead silence in the room.

Cleve Lambert snatched up the receiver, gesturing for the others to remain quiet. He answered with a tentative hello. He felt the relief flood through his body. The voice on the other end belonged to Jim Alexander, one of his agents at the L.A. office, who informed him he had an urgent incoming call.

"I don't care who it is," Lambert said brusquely, "he's just going to have to wait. Get a number, whatever."

"All right, Cleve," Alexander said, "but he said if you don't talk to him he's going to call J.B., whatever that means."

Lambert covered the mouthpiece while he cleared his throat, using the time to think furiously. J.B. had to mean Joshua Bain. "Okay," he said, "put him through on a closed line." A few seconds later, a man's flat voice came on the line.

"This is Tony Seastrom, Mister Lambert."

Cleve Lambert had to fight for control of his voice. "What do *you* want?" he demanded, his voice deadly.

"Well, Mister Lambert, I kinda figure we got something serious to discuss. I mean, since I'm in town and like we both know who pulled the string on Joshua Bain's girl—"

"I don't know what you're talking about," said Lambert sharply, and he was conscious of the other witnesses behind him. "In fact, I've just about—".

"Don't jive me, super-fuzz," Seastrom warned him. "If you hang up, then I'm placing a long distance call to Mister Bain. There's also the matter of one Fred Bingston, a sad—"

"All right!" Lambert snapped. "You've made your point."

"Not yet, I haven't," said Seastrom. "My point is ten thousand big ones."

Despite the cool air around him, Lambert felt himself starting to sweat all over. He knew he somehow had to terminate the conversation. There was too much at stake now. "You're aware," he said then, "that my divulging that information was not an illegal act. So, you see, you haven't any case to base—"

"I'm going to hang up now, Mister Lambert, and place a call to Joshua Bain. He gave me his number yesterday, in case I should remember anything."

"Wait!" Lambert screamed before he could catch himself. "When and where can I meet you?"

"With the money?"

"Yes, yes, man."

"I'll call you this afternoon."

The line went dead, and Cleve Lambert placed the receiver in its cradle, noticing that his hand was shaking. While he'd never met or talked to Tony Seastrom before, he knew enough about the man now to assume he was a gigantic fool. Typical stupid punk. It was all probably a Huey Orville ploy, anyway. By this afternoon, it wouldn't matter whom Tony Seastrom tried to call.

10:45 a.m. At mid-morning, the wind was less hostile on the promontory than it was later in the day. Joshua remembered that when he and Jerrie had been up here before it was like this in the morning, the shadows falling the same. He walked up to the cliff's sloped edge, stopping about where Alan had stood, to look down on the panorama of the Coachella Valley. He raised the ten-power binoculars, focused them on the area of the Bermuda Dunes Airport. In addition to Britt Halley's Lear jet, he could make out at least two other executive jets parked near the ETC hangar.

"How about that," he said under his breath. "It looks like we might just hit the jackpot."

He let the glasses go to hang down his chest, and he stood motionless for a few more minutes. There was less of a lump in his throat now, and it grieved him to think that the passage of time, plus all that he was trying to do, had combined to make the memory fade by some perceptible degree. Or, was that really what was happening, he wondered, remembering again yesterday and the motel room and the trade-off he had made of a Gideon Bible in lieu of a fifth of vodka.

He turned away to another quadrant of the valley floor, tipping his head up to breathe deeply of the sudden, intensifying breeze. He was conscious of the wind's strength then, widening his stance in a kind of reflex action. The very terrain around him seemed to be waiting, measuring him, and he closed his eyes, knowing he was stalling now.

The wind shifted abruptly, causing him to nearly lose his balance, and he sensed that it was time to simply turn and walk away.

But he stood fast a little longer.

The muscles along his jaw tightened up as he struggled with himself, and he realized he was biting down hard on his teeth. It won't work now, he finally said inside. It was all in motion now, and it couldn't be stopped.

At that moment, he noticed that the wind had ceased, and that it was quiet again on the promontory. And he turned away, not looking back, to start down the steep trail, passing near the rocky stream bed of the gully with its stand of delicate smoke trees.

11:00 a.m. It occurred to Britt Halley that she was finding it increasingly more difficult to keep her mind on things official. For the past few days, she had allowed her incoming basket to get behind every day, so now it was stacked up over its sidewalls. She also had been shopping for clothes three times in as many days. She caught herself calling the estate house two or three times a day, checking on some trivial subject that she would normally ignore. She knew much of it evolved from her feelings over Joshua Bain. But what concerned her the most was her lessening interest in the daily ETC business, which, up until a few months ago, had dominated her being for over two years. She was changing, and she was glad that she had the common sense to notice it.

Gus, too, had noticed it.

She would talk to Calvin Price later on in the day, after the ex-com meeting. The tension was getting to them all. Some tough, professional advice right now could do much to renew her sense of purpose.

It had even occurred to her last night, while she had been eating alone, that the table needed a man. She realized she was getting soft. What an absurd proposition: that she needed a man. She wanted Joshua Bain, and she would have him. But she would at the same time maintain her perspective. She leaned forward, reaching determinedly for the incoming basket.

11:20 a.m. Parking the Ford wagon in the lower first-level, Joshua used the main entrance to the ETC headquarters. The only access to the second floor was through the one security post servicing the executive parking level. He cleared the crowded cafeteria, which was handling the first-floor luncheon traffic, using the executive entrance, to move along the narrow walkway leading to the first guard station. There were a few employees in the area, but not many, because most on the second floor were at their work stations. The second floor broke for lunch at noon.

The bell for lunch today was going to be one big bang, and about two minutes early.

Showing his ID, he was admitted to the second floor. He set his watch to match the exact time shown on the clock over the guard enclosure. He was dressed in a light green wool sportcoat over a long-sleeved brown dress shirt, with a heavy knit dark green tie. His slacks were dark brown double-knit. His shoes were lowcut, string tied. The clothes were functional for what he would have to do. The jacket covered the three pairs of handcuffs, tucked inside his belt at the small of his back to keep them quiet when he moved. The Viper was in its usual thigh holster.

As he walked the first hallway, he felt his belly starting to act up. Then left up the critical hallway to the second guard station. He was passed through. A few seconds later, at exactly 11:30 by his watch, he was shown into Britt Halley's office.

She came out from behind her desk, an open, pleased look on her face. She had on a white, high-necked blouse, long sleeves, with frilly lace. A dark brown medium-length skirt. She approached him with her arms extended, and Joshua was careful to slip his arms under hers. They embraced, and Joshua played out this final act as best he could. She kissed him hard, and he attempted to respond.

She took a step back, held him at arm's length. "You know, Joshua," she said softly, "it's been months since I last saw you dressed up, and I've forgotten how good you look." She turned away, back toward her desk. A few steps short of the desk, she pulled up, moved instead to one of the nearby chairs. Joshua sat down also, at the other end of the desk. She crossed her legs, the nylon making a soft swishing sound. Looking at her, seeing how very beautiful and alive she was, Joshua began to feel something inside that he didn't like.

Don't let her get to me now, he warned himself.

"Why are you so fancied up?" she asked lightly.

Joshua shrugged, smiled back at her. "We're going to lunch, remember? And I thought we might go to the club at La Quinta."

"Sounds fantastic," she said, obviously pleased with his thoughtfulness.

He had at one point in his planning thought he might bring her flowers on this morning, but somehow that had not seemed right at all. Discreetly checking his watch, he tried to get to the subject, but the words were frozen.

"What's the matter, Joshua?" she said with concern. "You seem preoccupied. I could tell when you kissed me. What's wrong?"

Feeling relieved that she had made the opening, he found the right words finally. "Well, I don't know exactly how to begin," he said, "but I've worked myself up to a pretty bad state, I guess."

"About what?" she asked, her brow starting to turn down.

How clever she was, he thought admiringly. The pretense of concern. He swallowed hard, remembering back an hour ago, back to the promontory, and he settled down. "It's hard for me to say, Britt, but you're the only one I feel I can trust.

You see, I think that someone in the ETC was actually responsible for Jerrie's death."

"Oh, Joshua," she said, seemingly relieved. "That's ridiculous. Why, Calvin Price himself put Gus to work on that, and everything he has found suggests it was an accident. There's not one shred of evidence."

"That's the point, Britt. I'm convinced that Gus had something to do with it. You know, he never did like Jerrie anyway."

"Is that all you have, that kind of suspicion?"

"No," said Joshua, and he felt the butterflies starting now. "Last night, Alan Hunt finally broke down and told me that Gino Malone actually drove her to the airport. I guess Alan's conscience finally got to him."

"Alan Hunt?" she said disbelievingly.

"That's right."

"No, it's absurd," she said, and for the first time, Joshua saw in her carefully controlled face a kind of malice. "You can't believe it," she said then.

"Yes, I do," he told her gravely. "So much so that I've decided to quit the ETC." He had just played his ace, and he watched her for her reaction.

"Oh, please, Joshua, you can't be serious," and she got up then, her hands on her hips as she started to pace over the thickly carpeted floor. "Joshua, all we have to do is resolve this. I'm sure—"

"Last Saturday, while Gus was interviewing me before the screening, we talked about Jerrie's death again. At that time, he dropped the remark that it was too bad that she didn't have any next of kin. Now, he had no reason to know that. I certainly didn't tell him."

"Joshua, Gus has every reason to know that," she said, obviously trying to be convincing, almost pleading now. "We have a dossier on Jerrie McKennan. It's part of the routine with all our prospective elders. We know more about their personal families than they do."

"You have a file on Jerrie?"

"That's right."

"And it's maintained by Gus Holliman?"

"Yes," she said, making a move toward her desk. "I'll have him bring it in."

"Wait a second," Joshua said, and he frowned thoughtfully. "I think he might be behind it, Britt. If he is, then he'll strip that file clean before he brings it to you."

"A valid point," she said flatly. "I'll get it myself."

"Let's go together."

On her way to the elevator, she stopped, turned to face him, and she looked as if she might be appraising him. "You don't trust me?"

"You know better than that; otherwise why would I be telling you what I suspect. But you're loyal to the ETC, right up to your beautiful little ears. I don't think you would remove anything, especially to protect Gus, but there is the temptation to protect the corporation. Whether I'm right or wrong, why don't we find it out together."

"Fair enough," she said. "I'll show it to you right out of the file. Will you promise to drop this nonsense if the file is clean?"

He stood up to move up to her. He put his right forefinger under her chin, tilted her head back. "You better believe it," he said gently, and he kissed her.

A few seconds later they were in the Sanctuary hallway.

"You should've come to me earlier," she told him as they strode quickly down the hallway, side by side. "I guess Alan has some motive for making up a story like that. You know, I wondered about the wisdom of your bringing him in on the property deal. But, it's probably as much my fault. When you first brought up bringing him in with you, I had Gus check him out. He has a bad record, and I should've told you."

"You could be right," Joshua admitted.

"I know I am. Why, his motivation might be to turn you against the ETC so that he can profit on the ranch deal in some way."

They were now at the door near Gus Holliman's private elevator. There was a small square of nine lighted buttons beside the door, and Britt sequenced three of them, so quickly that Joshua was only able to catch the first one. The door slid open with a hydraulic sigh, a plaintive, almost human sound. The door opened to a long, totally bare room which Joshua estimated was about forty feet long by twelve feet wide. He was disappointed that there were no signs of any records.

"This is the foyer to Gus Holliman's library, as we call it," she told him while they were standing in the hallway. "Actually, the library is formally called the Documents Room. This foyer is scanned by two closed-circuit TV cameras which report to the guard station you passed before you got to my office." She stepped inside the door, turned a quarter turn to her right.

Joshua leaned in the doorway to see that she was activating an intercom switch located under a recessed screen opening.

"Station two," a distant voice reported.

"This is Mrs. Halley," Britt said into the intercom. "I'll be here for a few minutes with a visitor, Mister Joshua Bain. Will you please log it."

Looking into the unerring eye of the camera at the far end of the room, Joshua felt his heart thumping now. He was tempted to shake his arms down, to loosen up, but he stood beside Britt, appearing indifferent, even a little bored. As she started toward the middle of the room, he asked her, "Does Gus know we're in here?"

"No; but he will know when he checks over the log tonight." She slowed to look at him over her shoulder. "Please wait there."

He did so obediently while she moved on down about two-thirds the length of the room. He saw the door then, a massive offset sliding arrangement, not unlike a large elevator door. She stopped to the right of the door, sequenced another series of buttons. The huge door slid open. "Okay," she said, "come on in."

Joshua moved forward, feeling himself on the balls of his feet. He nervously checked his watch again; they had exactly eight minutes to go. He turned the corner of the doorway, stepped into the Documents Room.

He was startled briefly by how small and bare the room was. To his right was a single mantle resembling a work bench, waist level, running the width of the room, which he estimated to be about nine feet. A small wooden cabinet was on the shelf, looking like a part of a reference file of a library. He saw the viewer then, and he immediately knew the file cabinet held some kind of film, microfilm or microfiche. Directly to his front was a standard four-drawer filing cabinet, also made of wood. To his left was what looked like an old-fashioned wooden typing desk. One straight-backed chair was tucked into the desk opening. A little let-down, he saw that Britt had opened one of the filing drawers, was thumbing through the tightly packed folders.

Joshua reached around behind his back, pulled out the first pair of handcuffs. He quietly walked up behind her, stopped. He could smell her perfume then, an exotic and very expensive special blend which she told him she brought in from a small shop in London. He reached for her right arm, turned her slowly to face him. He had worn the necktie because he guessed he might have to tie her ankles, but coming in he had noticed that the bench along the right wall had two heavy stanchions supporting its forward edge.

He snapped the first cuff on her left wrist.

She stared up at him, her mouth partly open, an honest look of disbelief on her face. "Joshua, what in—"

"Shut up," he said sternly. "And if you say another word I'll have to gag you," and he led her to the bench, looped the loose cuff around the stanchion, clipped it to her right wrist. He noticed that the long sleeves on her blouse would protect her wrists.

He checked his watch. Six minutes. He was right on schedule.

"So you're with them," she said then, her voice remarkably controlled. "You know, you can't possibly get out of here." She shook her head then, laughing bitterly. "You're good at your job though; I have to admit that," and she looked away, her hair falling over the right side of her face.

"I said shut up!" Joshua snapped, and he reached into his jacket pocket, pulled out a roll of two-inch adhesive tape. Checking his watch again, he quickly and a little roughly taped her mouth. "You can breathe through your nose," he told her as he turned to inspect the small film storage cabinet.

"You organized it pretty well," he said after a moment. "But you made a couple of mistakes, Mrs. Halley. First, that you underestimated how far I'd go to find the truth, and, secondly, that you left Alan Hunt on the scene. You couldn't be blamed for the last error, because it made sense that you had to keep Alan on my tail to keep you informed. So, if I ever did start getting close, you could've used him as an early warning device. That's why you really didn't object when I asked to bring him in on the property deal. But, then, Alan Hunt presents a special kind of problem, one which is simply beyond your comprehension; that he in fact answers to a higher authority." The cabinet was secured to the bench, and Joshua could not break it loose. Removing one of the narrow drawers, he turned to the filing cabinet, where he pulled out the bottom drawer. He stared stupified for a moment. The filing drawer was half filled with money! Composing himself, he dumped the contents of the microfiche drawer on top of the money. He quickly began to transfer the rest of the film to the drawer. "Another mistake was the heroin," he went on. "I realize you needed that to really lock it up with the authorities. But, it was that which set me on the trail. You see, I knew my wife. I knew her like I knew myself . . . ."

Finished transferring the microfiche, he tried to move the filing cabinet, but it, too, was secured. He slipped the bottom drawer off its runners to see that there were four bolts holding the cabinet to the floor. He anxiously checked his watch again. Four minutes. He put his shoulder to the filing cabinet, began to push. Holding solid at first, the cabinet began to loosen after three or four hard thrusts with his shoulder. He stopped then to catch his breath.

"But all that was just clever smoke to cover the real truth, the terrible disgusting truth, Mrs. Halley," he said then. "Because you had planned to kill Jerrie from the very beginning. By my estimate, at least three weeks before. That was just about the time Jerrie and I were married. The WAR clowns stumbled in, though, and almost did it for you. But, somehow, they failed to finish her off. She was alive. And Gino, with your help probably, had to make the decision whether to finish her off on the spot, just leave her, or to go with the plan. There was Alan Hunt to complicate the matter at the house, because at the time Gino didn't know how long it would take Alan to get back there. The surest and cleanest way was to go with the plan. After all, besides Alan Hunt, there was the prospect that the WAR assailants could be arrested and made to talk, revealing the fact that they had left her alive." Joshua was back against the wall now, glaring at the ceiling. He turned to face the cabinet, lowered his shoulder to hit it savagely. The cabinet tipped over, falling heavily to the floor.

Britt Halley flinched as the cabinet hit the floor. When she had opened the door, she had programmed the first button to level three, allowing up to four hundred pounds additional free weight on the floating floor. Her weight and Joshua's combined was only about three hundred pounds. The one-hundred-pound leeway would normally be adequate for the brief time they were going to be in the room. Now, she looked with fright to the pair of small indicator lights over the door. She breathed easier, seeing the green light was still on. Apparently the heavy mass of the floor absorbed the bulk of the cabinet's impact.

"The timing was what did you in, Mrs. Halley," Joshua

was saying. "Only twenty-five minutes from the time Alan called back to Gino that he'd lost the getaway car to the exact moment the Avion hit that mountain. Far too short a time to have allowed you to ad-lib the whole deal. No one in the company, or even connected with it, is permitted to use dope of any sort. Yet you and Gino had a supply of heroin handy, with the equipment to administer it, because that was the only way you could justify as good a pilot as Jerrie to have an accident. Gino never packed his chute until right before a jump, yet, according to the duty mechanic at the hangar, Gino packed his chute three weeks before Jerrie was killed and put it in the trunk of your limo. The next day or so, Gino told the same mechanic to move the Avion around to the blind side of the hangar, because it would be better protected in the shade. Sometime in the next day or two, Gino then stored his packed chute in the aft storage compartment of the Avion. So then you were ready; all you had to do was wait for the right opportunity."

He checked his watch. One minute to go. "The rest is academic. After you got her into the plane, with Gino at the controls, you used the radio in either the chopper or the jet to talk to the tower, cranking the tuner off just enough to disguise your voice with heavy static. The reason Gino was in the chopper when I arrived was because he had to be. You dispatched the chopper yourself, not to check out the wreck, but to pick up Gino after he bailed out of the Avion. I checked the chopper's log, and it shouldn't surprise anyone to find out that McLean, the regular chopper pilot, returned the ship to the ETC pad. And, he hasn't been seen since. Reassigned, according to rumor, to your New York operation. I suspect that one of these days his bones will be recovered by a hiker, if Gino didn't bury him too deep, somewhere below the peak of Mount Diablo. It was a pretty good plan, Mrs. Halley. But, then, you folks are expert at killing people by accident."

He walked up to the open door, shaking himself down, loosening his arms. Looking up, he noticed the tiny, grain-of-wheat pair of indicator lights over the door. The one on the left was glowing green. Probably a general circuit report, or a power-source reading. Could even be an oxygen level indicator. It didn't matter, probably, since the color green meant a "safe" condition.

He stooped down to jam a clothespin between the door and its channel. Looking as natural as he could, he then stepped out into the foyer, where he turned sideways to the open door, making a motion like he was talking to Britt Halley. Under the eye of the two cameras, he turned then to stride out of the room.

In the hallway, he checked his watch again. Closing his eyes briefly, he realized that he had just offered up a brief prayer.

Chapter twelve

It was 11:55 exactly.

The gas company repair truck careened up the cement ramp leading to the second-floor parking area. Its emergency lights flashing, it pulled up with a screech of rubber not more than ten feet away from the guard station to the second floor. Cleve Lambert, dressed in heavy field working clothes and a white hard hat, jumped out of the passenger door. Like the rest of the crew tumbling out of the truck from both front and back, he was loaded down with shoulder satchels and other equipment too confusing to comprehend at first glance.

Cleve Lambert had no illusions about the difficulty of their task. The guards from this point on were the cream of the ETC security force, tough and well-paid mercenaries. One they were going to finesse, the other they would probably have to kill.

He rushed to the guard station, shoved an ID through the small window opening.

"I'm Inspector Graves," he said breathlessly. "Where's the leak at?"

The security guard stared at him, started to frown.

"Come on, man!" Lambert screamed. "A Mister Holliman called us a few minutes ago to report a massive gas leak in this building—this place can go up at any second!"

"Mister Holliman," the guard repeated haltingly, and he reached for the telephone near his right elbow.

"No, you idiot!" Lambert screamed at him, his face twisted in a combination of fury and exasperation, and he reached through the opening to grab the guard's arm. "Don't touch anything that might open an electrical circuit! Not a button, not a switch, nothing! The spark could blow us all sky high!"

He lurched off to his right, yelling back over his shoulder, "We'll find it ourselves!" and he was gone down the hallway with three of the four men following him.

Burt Ingstrom stepped up to the enclosure, pushed what looked like a cylindrical probe through the opening in the heavy protective glass. "Don't move," he warned the guard, and he moved the probe to and fro, reading something on an attached meter. "Not a muscle," he cautioned the guard. "Don't touch anything; static electricity is the danger now." He stopped the probe, frowned gravely. "Oh-oh," he said then. "Get out of there, fast!"

"I can't!"

"Move it!" Ingstrom screamed at him threateningly. "Do you want to be responsible for blowing this building apart?"

Faced with the ultimatum, the guard complied, releasing the inside lock on the door. As he stepped out, Burt Ingstrom pushed a snub-nosed thirty-eight into his belly. "In the truck," he said, his voice now low and sinister.

Behind him, Alan Hunt slipped out of the van, moved toward the nearby black limousine. Britt Halleys' chauffeur was out of the car, standing curiously by the open driver's door. A few seconds later, the chauffeur joined the security guard in the van.

Once in the hallway, Lambert and his men had slowed to a walk to avoid alarming anyone. About twenty-five feet in, the first man fell out to post himself. The second dropped out after another equal distance. Both men left behind began moving slowly in a circle, holding out identical cylindrical probes. The three or four people using the hallway eyed them curiously before moving on.

Agent George Adams pulled up about ten feet short of the hallway leading to the executive area. With Cleve Lambert shielding him, he pulled an M14 rifle out of its canvas cover. At the same moment, Lambert pulled a rifle grenade out of the satchel slung over his left shoulder. With the butt of the rifle on the floor, Adams took the grenade, tipped it upright, mounted it securely to the launcher attached to the muzzle of the rifle. He then pulled the loaded weapon close to his side, further shielding it.

There was a wall clock mounted over the entry door, and Lambert checked the exact time, comparing it with his own watch. "We've got one minute to go," he whispered.

"Oh, man," said Adams quietly, "that can be forever."

"Yeah," Lambert agreed quietly, "that can be forever. We got by that first guard quicker than I figured," and he again glanced nervously over his shoulder to see that Burt Ingstrom had taken up his position in the guard enclosure. From the waist up, Ingstrom was now dressed in the ETC security uniform. Lambert assumed that Alan Hunt had made it out with the limo. The next critical step was for Joshua Bain to nail Gus Holliman. Then, it was his turn again.

In the Sanctuary hallway, Joshua punched the button on Gus Holliman's private elevator. The door slid open immediately. With the Viper in his right hand, he stepped into the cubicle. He pressed the "Down" button firmly. There was the slim chance that Holliman might hear the elevator, provided he was in fact in his office, but it didn't matter to Joshua because he figured he would be on Gus before he had time to translate the situation. The single most important consideration now was to prevent Gus Holliman from reaching any magic buttons.

The door slid open.

Gus was not behind his desk!

With the Viper concealed behind his hip, Joshua took a tentative half step into the room, blocking the elevator door with the calf of his left leg. He at the same moment swept the room curiously. Sensing movement to his far right, he jerked his head around in that direction to see Gus Holliman standing in the open doorway of his private restroom. For a fleeting fraction of a second, it occurred to Joshua that Gus Holliman had certainly picked a most propitious time to be going to the bathroom.

"Quick man!" Joshua yelled, motioning with his free hand, "Britt Halley has collapsed in the Throne Room!"

Gus did not move. Riveted in the doorway, he looked totally bewildered.

"Hurry," Joshua implored, but he sensed by Holliman's further indecision that the ruse was a failure, and he thus started bringing the Viper out from behind his hip. Gus Holliman had already made up his mind, too, for he at the same instant started back into the restroom, pushing the door closed.

The Viper whispered once.

Shot hurriedly and without deliberate aim, the small-caliber slug missed its intended target by a wide margin, *thunking* harmlessly into the nearby wall.

The door slammed with an unaccountably heavy authority.

Joshua angrily stooped down, jamming the elevator door with his last clothespin. He then strode quickly across the room, thinking with disgust that he might just have blown it wide open. He stepped back, lunged forward to kick the door as hard as he could. The door was solid, obviously reinforced. Disappointed and frustrated, Joshua leaned against the jamb. There was still one chance, he thought desperately. "Gus!" he screamed. "She's in the room! She's with the records!"

Gus Holliman digested Joshua Bain's comment, which he could barely make out through the heavy door. A bluff, maybe. Yet how had Bain made it into the Sanctuary? His mind tumbled with the possibilities of the irregular situation, and he couldn't believe this was happening on this of all mornings. He had to have input. Though not as elaborate as his office, his dressing room was equipped with enough machinery to get the information he needed.

Stepping across the tiled floor, he opened the mirror-covered door to what functioned as his spare clothes closet, dressing room, and as known only to a selected few, the emergency entrance to the Sanctuary. Just inside the door to the small room, he turned to his right to yank open a well-disguised panel. He studied the controls briefly, before levering the intercom switch for Britt Halley's office. He called her name twice, without answer, before switching to the main security station located in the executive hallway. The guard answered routinely, "Station Two."

"This is Holliman," Gus said, trying to keep his voice calm.

"Yessir," the guard answered tersely.

"Status report," said Gus.

There was a slight pause, then, "Routine hallway action. Lunch about to start."

"Have you seen Mrs. Halley?" Gus asked impatiently.

"Yessir. She's in the library. A Mister Bain was with her for a few minutes, but he left."

Gus punched the foyer station next to the Documents Room.

No response.

He reached down to pick up the telephone from the vanity dresser. He hurriedly dialed the interoffice number for the Documents Room. He hung up after six rings. Finally, he reached back up to the intercom, punched the button for station one, the guard station located on the second level parking entrance.

No response.

Gus stood absolutely perplexed. Follow procedure, he thought then, and he mechanically reached up to push the general alarm button. Next, he threw the main power switch off. The overhead lights started to dim before picking up again as the auxiliary power system kicked in. Now, the only equipment operable in the complex was that which was emergency backed to protect the Sanctuary. Even if Bain had help, it would do him no good now. Gus figured he had time on his side. But he was at a loss as to how to proceed.

His feelings tugged at him, to and fro. On the control panel before him now was a single row of four lighted pushbuttons, which sequenced in the right order would trigger the destruct device protecting the Documents Room. Assuming that Britt was in fact in the room, he had ample time to get her out and then destroy the records, if necessary. He took a deep breath, trying to settle down. He could hear the alarm siren blasting through the main complex now. That plus the darkness out there. He realized he was chuckling, as if he was enjoying the confusing situation. Incredibly enough, it seemed that the decision making had been taken out of his hands.

Sensing the press of time, he yanked himself out of his thoughts to reach down to open one of the small drawers on the vanity dresser built into the wall. He gingerly lifted out a small automatic pistol, turning it once in his hand to make sure it was loaded and cocked. He then with reluctance placed the small weapon in his waistband. Turning to his left, he reached up to flip the tiny rocker switch located below what appeared to be a small wall-mounted mirror. He next placed his right palm squarely in the center of the mirror. There was a low hum as the analyzer read his handprint through the two-way surface. The back panel to his dressing room slipped aside, allowing him to step into the cement-lined tunnel leading to the Sanctuary.

With just seconds left, special agent Adams had dropped to the floor, where he had rolled up tight against the wall. With the M14 held out, he had froglegged forward until the corner of the wall was at his left shoulder. He had waited, then, listening to Lambert's heavy breathing. Unaccountably then, an alarm siren had commenced to wail, shattering the quietness. He had turned to look up sideways at Lambert, who was frowning. He realized that the overhead lights were starting to dim. Blinking once, he sensed that a whole lot of something had gone wrong.

"Shoot!" Lambert was screaming in his ear.

He obediently turned the corner, bringing the weapon down and in. The guard station was there, at the far end of the hallway, glowing eerily now like some space station, as if it had its own light source. He was prepared to use the side-mounted sighting aperture, but the light was so poor now he couldn't get a picture. He looked up over the rifle's barrel to see a dozen people rushing down the hallway toward him! He heard the screams then, mixing in with the siren, and then the voice of Lambert yelling at him to "Fire! Fire!"

He elevated the barrel slightly, hoping to clear the rush of bodies bearing down on them. The heavy anti-tank grenade bucked off the launcher, propelled forward by the exploding charge within the rifle's barrel.

In that split second while the grenade streaked down the hallway, Adams could actually see its silhouette, and he could tell that he had let it go too high and too far to the right.

Joshua Bain had given up trying to punch through the rest-room door. With the power off, he could not now activate the elevator either. In the dark no matter which way he turned, he had abandoned Holliman's office in favor of seeking help from Lambert's assault team. He was in the executive hallway, waiting in front of Holliman's office door, when the first grenade hit.

Angling in to the right, the grenade richocheted off the reverse curve of the security enclosure. Deflected, it started to keyhole through the adjacent hallway wall. Its shaped charge detonated upon impact.

The blast, confined and accelerated in the hallway, caught Joshua head on.

The muted, flat report of the grenade explosion reached Gus Holliman as he came abreast of the door to the Throne Room. He pulled up briefly, tipped his head to listen for further sound from the direction of the second floor. The ETC was obviously under attack of some sort. Probably the FBI. It came to him that he could restore the main power and possibly escape via Britt's office. He forced himself to turn toward the

Documents Room. The records were the key to all their survival. Including, foremost, the survival of Gustave Holliman.

Cleve Lambert tried desperately to sort out their predicament. Once more, he sneaked a quick look around the corner of the hallway leading to the guard station. The bedlam in the hallway had died down enough for them to get a second shot in. In the past few seconds since the explosion, most of the employees had either cleared the area or were laying low. The guard station was apparently still secure. Adams had been right, he noticed, for the enclosure was aglow with some kind of ambient light source, probably flourescent.

Squinting through the clearing smoke in the darkened hallway, he was enraged by the arrogance of the guard enclosure and his inability to deal with it on schedule. He was about to turn away when the lower portion of the enclosure erupted with a blinding light. Startled, he blinked once against the glare before realizing that an automatic weapon had commenced to operate. He jerked back behind the safety of the corner. He ducked then as a hail of slugs ripped into the opposite wall. Retreating a few steps from the corner, he pulled Adams up beside him. The second man down the hall had come forward to put a lighted lantern down between them.

"He's kicked in a searchlight," Lambert shouted, "and he's got a gun port!"

The younger agent was nodding furiously that he understood.

"We've got one chance left," Lambert exclaimed, and he reached into the satchel slung over his left shoulder. "I'm going to put a canister of smoke right under his nose. We'll give the smoke a couple seconds to spread. He'll be blinded for a while anyway; that's when you hit him with the second grenade!"

It seemed workable to Lambert as he fumbled for his own gas mask. Looking into the smoke with that floodlight for the guard would be like looking into dense fog with high beams on. He begrudgingly had to give the guard credit, for while the man was fighting a losing battle, he was really winning the war right now because he had managed to hold them up, perhaps long enough to put Joshua Bain in the soup.

An enormous sense of relief flooded over Britt Halley as she saw Gus Holliman enter the Documents Room. She motioned with her head for him to remove her gag, which he did quickly.

"What's going on?" Gus demanded as he stood up.

"Where's Joshua Bain?" Britt said, her voice hoarse and heavy with anger.

Gus shook his head before explaining what little he knew.

"Have you tried all the security stations?"

"Yes," he told her. "In the lounge just now, and the comm lines are all dead. The phones are all out, too. However, the executive station is still active because I could hear machine gun fire in the hallway," and he looked down to her handcuffs then. "How do we get you out of here?" he asked with concern. "We've got to destroy the records."

"I know," she agreed impatiently. "But Joshua has the key, so we've got to get him first."

Gus sat down heavily on the toppled wooden cabinet. "It seems," he said after a moment, "that every time I turn around lately I keep running into Joshua Bain."

"We'll get him," said Britt confidently. "Do you have a gun?"

"Yes."

"Good," she said, thinking that Joshua Bain would be there soon; if Gus could just hold up his end. Her mind was clearing now. "How much time do we have?" she asked, her voice now more normal and calculating.

Gus shook his head. "Could be quite a while," he suggested. "They've got to find the emergency tunnel, probably have to blast all the way through." He shrugged then. "Depends on how many people they have, what kind of equipment and explosives. Could be as long as another hour."

"Can you reset the weight control on the floor sensor? I'd like to move it to the max load."

"You know better. We can't override without returning to zero and closing the door."

"Get busy then," she told him, "and try to find something to pry me loose," and she swiveled around to study the thick metal stanchion holding her prisoner. "Are there any tools in the lounge area?"

"Not that I know of."

"Well, go look!" she yelled at him, getting angry with his seeming indifference.

As Gus left, she sat back down on her haunches. She figured they were at a stand-off, perhaps with an edge in their favor now. As long as she was manacled to the records, they couldn't blow them. But, they had the better part of an hour to work out the problem. She turned her head then, listening to the distant sound of another explosion. And she swallowed once, feeling the mobile floor beneath her shifting a small but yet still measurable degree.

She glanced up, reassured to see that the green light was still on.

Alan Hunt parked the limo directly in front of the main entrance to the Halley estate. He casually got out, walked slowly and deliberately across the flagstone landing leading up to the massive front door. Depressing the door bell, he then stepped aside, waiting.

Gino Malone opened the door, stared at him indifferently for a second. Gino was out of the hospital now, an ambulatory patient, and still had a way to go before recovering, as evidenced by the solid cast enclosing his neck and lower face, the stainless steel wires. Alan caught himself wondering how the man managed to eat.

"I have an urgent message from Mrs. Halley," Alan said easily, and he moved into the foyer. It was a time for taking charge, of even bluffing, because right now every second was vital. The telephone lines to and from the estate had been cut nearly eight minutes ago, and if someone on the grounds had tried to dial out . . .

Gino took his arm.

Alan almost took him on the spot. "It's all right, Gino," Alan assured him instead, smiling as best he could. "I have to report directly to Senator Price, and I mean, right now," and he pulled away from the other man's grasp.

Gino frowned, shook his head negatively.

"You mean the Senator's not here?"

Gino nodded his head yes.

It was Alan's turn to frown. On his way in, he had used the limo's mobile phone to confirm with the airport operations that three ETC jets had landed within the past two hours. "Then I'm to report to Mister Fleming," he said, pulling out the only other name he had to work with. "And you best get with it, Gino," he added, "because what I've got to do is more important than you can realize."

Gino nodded once again, pointed down the hallway toward the study. Alan followed behind as Gino led the way, worried about what had happened to their most important bird, Calvin Price.

With the guard station finally immobilized, Cleve Lambert led his last two men up the hallway. Adams was on his way back, to the van, having suffered a gunshot wound in his right arm. Lambert dropped one man off at the operations doorway. At the intersection of the executive hallway, he pushed the second man off to the left toward Britt Halley's office. Both men were under orders to clear the area and then to set their satchel charges. He hesitated only briefly before the shattered guard station, and he had no way of estimating where the last anti-tank grenade had hit; the enclosure was totally destroyed.

He loped off to his right then, heading toward the office of Gus Holliman, and he had no knowledge of what to expect, beyond the two-dimensional graphics of a hastily drawn floor plan imprinted in his mind.

At the end of the hallway, he pulled up before the door to Holliman's office. He quickly stripped off his protective helmet, pulled out of his gas mask. Holding his breath, he turned the door knob enough to release the catch. Standing back a half step, he kicked the door open, lunging into the room at a half crouch. Inside, he swept the room once with his lantern, seeing that he was alone in the office, except for Joshua Bain, who was down in front of him, on his knees, his head down.

The air in the office was clear; Lambert pushed the door closed behind him. He then put his lantern on the desk before reaching down to help Joshua to his feet.

"Where's Holliman?" he rasped, hearing the coarseness in his voice, as he helped Joshua into the nearest chair.

Joshua rolled his head back and forth several times before leaning forward to stare at him in a distant, confused way, suggesting he was in shock. "How long has it been?" Joshua asked, and he coughed once, leaning his head back once again. There was a drying patch of blood under his nostrils.

Lambert turned his watch to the light. "We've only been in here a little over nine minutes." He looked impatiently around the office again, spotted the small bar behind the desk. In the next few seconds he managed to get enough brandy down a protesting Joshua to get him on his feet.

"Now," he said brusquely, "just what is going—"

"Okay," said Joshua as he straightened himself up. "Britt

Halley is handcuffed in the Documents Room. I came down here, right on schedule, but Holliman got away," and he gestured toward the restroom door, "into that room."

Lambert started toward the restroom door.

"Forget it," Joshua told him. "We'll have to blow it."

Lambert pulled up, turned toward the open elevator.

Joshua was shaking his head. "You can forget that, too. I've been over this office twice, and it's a big fat dead end," and his voice trailed off.

"Do you think Holliman is still in there?" Lambert asked skeptically, and he felt himself getting angry with Bain's negative attitude.

"I suppose he's still in there," Joshua was saying.

"Come on, man, use your head," said Lambert irritably. "As important as that Documents Room is, and the Sanctuary, don't you understand? There has to be another way in."

"You could be right," Joshua admitted. "It makes sense."

Cleve Lambert was now pulling on his right ear. "The power failure was a defensive shot, freezing all the normal routes, including the elevator."

"What explosives do you have?" Joshua asked, and he was more alert now, up on the balls of his feet.

"A satchel charge."

Joshua shook his head. "No, too much. That'd bring the whole place down around our ears."

"We've got plastic in the truck."

Joshua shook his head again. "Take too long."

"A couple frag grenades," Lambert offered, rummaging in his bag.

"Dump the bag in the elevator," Joshua told him as he took the two frag grenades. Stuffing one into the canvas bag, he hurried toward the restroom door. Passing the desk, he picked up the lantern. At the door, he looped the shoulder strap over the knob. Looking back once over his shoulder, he saw that Lambert was in the blind corner of the elevator and out of the direct blast line. He pulled the pin on the first grenade, released the safety lever, dropped the armed grenade into the bag. He then dashed back toward the open elevator.

Four and one half seconds later the restroom door was blown off its hinges.

In the Sanctuary hallway, the sound of the explosion caused Gus Holliman to pause briefly. On his way back to the Documents Room, he stood still for a moment longer, trying to pin-point the exact location of the blast. Satisfied, he moved on, taking his time now. He realized that he was actually enjoying the moment, and in the Documents Room, he had the distinctly happy chore of telling Britt that he had not been able to discover any device to help free her of the handcuffs.

"It's all right," she assured him. "Joshua has the key."

Gus shook his head. "There'll be a mob in here when they finally make it," he protested.

"No, Gus," she said soberly. "He'll come in first and he'll come in alone."

Gus shook his head wearily. "But what if he doesn't? Don't you understand?" And he gestured toward the filing cabinet. "We've got to destroy those."

"I know better than you do," she said evenly, and she shifted her weight, relieving the pressure on her other hip. "Now, what was that last explosion?"

He shrugged indifferently. "I'm pretty sure it was the restroom door in my office." He drew a deep breath. His thoughts spun aimlessly. He could not comprehend how Britt could remain so calm now that she must be aware that it was her life against the records. An hour ago, he had been ready to scrap the whole program, especially to get at Britt Halley. But the records were something else; he was not about to spend the rest of his life in prison. He looked down at her then, saw that she was studying him closely.

"He'll come in alone," she said then, "because he knows that I was the one who planned Jerrie McKennan's death."

He stared at her disbelievingly, aware of the doubt showing on his face.

"It's true," she went on. "Gino handled it for me."

Looking aside, Gus realized she was adding on another bit of confirmation. Closing his eyes, he thought that there was nothing, no limit, to what Britt Halley might do to further her own interests. *Dried grass*, he thought bitterly. And how she had used him, too. He slumped against the nearby wall. "So," he sighed, "what do we do now?"

Britt Halley figured the disclosure had been worth it; at least she had Gus turned around. "You're positive he'll come in via the tunnel."

"Yes, because he'll have to. The main power is off and can only be restored at the same switch, which eliminates the elevator. They'll eventually find the door leading to the tunnel, but they'll never find that power switch."

"The tunnel opens in the men's lounge, right?"

He nodded once.

"Joshua knows the area," she said thoughtfully, "so he'll take the shortest line, right out the lounge door into the hallway, then into here."

Gus nodded again.

"So you wait in the women's lounge, with the curtain drawn. As soon as he passes, you step out and take him from behind."

Gus contemplated the simple plan for a few moments, pursing his lips appraisingly. He was acting now, and he suspected that this new dimension was helping him to keep going. "It will work," he admitted. "Provided he is alone."

"Play it by ear, Gus," she said, encouraging him. "And don't kill him," she warned. "I want him brought in here alive," and there was an edge in her voice which caused Gus Holliman to flinch.

The area of the restroom near the door was in a shambles. Protected by his flak vest, Cleve Lambert had entered the room first. The undamaged few lights away from the door were still lit, and Lambert realized they had finally pushed through into the forbidden domain of the complex. Finding the room empty, he gestured an all-clear signal.

Joshua pulled up next to his shoulder. They both moved to face the only other door in the room. With his revolver ready, Lambert stepped forward to kick the mirrored door open. Both men dropped to a crouch. Lambert then stepped into the empty dressing room. He kicked the nearby wall, shaking his head.

"Can you believe it," he said disgustedly. "I went through D-Day, at Normandy," he commented. "And it was a lot like this—one rotten bunker after another."

"It's got to be there," Joshua insisted as he pushed past him. He started to pound on the back wall with his fist.

Watching him impassively, Lambert began to sense there was more to Joshua's enthusiasm than met the eye. "I know why I'm here," he finally said, "but you've already done your part, Joshua, so why keep pushing?"

Joshua turned to face him squarely. "Would you believe," he said evenly, "I'm not altogether sure anymore," and Cleve Lambert thought he could detect a note of sadness, almost melancholy, in Joshua's voice. They were both walking disaster areas. Joshua's face was covered with grime and soot, streaked with his sweat. The left sleeve of his sport jacket was nearly torn off. And both of them were breathing hard, showing signs of near exhaustion. Lambert forced himself to stand erect, gestured toward the back wall.

"Is that it?" he asked, renewing his interest.

"Sounds like it."

Using the butt of his revolver, Lambert tapped the wall several times in widely spaced places. "You're right," he conceded. "But it'll take explosives, like another bunker," and he wondered how many more they had to go.

"Get Ingstrom on the horn," Joshua told him, "and have him bring in all the plastic you've got left."

Lambert reached under his jacket, pulled out the powerful transceiver. He moved out into the main hallway in order to guarantee a clear signal. Burt Ingstrom, standing by at the garage guard station, responded immediately.

Joshua ran his fingers inquisitively around the perimeter of the back wall, searching for the device to trigger the door. He finally noticed the small rocker switch under the wall mirror. He levered the rocker several times, to no avail. He turned then, hearing Lambert returning. The older man had the hint of a smile around his mouth.

"The plastic is on its way in," Lambert reported.

Joshua grunted once, apprehensive over the delay. It would take several minutes at least, giving an inventive Gus Holliman perhaps all the time he needed.

"Guess what?" Lambert said then.

"I can't imagine," Joshua mused, prepared for another letdown.

"We should've checked in with Burt earlier," Lambert proposed. "It seems that about five minutes ago, he took Senator Calvin Price into custody."

Joshua felt himself reacting to the news, and he realized that he was staring at Lambert and that his own mouth was hanging open. "Well all right already," he finally blurted. "Get him in here on the double!" It was time, he thought excitedly, it was time to grind a deal with the senator.

"He's on his way," said Lambert. "As soon as they get the plastic together."

Sensing they were finally on the gun lap, Joshua turned the Viper up, pointing it directly at Lambert's throat. He then extended his left hand. "Give me the gun, and be careful, very careful."

Lambert stood stock still, caught totally by surprise.

"Don't bat an eye," Joshua warned him. "It's almost over, and with any luck, you'll get your lousy records out." He gestured once more with his left hand.

"It's up to you, Lambert," he offered.

Lambert obeyed, turning the butt of the weapon up. "So now you tell me."

"Get out of the flak vest," Joshua told him. Watching him comply, Joshua finally said, "I'm not going to tell you much. I went to the trouble of explaining it all to Britt Halley, because, I guess, I thought it would make me feel better. With you, though, I don't care one way or the other," and his voice lost its edge, turning down on a weary note.

The older man dropped the vest to the floor. Joshua moved in quickly to shake him down, very carefully and very thoroughly.

"Now will you tell me what you're talking about?" Lambert asked, and he appeared his usual confident self, actually unperturbed.

"Just one thing," Joshua told him. "The phone call you got from Tony Seastrom this morning. Well, Mister Lambert, that call was made by Alan Hunt. And I was on the extension. We've got it on tape, for your information."

Cleveland Lambert seemed to wilt slowly. His shoulders sagged, his right hand twitched once, and he looked down to the debris-covered floor.

"What makes it worse, even," Joshua said then, "is that I was going to stay. I was going to move Jerrie to the coast."

After a quiet passing moment, Lambert shook his head once, slowly. "She would have sucked you out, Joshua."

Joshua drew a deep breath, exhaled heavily. Lambert showed no remorse, no sorrow, only a kind of defiance, as if killing someone had become an acceptable thing now. Terrorists in the streets did it, like Huey Orville. And even the elite, the alligator-shoe gang, like the executive committee, did it. Maybe Cleve Lambert figured he had to fight fire with fire in order to come out on top.

"What about the records?" Lambert asked.

Shaking his head sadly, Joshua flipped the cylinder open on Lambert's revolver. Moving a step away, he ejected the six rounds, dropped them in his jacket pocket. He handed the empty revolver back to Lambert. "It's up to you," he proposed then. "You can go in with me, unarmed. And, after it's over with, I turn you over to Burt Ingstrom."

"Fair enough," Lambert responded, taking the revolver. He reached up to pull on his right ear. "So I get the records, and you get Britt Halley," he said reflectively.

"If we're both lucky," Joshua answered, and he remembered again that Alan Hunt insisted that luck indeed was the will of God.

Britt Halley realized she was working herself into a rage. Waiting was enough to normally upset her, because she had not had to wait for anything for as many years as she could remember. She yanked once again at the handcuffs, cursing the circumstances, her own impotence, and especially the weakness that had led her to her present predicament. Her only calming observation was that she personally was going to kill Joshua Bain, somehow, regardless of the consequences. She turned once more on her hip, feeling that she was numb there now.

She jerked her head upright then, hearing the one sound that caused her to gasp unbelievingly. The elevator door to Gus Holliman's office!

It must be Gus, she thought hopefully.

The form took shape then, in the doorway.

Joshua Bain stepped into the Documents Room, followed by another man!

The tiny red indicator light over the door began to glow.

"Oh, no!" Britt cried.

Joshua looked down at her, frowning at her sudden reaction.

"Gus!" she screamed.

Joshua bent down, grabbed her by the hair to steady her head. She tried to say something, but he jammed her mouth closed before firmly replacing the tape.

As the two men's weight had registered, the sensor below the floor dispatched its signal at the speed of light to the timer wired to the ignition matrix covering the room's walls from floor to ceiling. The tiny red light over the door would glow continuously for the first thirty seconds. At thirty seconds, the light would commence blinking, at an accelerating rate.

Standing up, Joshua stared briefly at Britt Halley, and he realized he was burned out inside. There was nothing left now, no triumph, no feeling of victory, nothing that he could identify. He had felt the same way at the motel yesterday. And even earlier, back on the oiled road after the screening exercise. The emptiness was becoming like an old friend . . .

"Is this all there is?" Lambert was asking skeptically.

"It's all here," Joshua assured him. "Most of it's on microfiche," and he turned to look out the door toward the hallway. "We're probably going to have to deal with Gus Holliman," he suggested wearily.

"The records first," Lambert said, and he shoved the empty revolver in his belt before lifting his end of the cabinet. He started moving the cabinet toward the open doorway.

Fifty-one seconds, fifty seconds—

Neither man noticed the tiny red indicator light.

Gus Holliman worked his way cautiously out of the women's lounge. He had been waiting for the one final explosion, the one opening up the emergency tunnel, when Britt's scream broke through the silence of the Sanctuary. At the lounge doorway, he squinted down the length of the hallway, and it took a full second for it to register: his elevator door was open!

Somehow, he thought, they got the main power back on.

Not knowing what else to do, he started down the hallway, the automatic pistol out in front of him. He moved silently over the heavy carpet.

Forty-five seconds, forty-four—

The heavy cabinet caught on the door channel, and Cleve Lambert stepped into the foyer, leaning the cabinet into his chest. Still inside the room, Joshua leaned down to lift his end of the cabinet over the channel.

At that instant, Gus Holliman reached the foyer door. The blood pounded in his temples as he looked into the doorway. He saw a man he didn't recognize holding up the tipped cabinet. *The records!* Gus swallowed once, again totally confused.

The automatic was up, shaking violently.

Cleve Lambert spotted the movement out of the corner of his eye. He dropped the cabinet, turned to his left in a reflex action, bending down into the crouch, the only position he knew. Instinctively too, he palmed the thirty-eight out of his belt.

The automatic popped in Holliman's hand, surprising him.

The twenty-five caliber bullet passed cleanly through Lambert's throat.

Startled, Joshua reacted slowly, seeing that Lambert was down, pinned under the heavy cabinet. With the Viper up, he stepped up next to the jamb of the doorway. He vaguely heard Britt groaning, and he figured she was getting hysterical in reaction to the gunshot. A few seconds passed before he realized he had to make a move.

Gus Holliman walked slowly into the foyer.

The red indicator light had started to blink.

Thirty seconds, twenty-nine—

Gus walked up to the man pinned under the cabinet. The bright red blood soaking into the carpet turned his stomach. Looking aside, he was numbly aware he was looking into the barrel of another gun. He glanced up, blinking to keep his vision clear, and he was not surprised to find himself staring at Joshua Bain.

"Drop it!" Joshua snapped at him.

Gus looked down to his right hand, remembering then that he also had a gun. He immediately dropped it. He stood still then, closing his eyes, still unable to comprehend what was really happening.

Twenty seconds, nineteen—

Joshua rolled the cabinet away from the door and off Cleve Lambert. Gus simply stood nearby, his arms slack.

Joshua stooped down to inspect Lambert's throat wound. Only the exit hole appeared to be arterial. He stripped off his tie, folded it several times, placing it as a pressure bandage over the opening. "You're going to have to hold it," he told Lambert as he put the other man's right hand over the makeshift bandage. Unable to answer, Lambert blinked weakly that he understood. "And don't pass out on me," Joshua warned him sternly.

Twelve seconds, eleven—

Gus was aware then that Britt Halley was kicking the side of the wall. Glancing up, he saw that she was motioning frantically with her eyes and head. As Joshua helped his wounded companion to his feet, Gus stepped around the cabinet into the Documents Room. Inside, he turned to look up to the now rapidly blinking red light.

Nine seconds, eight—

Gus Holliman was familiar enough with the cycling rate to know he stood an outside chance of going after the key and freeing Britt Halley. But, there was no way he could get the records back into the room in time.

He turned to look down at Britt Halley, who for the first time showed in her eyes that she was begging him.

"Dried grass," he whispered.

The walls turned to fire.

The massive steel door, hydraulically operated, closed irreversibly, crushing the fragile clothespin.

The room became a crucible.

Epilogue

By eleven o'clock on Friday night, there wasn't much activity in the Pan-American VIP room. Most of the heavy overseas flights had already departed, and the flight line was also settling down. Joshua Bain was in one of the window booths, alone, a half-filled glass of iced tonic water in front of him. He had been reading a newspaper, and he folded it up now, putting it down on the seat beside him. He supposed that the Government had a hand in relegating the news report to a page near the back of the paper. According to the brief release, the Indian Wells headquarters of the ETC Corporation had been raided at noon, yesterday, in follow-up to a warrant issued claiming intent to commit conspiracy. The local FBI agent in charge, Cleve Lambert, had been seriously wounded in the raid and at last report was still listed as critical. The desert complex had been completely destroyed by several explosions and fire, a conflagration attributed to careless ignition of natural gas. Several executives of the corporation were also missing and presumed dead.

Covering up had become Standard Operating Procedure.

So be it, he thought dejectedly.

But, things would be different in the Monday morning edition.

Cleve Lambert would get his final gold star, even though it might yet have to be a posthumous award.

He looked around from the flight line to see a man standing by his elbow.

"Mister Bain?" the man was asking him.

Joshua nodded once, gesturing for him to sit down across the table. The slender young man was dressed in a nicely tailored vested suit, and he seemed to move self-consciously as he opened his jacket before slipping into the booth seat. He told Joshua that his name was Ben Caplan. Joshua reached forward to shake his hand, noting that both the man and his clothes seemed appropriate for an attorney on the payroll of the FBI.

"Did Mason brief you?" Joshua asked him quickly.

"He didn't say much," Caplan said, "except that I was to be a witness in a meeting under your charge."

"That's about it," said Joshua. "Just remember that what happens here is strictly confidential, to be reported to Jerome Mason only." He hesitated before adding, "Your only function is to listen."

"I understand."

"And you have no recording or transmitting gear on you—"

Ben Caplan smiled thinly, opening his jacket. "The Director made it clear that I am to be here clean."

Joshua relaxed back into the booth. "They'll be here in a minute, and it won't take long." He studied Caplan for a moment, before asking, "Any further news out of Indian Wells?"

Ben Caplan shook his head. "I talked to Burt Ingstrom about an hour ago. They think they found what was left of the Documents Room, which, essentially was nothing. A molten cavity in the ground. No bodies or remains, no records. Not one molecule of evidence." His voice trailed off on a discouraged note.

After talking with Calvin Price, Joshua was not surprised at the report. Gus Holliman and Britt Halley had been simply vaporized; it was as if they had never existed. Remembering how close he had come brought a crawling sensation to the back of his neck, and he turned to look down at the flight line. A lone 747 was being groomed by its pre-flight crew, men in white coveralls dwarfed by the huge aircraft, and Joshua knew he was looking at the midnight flight to London. Preoccupied now, he didn't notice the two men moving toward the booth until they were nearly on top of him. Coming out of his thoughts, he looked up to see Alan standing next to the table. Joshua lifted the thin-line vinyl briefcase off the seat beside him and put it on the table, making room for the two men moving into his side of the booth.

"Phone call made?" he asked, not bothering to introduce Ben Caplan.

"Yes," Alan answered. "To his stock broker."

"That figures," said Joshua, and he was smiling absently. He squeezed the briefcase, dumped its contents on the table. "Your passport, Senator, and an airline ticket, one way. Shot records. And all properly dated, sworn to, and so on."

"Thanks to Gus Holliman," growled Senator Calvin Price.

"More probably Morgan Halley," Joshua suggested. "From what we can tell, the old man had it figured that someday this kind of unhappy situation might develop, so the documents I just gave you have been waiting for just this moment. Gus, you might say, was merely the custodian," and he paused for a moment. "You'll notice your new name; you best start getting used to it."

"You don't really think," the Senator said caustically, "that you can get away with this. You're aware of the power I still possess—"

"Don't try to bluff us," Joshua warned him. "You especially should be aware of the existing evidence. The gentleman sitting across from you is a special agent from the FBI, here, to this point, in an unofficial capacity. If you prefer, I'll give him the green light to take you into custody right now."

Calvin Price glared at Ben Caplan.

"He's telling you the truth," Ben Caplan was saying as he produced his ID, flashing it to the Senator.

Joshua started to reach for the papers in front of Price.

"Never mind," the Senator conceded. "But I figure you owe me an extra forty-eight hours. Our deal was to show you the power switch. However, I also helped you by showing you the freight elevator—"

"Forget it," Joshua snapped. "A deal is a deal," and he held firm despite the fact that the Senator had volunteered to return to the Sanctuary to help him retrieve the records. Despite the fact, too, that the Senator had then led them to safety via a freight elevator, enabling Joshua to slip the records out without detection. The Senator's real motive, of course, had been the escape documents now before him on the table, without which his two-day headstart would be largely futile.

"Okay," the Senator said, "you'll have to forgive me."

Joshua glanced aside to Alan Hunt. "Yes," Joshua said then, "that has already been suggested to me."

"So what now?" the Senator asked.

"You've got exactly forty-eight hours," Joshua told him. "The first thing you're going to do is to board that airplane out there, destination, London, England. After that, you'd best get busy trying to disappear, because at precisely midnight, Sunday, we turn the records over to the Justice Department." He noticed out of the corner of his eye that Ben Caplan's expression had shifted from apparent boredom to one of obvious interest.

The Senator nodded that he understood. "What about money? I'm going to need a lot of cash."

"Come on, Senator," Joshua said. "The ETC already owns

half the banks in Zurich. Think of it as a challenge."

The Senator chuckled once, as if he appreciated the comment.

"That's about it, Senator," Joshua went on. "I suggest you right now make your way to the nearest gift shop and buy yourself a pair of the biggest dark glasses you can find." He shrugged then. "As far as I'm concerned, you can get lost." He turned to look out across the flight line. He looked back after a few seconds to see that Calvin Price was still seated.

"I've already got a pair of big dark glasses," he told Joshua.

"We've got nothing to say to each other," Joshua commented.

"You know," Price started anyway, "I started thinking about you yesterday morning."

"You were a little late," said Alan.

"Yeah," Price agreed reflectively, "but just by a few minutes," and he shook his head then. "By just a few lousy minutes. And, you know, handcuffing Britt in that room was sheer luck on your part. That place was an impregnable fortress, yet—"

"Luck, you say," noted Alan with a knowing turn in his voice.

"Pure and simple," the Senator said.

"You couldn't be more right," Alan agreed.

There was a pause, until the Senator commented, "You both know that this country is going down the tubes."

"And the ETC was the last surviving hope," said Joshua.

Calvin Price shrugged. "What else?"

"Perhaps we should try God," said Joshua Bain, and he looked aside to see that Alan was grinning broadly. Encouraged, Joshua went on, "During the past few days," and he enunciated his words slowly, almost painfully, as if concerned he might be misunderstood, "I've finally had it knocked into my head that not only is there a God but that He is also actively involved in our lives. It took some doing, but it's finally starting to sink in." He looked out again to the flight line, taking a further moment to arrange his thoughts. "Apparently this understanding comes to each of us at different times, or something. I don't really know," and he turned back again to the Senator. "But it seems reasonable to me that if there is in fact a God, then we each ought to come to terms with Him, somehow, in some way . . ."

Calvin Price was nodding slowly, his eyes averted. "So you've got it all figured out?"

"No," Joshua admitted frankly, "not by a long shot."

"We're hoping he might continue to be lucky," Alan observed wryly.

Calvin Price pushed himself up from the table. In a wearying, final kind of gesture, he reached up to try to smooth down his unruly hair. "I guess you are serious, after all," he remarked as a kind of afterthought.

"Good luck to you, Senator," said Alan Hunt.

Watching the old man move away, Joshua understood that Alan's last remark was his way of saying he was going to pray for the Senator. He turned to face Ben Caplan. "Tell Mason that the records are safe, that you can have them Sunday at midnight."

Ben Caplan stood up, looking a little grave as he slowly and methodically buttoned his jacket closed. "I presume the Director is aware you have the records."

"No," said Joshua, "but I'm sure he'll be pleased to hear you've found them."

Ben Caplan lifted his eyebrows appraisingly, before he chuckled once, a brief exclamation which to Joshua seemed to be one of bewilderment.

"It will all fall into place," Joshua assured him, and he stood up to shake the young agent's hand. "Besides, a day or two will make no difference to the outcome anyway."

Ben Caplan moved away wordlessly, showing his discipline, but still shaking his head.

Sitting back down, Joshua hoped that Ben Caplan would ultimately understand why, that the records of the ETC Corporation had to be made public, and the only way he knew how to guarantee that disclosure was to turn them over in the presence of a crowd of news reporters.

"So," Alan said after a moment, "where to now?"

"Rancho Canaan," suggested Joshua. "We could tidy the place up a bit, since we're going to have a mob there Sunday night."

Alan chewed briefly on his lower lip, and Joshua sensed that his friend was having trouble saying whatever was on his mind. "Well," Joshua offered, trying to prompt him.

"I wonder about Rancho Canaan," Alan finally offered. "Do we really have a right to it?"

Joshua grunted once, thinking that Alan could be a little

less forward in bringing out that which affected their apparent mutual conscience. "An interesting question," he observed. "The morality of it has occurred to me also," and he paused for a moment, arranging his argument, for he was not about to give up the ranch. "We have survivor's rights to take it over completely, legally that is." And he got up, headed for the door, as if closing the matter.

"Sure," Alan admitted as he followed behind. "Like I can legally cheat on my income tax."

In the hallway, Joshua declared, "As you yourself told me, it says in the Bible that we are to obey the laws. And, the law says that we have the right."

The argument continued, until by the time they reached the street, Joshua Bain had his hands stuffed angrily into his pockets.

"I agree we earned the right to take title," Alan said a little breathlessly, having practically run the full distance from the VIP lounge in order to keep up with the rapidly striding Joshua. "But we must pay for it," he insisted.

"A quarter of a million bucks!" Joshua exclaimed incredulously.

"We'll find the way, Joshua."

Joshua turned to look at his friend, and for a passing moment he sensed that they indeed would find the way. "You're on," he consented abruptly. "But, we take title to the aircraft as well."

Alan contemplated the counter-proposal. "On one condition—"

"So we'll pay for it," Joshua added, throwing up his hands.

"Plus," Alan went on, "that you agree to burn the Cleve Lambert tape."

Joshua Bain could not help but smile. *Finally*, he thought, *finally it's my turn.* "Like the Senator," he said affectionately, "you are too late, my friend, because I burned it this morning."

Alan Hunt laughed once, extended both his hands, palms up.

Joshua slammed them with his own.

Thus agreed, the two men moved out side by side, and their hands were not weak, their knees were not feeble.

Merrill Wesleyan Church